# ANDRE GONZALEZ

# Secrets in the Vault

*For Bruce and Mer.*
*Thank you for the idea, and for always being supportive!*

"Don't be afraid to give up the good
to go for the great."

-John D. Rockefeller

# Contents

# GET EXCLUSIVE BONUS STORIES!

Connecting with readers is the best part of this job. Releasing a book into the world is a truly frightening moment every time it happens! Hearing your feedback, whether good or bad, goes a long way in shaping future projects and helping me grow as a writer. I also like to take readers behind the scenesw on occasion and share what is happening in my wild world of writing. If you're interested, please consider joining my mailing list. If you do, I'll send you four FREE novellas as a thank you!

You can get your content **for free,** by signing up at https://an dregonzalez.net/join-newsletter/

# Chapter 1



*June 16, 1991*

The man stared at his blurred reflection in the steel doors, a new life awaiting him on the other side. He faced the freight elevator of the United Bank Tower in downtown Denver, having just paged the guards through the intercom, where he posed as the bank's vice president. They didn't question the ruse, and why would they? Who else could possibly want access to the building on Father's Day at nine o'clock in the morning?

He listened as the gears whirred on the other side of the doors, and tightened his grip on the pistol. *It's go time.*

His leg bounced as time seemed to drag. The sounds stopped, and he braced for the doors to open.

Seconds later, they parted, revealing an older bank security guard, coffee cup in hand, not a worry in the world until he looked down and saw the Colt Trooper pointing directly at his chest. He dropped the coffee and reached for his baton.

"Don't even *fucking* think about it," the gunman snarled. "Swing that thing and I'll blast your brains all over this elevator."

The guard—McDowell, according to the name tag clipped

to his navy blue uniform jacket—released his grip from the baton and held his hands above his head.

"Better," the man said, looking over his shoulder to make sure no one was around. McDowell had coffee splattered all over his pants, or maybe the dark stain was piss. His eyes bulged with terror, hands trembling in the air. "We're going for a ride. Do you understand?"

McDowell only quivered like he had just stepped into an ice bath.

*What a chickenshit!*

"I said, do you understand?!" the man shouted, stepping into the elevator, shoving the gun into McDowell's pudgy gut.

"Yes, sir," McDowell said in a wavering, cracking voice.

"Good. Take me to the subbasement, and don't get any cute ideas. This gun will be on you the whole time."

McDowell nodded, but didn't move.

"Push the damn button!" the man barked, whipping McDowell across the face with the revolver. Blood spurted from his nose while he stuck out a wobbly finger and pushed *SB*.

The doors finally closed, and the elevator descended.

"Give me your keycard," the man said, having seen it clipped to McDowell's belt.

"Please," McDowell begged. "Please don't kill me."

"Give me the keycard!"

The elevator stopped, and the man pulled the trigger before the doors opened, knowing the sound wouldn't be heard in the guardroom on the basement level above.

McDowell collapsed to the floor, blood spreading across his chest while his arms lay lifeless by his sides. The keycard lay pinched beneath the guard's dead weight, so the man rolled him over and plucked it off the belt just as the doors opened.

He jumped to the side wall and peered out, relieved to find the coast clear.

The man stepped out and turned left to the lone door next to the elevator, entering a stairwell. He climbed up one flight to the bank's basement level, which was host to the guardroom and vault. He tapped the keycard on the scanner and opened the door, leading out with his pistol in front.

*No one heard*, he thought, once more relieved to find an empty hallway. The vault waited at the opposite end, but he'd have to pass the guardroom first.

He crossed the hallway and strolled ahead, his baggy sport coat whispering against the concrete walls. Cameras lined the hallway, so he needed to move quickly and with confidence. With a little luck, he could still catch the guards daydreaming before they realized what was happening—his disguise would definitely help.

The man was nearly jogging when he reached the guardroom's door and threw it open, the door banging against the wall and causing the two guards inside to jump up from their desks. He saw another door behind the two men marked as *BATTERY ROOM – CAUTION*.

Both guards whipped out their batons and held them out in front.

The man moved his pistol back and forth between the two, letting them know he could take them both out within seconds. The door glided shut behind the man, and that's when he pulled the trigger again.

"Fuck!" the guard on the left shouted, dropping his baton as he clutched his arm.

The man shot the next guard, catching him in the shoulder and sending him tumbling backward. "Get in the battery room!" the shooter yelled. "Hurry!"

The guard who had fallen down crawled toward the battery room's door. The other did not, so the man shot him again, this time in the stomach.

"Right fucking now!"

Both guards pulled themselves toward the battery room, all fight having vanished. The man had made easy work of them and should have an even less difficult time robbing the vault.

He kept his gun fixed on the guards as they first opened the battery room door, still crawling on the floor. The other followed at a much slower pace, bleeding from his stomach. The man kicked this guard in the rear, forcing him face-first into the room, where his colleague grabbed his arms and helped him in. The man stood in the doorway and shot both guards two more times in the head. They lay dead below a row of batteries used to power the bank's computer system.

He reloaded the pistol.

The guardroom door swung open, and another guard entered. "What the hell?!"

The man spun around and fired, the first shot errant as the guard dove to the floor. The guard hid on the other side of the desk, and threw his baton over the edge, nearly striking the man in the head, but instead hitting the wall behind him.

"Bad fucking choice!" the man shouted, jumping on top of the desk and shooting downward. He fired six quick rounds, and each hit the guard. The man read the guard's name tag: *Harvey.* "Sorry, Harvey," the man said with a chuckle, reloading the pistol once more with one of the several speedloaders he had stuffed into his coat pockets.

He hopped back down and looked at the ten monitors splayed across the front wall of the guardroom. The vault was indeed open and had six employees inside counting and sorting cash. Not a single one of them seemed perturbed, so he knew none of them had heard the gunfire.

*Take your time*, he thought. *Clear the evidence.*

Scanning the screens one more time, he found no other guards anywhere else in the banking area. He was all alone with the employees.

He looked down and saw a set of bank keys, slipping them into his pockets. A two-way radio stood on the edge of the desk, and he stuffed that into his other pocket after turning it off. The guard logbook lay open, and he saw a note about a silent alarm going off at 9:20 A.M. from the subbasement stairwell. Wilson Harvey had gone to check it.

He grabbed a handful of the log's pages and ripped them out, stuffing them into the inside pocket of his coat. "What else?" he asked the empty room, scanning the desk for any other clues that he might have left behind. The glimmer of a shell casing caught his eye on the floor, so he spent the next five minutes collecting each spent casing from his rampage.

After collecting the casings, he found a paper grocery bag under the desk, and tossed them into it, bringing the bag with him to the front of the room where he ejected the video tapes for all the active camera feeds, dropping them into the bag. He repeated this process ten times until all footage was officially erased.

Excitement bubbled within the man. He had made it through the hardest part of this robbery, and only had to collect his cash from the white-collar workers in the vault. He'd be home free within the hour.

Brown bag in hand, the man scanned the guardroom behind him, a few splatters of blood soaking into the carpet. Aside from that, he cleaned up the area nicely.

"Sorry, gentlemen," he said. "It wasn't personal."

He turned and left the guardroom, butterflies fluttering in his stomach as he continued down the hall toward the vault. He tapped the keycard to unlock the first door, and stepped in to see the vault wide open, bright light pouring out. Two counters ran the length of the vault, and each had three employees working quietly among themselves, pulling wads of cash out of large black bags, and running them through a counting machine.

All six of the employees were so deep in their work, they never noticed the man creeping toward the vault, arm extended as he held the pistol. He rapped the barrel on the vault's door. "How are we all doing?"

A woman in the back gasped and dove to the floor. The two men closest to the entrance casually looked over, then immediately raised their hands. The other three workers, two women and a man, stopped what they were doing and froze, as if they thought maybe the gunman wouldn't see them.

"Let's make this easy," the man said. "And everyone can go home today. I want everyone to close their eyes and get on the ground calmly and quietly. If I see any sudden movements, I will shoot. If I see you reach for any hidden alarms, I will shoot."

Everyone obliged and eased themselves downward. Some covered their eyes with their arms, others simply squinted their eyelids shut. The man nodded toward the gentleman closest to him, presumably the manager, as he wore a suit and tie, while everyone else had dressed more casually for their Sunday morning in the office. "You. Keep your eyes open and load up one of these bags with all the cash you can fit."

The nervous manager nodded slowly and turned around to the counter he was working at, lowering his hands cautiously toward the piles of cash. He grabbed handfuls at a time and returned them to the black bag.

"What's behind that door?" the man asked, pointing his gun toward another door outside the vault's entrance, just to the side.

"It's a mantrap," the manager said. "Just a different access point to the vault." He continued filling the bag with cash, constantly looking over his shoulder.

"Okay. I want all of you to crawl out of the vault and go behind that door. And drop your keycards before you go in. Let's move, people!"

They all reluctantly crawled along the floor, three of them passing by the manager, who looked down and gulped.

"You're all doing so good," the man said. "Keep this up and we'll all be on our way in no time."

A few minutes passed while they crawled on elbows and knees toward the mantrap, each dropping their keycards by the man's feet as they passed him. "I only see four cards—there should be five."

One man started wailing. "I'm sorry, I forgot."

"No need to cry, cupcake, just toss it this way."

The sobbing man obliged and threw his keycard over his shoulder where it landed close enough to the rest.

"Very good," the man said, picking one off the floor and starting toward the mantrap. He tapped the keycard on the panel and pushed open the door. "Wow, that's a tight fit in there. You guys will be okay, though. In you go."

"You'll never get away with this," one woman muttered under her breath as they formed a line and crawled into the mantrap.

"Excuse you, ma'am. I didn't ask for your thoughts. You'll keep your mouth shut if you know what's best for you."

She said no more and entered the small space. The man backed away from the door, but kept his pistol pointed toward it, backpedaling until he could see the manager more clearly. "How are things going in there?"

"One bag is full, sir."

*Oh, he's definitely a bank manager. Even talks like one.*

"That's good news. Now bring it out here, drop it on the floor, and join your friends."

The manager did as instructed, carrying the bag in one hand while holding the other above his head. He dropped it on the floor just outside the vault, gave a quick look up and down of the gunman (probably to share details with the police later), and shuffled into the mantrap with the rest of his employees.

"You all have a good day. And thank you for your cooperation."

He pushed the mantrap's door shut, and pulled it to confirm it wouldn't open. Whether going in or out of the door, a keycard was required. He pocketed the one he had already used and left the rest on the floor.

A calming stillness filled the air as he crossed the room and picked up the bag of cash, slinging it over his shoulder. "Money is heavy," he said, and broke into a sprint down the hallway.

He called the freight elevator and anxiously waited for it come to the basement level. Another guard could have been in the bathroom or on a break, and he didn't want to stand inside this building any longer than he needed.

When the elevator doors finally opened, he stepped in, the

smell of blood and coffee blending in a nauseating odor. He sent the elevator back up to street level.

The doors parted and revealed the parking garage, the morning sunlight visible just thirty feet away.

"It's now or never." He dashed through the garage, and hooked around the corner of the garage's exit, sprinting down the sidewalk on Lincoln Street. He saw no pedestrians aside from a homeless man rummaging through a nearby trashcan.

This man would get away with this crime for decades to come.

Until one day. . .

# Chapter 2

*Present day*

The trio gathered at the headquarters to meet Commander Briar. After only one mission, the team of Arielle Lucila, Felix Francisco, and Selena Nicole had gained a reputation across the Road Runners organization unparalleled to anything they had seen before.

They were considered a super team. Rock stars. Arielle had already been a celebrity within the group—most top-ranked Angels were—but having worked with Selena and Felix on the last mission, the two had been elevated to a similar status.

"This is crazy," Selena said after they gathered in a private conference room, having pushed through the office where everyone gawked at them, or tried to chat them up as they strolled down the hallway. "Is this what it's always been like for you?" she asked Arielle.

"Not here in Denver. When I've visited offices in different cities, there is a little of it, but today felt like walking down the red carpet."

Felix laughed. "Some guy out there said he wants to do what I do. Can't say I've ever heard that before."

"I don't understand *why* this is happening," Selena said.

"Like, it's only been two days since we got back. How does everyone know we even went on a mission together?"

"Remember, we're in a time of peace," Arielle said. "Commander Briar has launched many initiatives to drive engagement from all Road Runners. His focus has been on building a sense of community. Since there is no more war for our internal news to report on, they just talk about the current missions. I think there's a newsletter that goes out once a week, too. And it covers the mission work."

"So it's just a matter of increased visibility?" Felix asked.

"I suppose. I haven't seen what's all been said about us, but clearly we're well-received by the organization."

"It's because we're badasses," Selena said. "I don't mind the fame one bit. It was the life I was going to have, anyway."

The door swung open, and Commander Briar entered. "Good morning, you three. How are things?"

He shuffled around the table and took a seat opposite the three Angels.

"Everything is great, Commander," Arielle said. "Ready for our next mission."

"Always so eager. And how about you two?" He nodded at Felix and Selena. "How are you adjusting to the new life? Have you seen the special report that's been streaming? It's a deep dive into all of your lives."

"Well, that explains it," Felix said. "How did they do that without even talking to us?"

"We're time travelers," Commander Briar said with a light chuckle. "Our team just goes back and follows different parts of your lives. I'm sure they'll be in touch for a live interview in the present time. You three are becoming the face of the organization."

Selena grinned from ear to ear. "Fantastic."

"It's just buzz," the commander said. "Give it a few weeks and it'll die down."

"Unless we keep crushing these missions," Arielle said. "It could get even worse."

"Fine with me. I've been the popular one for long enough. Time for someone else. Now, let's get to business."

Commander Briar turned on the TV hanging on the wall at the front of the meeting room. It revealed a standard PowerPoint, the opening slide reading *Father's Day Massacre.*

"This is a big one," the commander continued. "Not for having a wide reach, but for the popularity this received at the time. On June 16$^{th}$, 1991, a lone perpetrator entered the United Bank just down the street from us—the Cash Register Building."

The slides changed to show the iconic Denver skyscraper with a roof shaped like a traditional cash register. It quickly changed to show the inside of the bank as it looked in 1991.

"Four guards were killed, and over two hundred thousand dollars were stolen."

The slide changed to show a middle-aged white man with a buzz cut looking into the distance.

"This is Jacob Kennedy. They arrested him on July 4$^{th}$, 1991 as the primary suspect in this robbery. He was a retired police officer and former guard at the bank. His trial was nationally broadcast, and the jury found him not guilty. He was released, and they never found the money. There were a lot of holes in the prosecution's story, but also in Kennedy's narrative. Personally, I think he did it, but the evidence presented at trial was spotty."

The slide changed to another man, this one a grainy picture.

He had large-framed glasses and a receding hairline.

"This is Peter Young. He's another suspect who lived about a half-mile away from the bank. They found some questionable things in his apartment, but nothing connected to the robbery. He also had no alibi. He'll be worth a look when you travel back."

Arielle had opened her notepad and scribbled notes. "When are we expected to start?"

"You'll have some time. There are a lot of moving parts to this one. The scouting team still has about a week's worth of research to do, maybe a little less. Plan for five days at the very least."

"Wow, that's pretty much a vacation," Arielle said.

The commander nodded. "We're trying to put more time between missions. Anything you'll need from us before the mission starts?"

"Actually, yes. I want us to jump in right from day one. I think we could have learned a lot more on the last mission if we had access to the target's workplace. A lot happened inside that building during the daytime, but we had no way in. I want this to be an automatic request for all missions going forward. We need to get Selena inside the building, one way or another. Are we able to do that?"

Commander Briar leaned back and stared into the distance. "I think so. It will vary by mission, and we'll need to find jobs that fly under the radar, but I think we can make it work."

"That's fine. It's not the job so much that matters, but having access to the buildings. Maybe even a custodian-type role would work best. They have access to nearly every part of an office."

"Exactly my thoughts," Commander Briar said. "Everything good safety-wise on the last mission? Because I think this next one will be plenty challenging."

"Yes. We got lucky with the murder being late at night."

"Good. That one was pretty straightforward. A targeted attack. This one, assuming it goes all the way to the day of, won't be so easy. The perp will shoot anyone who tries to intervene."

"Maybe I should be a teller?" Selena asked. "Put me in the front row on the morning of."

Arielle raised her eyebrows, never expecting Selena to put herself in the line of danger. "That won't be necessary. We'll work on finding a good position for you. I wouldn't trust standing at the teller counter. Too much can go wrong."

"If you say so. Are we free to do whatever we want for the next week, then?"

Selena never hesitated to redirect a conversation back to her true agenda.

"Yes, actually," Commander Briar said. "One of our main focuses is to make sure you have time outside of mission work to yourselves. Travel. Relax. Visit family. Whatever you need."

The way the commander was speaking made Arielle uneasy. But she had also been hard-wired from her days in the CIA to work around the clock. She had never minded, especially after losing her family.

"You especially, Arielle," Commander Briar said. "I was looking through your records, and you've never taken off more than three consecutive days. And I'm not sure even those count. I know you take work with you on vacation."

"Commander," she said. "I'm the top Angel. I can't just go off the grid."

He raised a steady hand while shaking his head. "You can. I promise we'll be fine. And if we're not, we know how to get hold of you. We've always been driven by urgency—we had to be, during the war, because any wasted second would cost more Road Runner lives. We're past that now. This time of peace allows us to take a step back and enjoy life. We don't have to complete missions as fast as possible. The past isn't going anywhere. If we can wait a few days to make sure more of our bases are covered, then we'll become even more efficient."

"What's our success rate?" Arielle asked, wondering what the percentage of recent missions had been dubbed as wins by the teams who explored the aftermath.

"98," Commander Briar said. "Was 95 this time last year. We're headed in the right direction, and I just might see if we can push it to 100. Why not?"

A failed mission meant one of two things. Either the Angels in the mission didn't achieve their objective, or the aftermath revealed a situation had reached the same outcome a different way, or ended up worse. Every department pointed fingers at the others when a mission came back as failed.

The prep team received blame for not looking deep enough into the matter. The Angels had to answer questions about what went amiss. Even the clean-up crew took heat for possibly leaving clues behind. Despite the turmoil, the actual cause usually ended up being a bit of everyone's fault. There were far too many moving pieces to pinpoint a specific reason for a mission going awry, so no official blame was ever assigned.

"We can reach 100," Arielle said. "It'll take more work, but we have the right people—we always have."

"I agree. With a year left in my term, and no crises to worry about, this will be my top priority." Commander Briar checked his watch, a flashy Rolex. "I have another appointment to get to. We can circle back once we have all the files from the Scouting team. Otherwise, plan to jump into the mission when you three are ready." He knocked on the table as he stood.

"Thank you, Commander," Felix said.

The commander left the trio alone once more.

Arielle stood up and paced near the television still showing the last slide of Peter Young.

"What's wrong?" Selena asked.

"This just all seems so strange. Less structured. I don't know."

"It's a new level of trust," Felix said. "You already had that respect from leadership, and now all of us do. The commander called us a super team. We're not going to be watched over like a less seasoned team might."

"I get that. I just don't know why all of a sudden... It's never been this way. Not even close."

"You heard him. It's a new era. Things are changing, and it sounds like for the better. You just might find yourself with a little more control over your missions."

Arielle shrugged. "So what are you guys going to do with a week off?"

"Unwind," Felix said. "Might catch a Rockies game, but definitely need to catch up on sleep. Don't feel like I got much on this last mission."

"I'm gonna catch up with some friends," Selena said. "Spend the weekend downtown. Maybe head up to the mountains for a day. How about you?"

"I'll visit my grandma. She's down in New Mexico, and I haven't seen her since last Christmas."

"I'm sure that'll be nice," Felix said. "I lost all of my grandparents by high school, but still remember visiting them every weekend."

"I only have the two on my dad's side, but they live in northern France," Selena said. "I'm not even sure the last time I saw them."

"My abuela is my only living family left," Arielle said. "Well, immediate family. I have some cousins, but none I'm really in contact with."

"Definitely visit her," Felix said. "It'll help you unplug. I dare you to not even take your computer with you."

Arielle laughed. "We'll see about that. Pretty sure my grandma goes to bed around eight o'clock. I'll need *something* to do."

They all shared a laugh at this comment, oblivious to the grueling mission that awaited.

# Chapter 3

Arielle arrived in Las Vegas, New Mexico, the next morning. She flew into Santa Fe and rented a car to drive the hour east to her grandmother's hometown.

Las Vegas had a population around 15,000 and sat directly off the interstate. Arielle and her family had made plenty of trips to visit family during summer breaks, where they somehow crammed into the lone guest bedroom available at the house.

Her grandmother still lived in the original house, a small ranch-style home with a white adobe exterior. When Arielle pulled up, she smiled when she saw it all looked the same. Cars lined both sides of Fourth Street. Chain-link fences separated the properties, and the front lawns were dirt or xeriscaped.

Arielle turned her car into the driveway and parked right behind her grandmother's Cadillac.

"Oh, *mija*!" a voice called from the front door, and Arielle stepped out of her car to see her grandma standing on the front step, crouched over with a cane to support her.

"Abuelita!" Arielle called back, running around the car and throwing her arms around her grandma's shoulders. She looked a little older each time Arielle visited. Her once-gray hair was almost completely white, standing out in contrast to her dark skin.

"How are you?" she asked, poking a bony finger into Arielle's gut. "Too skinny. Come inside and let's eat. I made your favorite." She cracked a grin, her lips sunken in, eyes filled with joy.

Arielle followed her inside and let the nostalgia sweep over her. The house had rarely changed over the years, except for when her grandfather had passed away in 2010. The living room and kitchen looked the same as she could remember from her childhood. Magnets covered the fridge, making it impossible to see the color underneath. The smell of green chile and refried beans filled the air, and Arielle's mouth watered.

Two lounge chairs faced the television in the living room, a folding dinner tray standing between them, covered in magazines and newspapers. Family portraits decorated the walls, both in color and black and white. A large crucifix hung above the TV next to a family portrait of Arielle with her parents and brother, the pamphlets from their funerals tucked behind the frame's edges.

Emotions rushed to Arielle's chest and head, and she bit her lip to keep from crying so soon.

"I miss them, too, *hita*. Think about them every day. Do you ever go visit them?"

Arielle nodded. "I try about once a week."

"Oh, good. Keep their graves pretty. They deserve it."

Arielle wanted to change the subject. "What are you cooking, Abuelita?"

"You still like your smothered burritos, yes? I got special hatch chile just for you. You know I can't do all that spicy stuff. Sit down. It's ready."

Arielle shuffled around the kitchen table and sat down in the seat she always used—facing the window that overlooked the front yard. Her grandma pulled out plates from the cupboard and served the food, drowning Arielle's burrito with so much green chile, cheese, and sour cream, that she could barely see underneath it all.

"You been busy, *hita*?" she asked.

Arielle took her first bite and nodded. The flavors brought back so many memories, one of the few things that could tempt her into quitting the Road Runners and spending the rest of her life in Las Vegas.

"Yes, work's been very busy, but it's supposed to lighten up soon."

"That's good. You look tired. You shouldn't work so hard. Go out and enjoy life. Any boys yet?"

Arielle knew the question was coming—it always did. "No boys. I don't have time for a relationship. Not yet, at least." She hadn't introduced a man to her grandma since Kevin in college, not that there had been anyone of substance since then.

"I know you'll find someone. I pray for you every night."

"Thank you, Abuelita." Arielle took another bite and shook her head. She couldn't believe food this delicious wasn't available at restaurants.

"Well, what do you want to do while you're here? How long are you staying?"

"I can stay three days. Honestly, there isn't anything I *need* to do while I'm out here. I have a few days off work and just wanted to get away."

"That's fine. Maybe we can go into town one day."

"How have *you* been, Abuelita? What do you do every day?"

"Oh, the usual. I go to church every morning. Stop at the diner for breakfast. Come home and take a nap. Watch my novelas, then make dinner. After that I take a bath and read for an hour before going to bed."

"Sounds like a nice relaxing routine. Don't mind me if there is anything you need to do while I'm here."

Her grandma shrugged. "It keeps me busy. The days are yours. Have you gone to church?"

Arielle hadn't stepped foot inside a church since her family's funerals. The tragedy had rocked her relationship with God, and witnessing all the nastiness on her mission work didn't exactly restore her faith.

"You have to go to church, *mija*. I know it's hard, but if you talk to God, he'll talk back. He always does."

"I'm not saying I'll never go back, but it's going to take some time."

Her grandma reached out and embraced Arielle's free hand. "I know. And that's why I pray for you. I just want you to find happiness again."

"I am happy."

Her grandma raised her eyebrows. She always could read her grandchildren's emotions, no matter their age, no matter how long it had been since they'd last seen her.

"You're not happy. I can see it in your eyes. You're content, but it can be better, no? Life is too short, *mija*. If it's your job that's not making you happy, go find a new one."

"My job actually treats me pretty well. I make great money, and genuinely enjoy what I do."

"Not just your job. There are lots of factors that go into a happy life. Physical, emotional, spiritual. They all have to be fulfilled. They all take time and attention."

"Abuelita, I promise you I'm doing very well. I'm in the best physical shape of my life. My emotions are fine. And spiritually . . . well, I'm right where I'm comfortable."

"I'm not going to argue. But I know you're not as good as you can be. It's okay to admit you're hurting. I'll never recover from losing your Abuelito, and definitely not from losing your family."

All Arielle needed to hear was the crack in her grandmother's voice, and she let down her guard. The tears she had fought back earlier came roaring back as she broke into a heavy sob and pushed back her plate. She looked up, eyes red and drenched. "I *hate* it," she said. "I hate that this happened to me. I hate that a deranged man gets to live while my family doesn't. I hate God for letting it all happen."

Her grandmother stood up and circled the table, hugging Arielle from behind her shoulders, planting a kiss on the back of her head. "Let it out, *hita*. It's the only way."

Arielle understood she didn't speak of the tragedy enough. She had undergone years of therapy, but a void forever remained. The therapy helped her manage the rage that boiled up when she thought about that day, but the sorrow remained as stiff as it had the first day she returned to her family's empty house.

"I want to kill him," Arielle said under her breath. "I want to kill him twelve times, one for each person he killed. He should have gotten the death penalty. I don't understand why he didn't."

Her grandmother massaged her shoulders. "Don't you wish you could just go back to that day and stop it from happening?"

"Every single day." Arielle's stomach churned at the thought. She really did consider it every day. Her grandmother meant it figuratively, but didn't know how realistic of a possibility it was.

Angels at Arielle's level had few restrictions, but tampering with her own past was one of them. It was highly forbidden for a multitude of reasons. Tampering with one's own past would alter their present timeline. All of the mission work she had done could be wiped out by changing her past. Her very existence could come into doubt.

That's why she only fantasized going to the shooter's prison and killing him in the present day.

"I know everything about him, Abuelita. Nicholas Robert Fenton." The name tasted like dog shit in her mouth. "Born in 1987 in San Diego. Charged with twelve counts of first-degree murder. One hundred and thirteen counts of attempted first-degree murder. Found guilty on all charges. Sentenced to twelve life sentences, plus an additional 2,718 years. Incarcerated at the United States Penitentiary in Allenwood, Pennsylvania. He's in cell D-12."

"Oh, Arielle. It's not good for you to know all this. You're not going to actually kill him. Revenge won't bring our family back, and it won't make you feel any better. You need to erase all that from your head. You're obsessed, and that's unhealthy. I guarantee you he doesn't spend his days thinking about all the people he killed, so neither should you."

"I'm not going to kill him," Arielle said. "But I wouldn't mind having a word."

If Arielle could get inside that prison, then she would absolutely murder him without a second thought. It might not bring her peace, but it would make the world a better place. She could close her eyes and picture his psychotic mugshot that had been all over the news in the weeks following the massacre. How she wanted to wipe that smug grin off his face.

"This is something you're going to have to live with for the rest of your life," her grandma said. "Don't let it control you."

Arielle rarely let the thoughts of killing Nicholas Fenton consume her life. She was much too busy with missions to spend serious time on the subject. It became clear why she avoided taking time off from work. It only offered free time for her to get her emotions riled back up.

Arielle grabbed her napkin and wiped the tears away. "I'm okay, Abuelita. Thank you. I feel much better already."

She stood up and hugged her grandmother, thinking about how good it would feel to one day end the life of Nicholas Fenton.

# Chapter 4

Arielle returned to Denver three days later, relaxed and recharged. Her grandmother hadn't pressed her on happiness or other life issues for the rest of her stay. Instead, they chatted about old memories, spent a day in town, and ate loads of food. She was pretty sure she gained five pounds during her quick trip.

Her grandmother had given her a fifty-dollar bill when she left, convinced Arielle was poor and never ate. "Take yourself out somewhere nice," she had said. "And order dessert."

Arielle held the bill in her hand and grinned. She didn't need the money, so she put it in a box she kept with other precious family memories. After each visit she always worried it might be the last time she'd see her grandmother. Abuelita was pushing ninety years, but she was an active woman with lots to look forward to. Arielle felt plenty encouraged after leaving New Mexico.

Arielle had only spent a handful of days at her own house during the past month, having been torn between missions and different trips out of town. The place almost seemed foreign, and she wondered if she should downsize.

She often had this debate with herself, and always talked herself into staying. The house was massive, but maybe one day there would be a family inside of it. Or friends. Working as an Angel for so long often made her feel like a machine. But having a week off had since reminded her what it was like to be a regular 27-year-old. She remembered what free time was like, not having a care in the world.

It almost felt foreign, and part of her felt guilty. She was supposed to be helping people in need, stopping crime, killing bad guys. Not lounging in her bed at eight in the evening.

Her doorbell chimed, and she hopped out of bed, tumbling over the pile of clothes that had been scattered from her trip. She was expecting Selena to pick her up, but not so soon.

She opened the door to find Selena grinning with a bottle of champagne in hand. "Surprise!"

"What are you doing here so early? Is everything okay?" Arielle stepped aside to let Selena enter.

"That question is exactly why I'm here. You worry too much. Let's have some fun. Are you familiar with the term *pregaming*?"

Arielle scoffed. "Selena, stop acting like I'm some old lady. I went to college. I used to party."

Selena looked her up and down. "Sure. And this is also why I'm here. You don't know how to dress for a night out. Don't worry—I'll help you."

Arielle rolled her eyes. "I have plenty of outfits for going out."

Selena stepped further into the living room, looking up at the vaulted ceiling. "Jesus Christ, you live here by yourself? This house in insane. You realize you look like a filthy rich person with your mansion at the top of the hill?"

Arielle shrugged. "I suppose I am filthy rich."

Selena howled laughter. "Quiet confidence. I love it."

"Any Road Runner can make easy money. It's encouraged."

"Oh, I know. And I do. I just don't think I'd ever get so much space for myself. I spend all my money on cars and shoes."

"And that dress? Gucci?"

Selena wore a lacy black dress, nearly see-through to an imaginative eye.

"Wow, you know fashion, too? Maybe we aren't so different after all."

"I keep up," Arielle said. "Went to Fashion Week once in New York. Did you ever go?"

Selena grinned. "More times than I could count. Please, the wealthy go to those things just to make an appearance. I went so many times in Paris with my dad. I've been surrounded by fashion my entire life. But do you know who might know even more about fashion than either of us?"

"Who?"

"Felix. His mother is a fashion designer out in San Fran. Told me he grew up going to fashion shows all the time."

"No shit? Well, looks like we've found something all three of us have in common. Is he still meeting us tonight?"

"Of course. I told him it's a team-building event—which it is. But really we're just going to cut loose before the mission starts. Maybe we can make it a tradition if we keep having these long weeks off in between."

"Maybe. What did you end up doing the last few days?"

"Visited my mom. After hearing about your trip to see your grandma, I thought maybe I should catch up with the one woman who's always had my back."

"Oh? Is she still in New York?"

Selena nodded. "Yeah, and I asked her to move out here to Denver. She told me hell no. She loves the big city too much. I expected that response. My mom tells people she's a native New Yorker, but she's not. Just fell in love with the place and refuses to leave it for anything."

Ariella chuckled. "You do anything fun?"

"Oh, sure. Plenty to do there. Caught a show on Broadway—can't remember the last time I did that. Spent a day at Central Park just talking and catching up. And spent our final day at her apartment, just hanging out and playing board games. I think we both really needed it. I'm glad I went."

"Me too. Glad I'm not alone in feeling weird about having all this time to ourselves."

"Seriously. I can actually go out and have the next day to recover. I feel rejuvenated just thinking about it. Shall we get ready? I'll pour the champagne."

* * *

An hour later they arrived downtown and found Felix sitting at the bar of the very crowded Johnny's Tavern. He had a half-empty beer stein and a basket of hot wings in front of him while he watched baseball on the big screens behind the bartender.

"Hey, you two!" he said, standing up to hug Arielle and Selena.

"Feels like it's been forever," Arielle said. "How has your time off been?"

Felix smiled. "So nice. I've done exactly what I said. Caught the Rockies game yesterday. Been getting a ton of sleep and catching up on shows. It's been so nice to not have to think."

"Yeah, the commander might really be on to something," Selena said. "I almost feel excited to start the next mission."

"You girls already have some drinks?" Felix asked. "I smell it."

Arielle and Selena stared at each other and burst into laughter.

"Yes," Arielle said. "We might have had a bottle of champagne while we got dressed."

"While *you* got dressed," Selena said.

Arielle giggled and threw her arm around Selena. "Right."

Felix looked like he was trying to hold in a laugh. "Is everything okay? I don't think I've ever seen you this way, Arielle."

"What? Tipsy?" Arielle said. "I'm fine. Let's eat."

They found a table near the back corner of the restaurant, and over the next hour chowed down on burgers and appetizers, then shared a slice of chocolate cake smothered in ice cream. They chatted about their past week, mentally bracing for the mission set to begin in exactly two days.

"I did some reading," Arielle started.

"There she is," Felix said with a cheesy grin.

"This mission is quite interesting. Have either of you ever worked on a case like this? Because I don't think I have. Normally, they give us the file with a pretty good understanding of who's behind the crime. This one, though, it sounds like our Advance Team has no idea where to start."

"It's the first one," Felix said. "I chatted with some of the team. Commander Briar wants to expand our range of missions. He's also looking into present-day missions to prevent things from happening in the future. He believes heavily in this one as it removes the prospect of the past pushing back. Imagine the thought of doing a mission and only having to worry about the real-world obstacles."

"Hold on," Selena said. "Why do you know all this stuff? Your team?"

Felix laughed. "We *are* the tech team. We monitor all emails that come in and out of the office. Some are restricted, but this thread between the commander and the Council was not."

"Oooh," Arielle said. "What did the Council say?"

She knew they liked to push back, and sometimes wondered if they just did it for fun.

"They said his initiatives all sound fantastic, but they told him to pick one to focus on. He wants to launch all these new teams and projects, and move people around to fill the voids. They told him no, and he started on this one first. I guess it was a more seamless transition from what we already do."

"But why wouldn't he have told us?" Arielle asked. "Why didn't I realize this?"

"Technically, our last mission was a cold case, at least in the eyes of the local police department and community. This next one, though, is a true cold case, even to us. We're going in blind. Sure, we have a couple of suspects, who may very well end up being our targets, but our Scouting team wasn't able to confirm any details. They were just as confused as the jury, it sounds like."

"So he's easing us into it," Arielle said. "I'm not sure I like it. We're not detectives. I don't know that we're the right team for this experiment."

"What are we, if we're not detectives?" Selena asked. "That's what I've always thought of you as."

"Assassins," Arielle replied calmly. "I'm a trained assassin. And my job is to kill the bad guys."

Felix took a gulp of his beer and gave Arielle a look.

"What?" she asked.

"Commander Briar's been playing you. Remember your mission in Mexico a few weeks ago? The one where you wiped out the cartel?"

"Of course."

"That was part of him wanting to explore a modern-day mission."

Arielle leaned back and touched her fingers to her mouth, thinking. "That son of a bitch. He told me it was because they came across the opportunity and had nothing in the past for me to work on yet."

"Nope. And that's why he sent you by yourself to fend off, what was it, twenty cartel soldiers? He wanted to prove that one Angel could handle a mission like that if they didn't have to factor in the past as another obstacle."

"Well, that just seems reckless."

"But you did it. You were never even in danger. The proof is in the results. I think many Angels don't realize just how good they are at what they do. You've all been conditioned to work around the past, so when the past isn't present it's a walk in the park. Honestly, I'm surprised the commander didn't explore this route first. It's easy."

"So what am I supposed to do now? Pretend I don't know this is all going on?"

"I don't get the sense that it's supposed to be a secret. He just doesn't want to make a big deal out of it. I suppose it's *not* a big deal . . . we're doing the same work, just with an extra step added."

"I wouldn't make anything of it," Selena said. "We can do this the same way."

Arielle considered the comments and agreed. She wouldn't bring up the matter to Commander Briar.

Not yet, at least.

# Chapter 5

Later that night, the trio moved from dinner to a busy night-club. Arielle ordered bottle service so they could have a private area away from the masses.

Music boomed, and Selena found herself back in her element, drifting from their private table to dance on the main floor. She swayed her hips side to side, keeping her drink elevated in one hand, eyes closed while she belted out the words to the newest Ed Sheeran song.

It had been a few weeks (in real time) since she had gone out in downtown Denver, and she didn't want to squander the opportunity. She'd be out until the club closed, even if that meant Arielle and Felix left before her.

However, they surprised her by joining on the dance floor.

"Having a good time?" Arielle shouted over the music.

"You know it!"

Men swarmed around the two of them.

"Do you want me to pretend to be your boyfriend?" Felix asked Arielle.

"No, I'll be fine. Let these boys have their dance."

They stayed on the dance floor for the next ten minutes before settling back at their private table.

"Why don't you dance with any girls out there?" Selena

asked Felix while Arielle poured them a fresh round of drinks.

"This isn't really my scene," Felix said. "I don't think I'd ever go home with someone from a nightclub or bar."

"No one said you have to marry the girl," Arielle said with a laugh. "It's just a dance, and you can never see her again."

"Have you met Felix?" Selena asked. "The man doesn't do anything for the sake of doing it. If he's going to invest time in a woman, even a quick dance, there better at least be the opportunity of it being more than that."

Felix nodded.

"You need to loosen up," Arielle said.

Selena broke into a cackle. "Wow, Felix. The queen of serious just told you to loosen up. Who is this woman, and where did she take Arielle Lucila?"

Arielle grinned. "I'm just saying. I understand having rules in life and sticking to them. Like I never accept a drink from a man, no matter what. But if that guy over there in the next booth wanted to come over here and take me to the bar to buy a drink . . . well, I just might say yes."

They followed Arielle's eyes to the man in the pinstriped suit at the neighboring VIP booth.

"Um," Selena said. "That's Javonte Morris, the running back for the Broncos."

"Oh, I know. Isn't he just . . . dreamy?"

"He's been looking this way," Felix said. "When you're not looking."

Arielle shrugged. "Well, the ball's in his court then."

"Oh my God, he's coming!" Selena squealed.

The football player strolled over with a wide grin. His silver chain gleamed in the dim club, matching rings standing out against his dark skin.

"Good evening," he said, towering over all three of them. "Can I buy you folks another bottle?"

"Hi, Mr. Morris," Felix squeaked, standing up and sticking out a hand to shake. "I'm a big fan. Glad to have you in Denver."

"Thank you. I'm enjoying it as well. That's why I bought ownership in this club. Anything at all I can get for you?"

His eyes didn't move from Arielle while he spoke, so she stared right back and replied. "Another Grey Goose would work."

Javonte nodded, the grin having no chance of disappearing from his face. "I can arrange that. Would you three want to come to my suite upstairs? It's quieter so we can actually talk."

"Sure," Arielle said, standing up. Selena and Felix followed, grabbing their cups from the table and trailing behind Javonte.

"I didn't even know this place had an upstairs," Felix said.

"Just be cool," Selena snapped back. "There are probably more famous people there."

They all followed Javonte to a private door with a bouncer standing guard. The bouncer nodded and stepped aside, pushing the door open to reveal a stairwell illuminated with purple lighting. As soon as the door closed behind them it became immediately quieter. Their shoes echoed with each step as they climbed and entered another room roughly the size of the dance floor they had just left.

A bar lined the wall to the right, circular tables and seats scattered across the rest of the space. There were indeed more famous people in this private area, including more Broncos players, a local rapper and his crew, and plenty of beautiful women sprinkled into each of the groups.

"Grab a table," Javonte said, nodding to an open one near the far end of the bar. "I'll grab us some vodka."

They crossed the room, passing the local celebrities. Felix gawked in every direction. When they sat at the table, he leaned forward. "Do you guys realize who all's in this room? This is nuts!"

"I said be cool, Felix," Selena muttered under her breath. "Don't embarrass us."

Javonte returned to the table with bottles of Grey Goose and soda. "Drinks have been served," he said, placing them on the table. He waved a hand toward the bar and the bartender slid over four glasses. "So what's your story? Friends? Siblings?"

"We're friends," Selena said. "By the way, thank you for bringing us up here."

"My pleasure. You looked like you were having a good time. What do you all do for a living?"

They exchanged glances around the table before Arielle spoke first. "We work in finance."

"Very nice. I have a few friends who do that as well. I'm sorry—I just realized I never asked your names."

They shared their names, and Javonte sat down with them at the table.

Selena felt Felix's leg bouncing uncontrollably, so she kicked him in the shin to stop.

"So Javonte, what do you do during the summers?" Selena asked.

"This," he said, raising his hands at the club around them. "I bought ownership in a couple of clubs around town. Seems to be a good investment so far. They always tell us athletes to have a back-up plan. Injuries can strike any time, and a football career can be over just like that." He snapped his thick fingers.

"Wise advice," Arielle said, knowing there were far better business investments than bars and nightclubs.

"I hope you don't mind me being honest," Javonte said to Arielle. "But you are one of the most beautiful women I've ever seen."

"And I'm sure he sees a lot," Felix said. This time Selena's heel jabbed him, prompting him to grimace.

"Excuse our friend, he's a little star-struck," Selena said.

"Nothing to apologize for," Javonte said with his charming grin, returning his attention to Arielle. "Would you be interested in going out to dinner sometime?"

Arielle smiled. "Yes. I would like that."

"I look forward to it," Javonte said, reaching into his suit pocket and pulling out a business card. "I don't start training camp until July, so I'm pretty available until then."

"I can get pretty busy with work—" Arielle began.

"But she'll call you," Selena interrupted, putting her hand on Arielle's back. "I'll make sure of it."

"Well, thank you," Javonte said, tipping back the rest of his drink and standing up. "I'll look forward to your call, but I have to get back to mingling with guests here tonight. Part of the job." He rolled his eyes and smiled. "You're all welcome to stay up here as long as you'd like, and if you need anything, just let Ronnie behind the bar know. He'll take care of you."

They thanked him, and he disappeared to another table, chatting with the rapper.

Felix couldn't stop smiling, even as he sipped from his glass. "So Arielle has a date with Javonte Morris. I'm speechless."

"You're also a clown!" Selena said, slapping Felix on the arm. "Why are you sitting over there acting like a total fanboy?"

"What? He's on my fantasy team. Would you have preferred if I talked to him about that instead?"

Now Selena rolled her eyes.

"You two both need to relax," Arielle said. "I'm glad this played out the way it did. Who knows what will come of the date, but now Selena has a connection in the nightclub industry."

"A *VIP* connection," Selena added.

Arielle smiled and shook her head. "Let's get out of here. I'm getting tired."

Selena wanted to rebuke, but decided the excitement of the last few minutes was enough. She could leave happy knowing the uptight Arielle Lucila had landed a date with a rising football star.

They left the club fifteen minutes later and returned to the warm summer night.

"Is anyone okay to drive?" Felix asked.

Arielle and Selena looked at each other and laughed.

"I'll take that as no," Felix replied, joining in on the laughter. "I guess we need to call for a ride."

"Or we just hang out until we get sober," Selena said. "Let's grab a greasy slice of pizza—that will help speed it up."

"Deal," Arielle said, and started down the sidewalk.

Shouts came from across the street, and they all spun around to see a crowd of people huddling around two men holding their fists up, ready to fight. They were in front of a neighboring bar, Swanky's.

One man shoved the other in the chest, and they both charged at each other.

"Should we go break this up?" Felix asked.

Arielle sighed. "We probably *should*, but do we really need to?"

Fists were being thrown across the street.

"Dammit," Selena said, running across the street in her high heels. She looked over her shoulder to make sure Arielle and Felix were trailing behind her.

The crowd had nearly doubled since the fight started, everyone watching the two drunks swing at each other. One man had blood oozing from his forehead, and the other had a bruise forming around his left eye.

"Stop it!" Selena snarled.

The two men spun around, confused. The one with the swollen eye looked Selena up and down, grinning. "Get out of here, princess—we've got business to handle."

"Excuse me?!" Selena cried, leaning down to take off her heels and toss them aside. "I was just out trying to have a good time with my friends, and now I have to deal with your bullshit!"

She charged the man, who reared back and landed a punch squarely on Selena's stomach. Pain ruptured from her insides and shot all the way throughout her body. She tumbled backward and needed a moment to catch her breath.

She hadn't expected such a forceful punch. This time, she was ready.

"Hey, asshole!" she shouted.

The man turned back around, his eye almost completely shut. "Oh, you want more, bitch? Let's dance."

The man rushed toward her, fist reared back again. Selena dropped to the ground and swung her leg out, connecting with the man's ankles and sending him flailing forward. He landed face down in front of a spectator and hurried back to his feet.

It was too late.

Selena had already lunged his direction and rammed her knee into the man's face, sending a spurt of blood out of his nose. He fell back to the ground, wailing as his hands cupped his nose.

The second man slithered toward Selena and wrapped his arms around her throat. The move caught her off guard, white spots sparkling across her vision. Sensing her strength on its last limb, she raised her right foot and kicked backwards as hard as she could. Her foot skirted to the side of his shin, but she felt it.

*One more*, she thought, and raised her foot again. This time she landed the blow directly onto his kneecap, bending the knee in the wrong direction.

"Fuck!" the man screamed, hobbling away as he tried to balance himself on the good leg. Selena jumped toward him and swung a fist to the back of his head. The man dropped like a boulder, a nine-millimeter pistol falling out of his waistband.

"Gun!" someone in the crowd shouted, and nearly everyone started running away.

Neither man had attempted to stand up. Selena hunched down with her hands on her knees, panting for breath. Arielle and Felix ran to her.

"I knew we needed to stop it," Selena said. "I saw the gun. His shirt came up after he threw a punch."

"Selena," Arielle said, placing a hand on her back. "That was incredible."

"It really was," Felix said, shock smeared over his face. "You know how to fight like Arielle."

"Not quite," Selena said, standing upright. "Arielle

wouldn't have taken that first punch, or been put in a chokehold."

Arielle nodded. "It's true."

They all broke into laughter and left to grab their pizza, supporting a slightly bruised but mostly unscathed Selena between them.

# Chapter 6

To Arielle's surprise, after reading through the mission report, she discovered she would leave for her own preliminary mission before the main one started. Their primary target—the man who stood trial, Jacob Kennedy—didn't pass away until 2009.

The Advance Team thought it would be wise to pry information from Kennedy, if possible. Perhaps some questioning two decades after the trial would reveal never-heard-before details. But Arielle would need to rely on her interrogative skills.

They scheduled Arielle to jump back to January 2008 at eight o'clock in the morning.

She drove downtown after an early breakfast, and planned to take her time-traveling Juice from there, since that would put her closer to her 2008 destination in Denver. The office was rather deserted for a Monday morning, but most Road Runners didn't arrive to work until ten. A handful had slept there overnight to monitor events, but the bullpen would soon bustle with the energy of a new day.

Arielle went to the conference room next to the kitchen, placed her luggage next to the door, and took a quick swig of her Juice. She didn't need to bring anything besides the file for the preliminary trip into the past, so tucked the papers into a backpack to sling over her shoulder.

*Packing light always makes an easy trip*, she thought as she stood in the middle of the room waiting for the past to take her away. All Road Runners were grateful Commander Briar had discovered a new formula for the famous Juice, one that allowed those jumping through time to have their physical bodies transport.

That lone change had removed a lot of hurdles and nuances from the process, making the Angels more efficient. The secret had been in the Book of Time, and had only come into the commander's possession after the war against the Revolution had ended.

Aside from that, everything else about the process remained the same, and Arielle fell into a void of darkness, a sensation of floating on a cloud until she lightly hit the ground in 2008.

The conference room looked mostly the same, only different furniture and technology. Arielle opened the door to peek outside, finding the bullpen emptier than when she had arrived in her present-time.

*Still before this place was a headquarters.*

The three people in the bullpen didn't pay her any attention. Most Road Runners in the small offices had grown accustomed to people from their future walking out of the conference rooms to go about their business.

A young girl nodded at Arielle, but offered nothing more beyond a polite smile.

Arielle made her way outside, where she had instructions to find a silver Mercedes waiting for her parked on the sidewalk, the keys hidden inside the front wheel.

She found the vehicle and keys without issue and dropped

into the driver's seat to open the map provided in her mission report. Jacob Kennedy had never left Denver after receiving a not-guilty verdict in 1992.

Arielle had a map with the route drawn to his house in Golden, about a fifteen-minute drive from the office. All reports suggested that Kennedy rarely left his home in the decades that followed his trial. Kennedy lived like a hermit after having been disowned by his friends and even some family members.

Arielle thought of the darkness surrounding this mission while she drove across town, and how the facts made no sense.

Kennedy had an alibi the morning of the murders and robbery. On their trip to 1991, they would specifically watch for the moment he claimed to have said hello to a neighbor, an act of one of several counterpoints brought up by Kennedy's attorney at trial. On the flip side, he was a former police officer who had investigated crime scenes, and had once worked at the very bank in question as a security guard. No weapon had been found. Neither had the 200,000 dollars of stolen cash. Kennedy's modest life never suggested he had come into extra money at any point since the trial.

As easy as it seemed to place blame on whoever might attract the most suspicion, Arielle had seen plenty of times where the main suspect was indeed innocent. Sometimes people were just in the wrong place at the wrong time and got saddled with the blame.

Arielle turned into Kennedy's neighborhood, a block of single-level homes, all with beautiful, small yards practically on top of each other. The narrow street offered little parking, but she found a space at a house three down from Kennedy's.

Arielle parked and walked up the sloped driveway until

stopping in front of Kennedy's house. He had a bright green lawn, even for January, with a long bench on the front porch. A windmill spun near the fence where Arielle stood as she examined the house.

They had studied this moment in time enough to determine Kennedy was home alone.

Arielle strolled right up to the front door and knocked, taking a step back to observe the surrounding neighborhood. Most of the other houses looked the same, and she wondered if this was a retirement community.

The door creaked open, and an old man with a white buzz cut poked his head out. "May I help you?"

"Are you Mr. Kennedy?" Arielle asked, offering a polite smile.

The man looked behind Arielle, his eyes darting in every direction before focusing back on her.

"Who wants to know?" His voice was rough and demanding, obvious hints at his former life as a police sergeant.

"My name is Arielle, sir. I go to college at Metro State. I'm taking a Colorado history class and learned about your trial in 1992. I'm sorry you had to go through that, but I was hoping you might answer a few questions for a paper I'm writing."

"I told you already, I'm innocent!" Kennedy stepped back and slammed the door shut.

Crows cawed from the power line, and Arielle thought they were laughing at her.

The door swung back open, and this time a middle-aged woman appeared, her face tight in a frown. "I'm sorry, young lady. Mr. Kennedy doesn't take questions about his trial anymore."

"I'm sorry if I upset him. I didn't mean any offense. I just genuinely had questions for my paper I'm writing."

"I'm sure that's true, dear, but in the years following the trial, Mr. Kennedy received requests like that every day. And some of them weren't real. The FBI watched his every waking moment. All these years later, I'm sure they've moved on, but it's been a constant hell for Mr. Kennedy. Even if things like this only happen every few years now."

"He still gets people knocking on his door to ask about it?" Arielle asked, faking her surprise.

"*You're* here, aren't you? You kids have your internet and can look up everything. Finding someone's address is pretty easy, from my understanding. What isn't easy is finding information on Mr. Kennedy's trial. It happened before the internet, so I'll tell you what I tell everyone else who comes here. The Denver Public Library is your best bet. They have records of everything from that trial, and might even have video footage of it. That I'm not sure about, since I've heard mixed information. But they'll have your answers. Mr. Kennedy won't."

"May I ask who you are?" Arielle said, almost blurting out that she expected Jacob to be home alone.

"I'm Mr. Kennedy's nurse," the woman replied. "He needs some assistance throughout the day."

*How did the team not catch this?* Arielle wondered.

"I see," Arielle said. "You know, ma'am, I've been reading so much about this trial and robbery. I, for one, believe Mr. Kennedy is innocent. Don't get me wrong, there were definitely some things that could *suggest* it was him, but there was far more evidence otherwise. If I can have even five minutes with Mr. Kennedy, I'll be out of your hair."

The nurse studied Arielle with her beady brown eyes, looking her up and down. "Innocent, huh? Well, that's a first. Most people come here trying to find the piece of evidence that makes him guilty."

"Not at all, ma'am. For God's sake, he had an alibi. He chatted with his neighbor that morning of the crime. While it was supposedly happening."

The nurse narrowed her eyes. "You really have been doing your homework. Everyone else says he paid off the neighbor to say those things. Offered her a cut of the stolen money. What do you say to that?"

Arielle shrugged. "I suppose that's possible, but we don't even know what happened to that neighbor. I'm sure if she had come into some extra money, the FBI would have known about it and tied it all back to Mr. Kennedy. But they couldn't. Another reason I believe he's innocent. It's almost impossible to get by the FBI. Beat the police department in court? Sure, that happens. But getting by the FBI monitoring you for *years*? Impossible."

The nurse grinned. "I like your style. What did you say you're going to school for?"

"History. I have a Colorado history class, and we had to choose a topic to investigate and write a term paper about. This one caught my eye."

"I wish you the best of luck, dear, really I do. And I hope you accidentally find something that will truly clear the guilt everyone associates with Mr. Kennedy. I suppose under normal circumstances Mr. Kennedy might actually sit down and chat with you, but this is as far as you'll get these days."

"Why is that?"

"Mr. Kennedy has dementia."

# Chapter 7

"I'm glad we don't have to travel anywhere," Felix said. "That's always a nice bonus."

The three had gathered at noon at the headquarters, ready to make their jump back to 1991.

"It's also a bonus knowing what the hell we're doing on a mission," Arielle said. "I traveled to 2008 to try to speak Jacob Kennedy. What a disaster. I don't understand why we're doing this—going in blind. Our own Advance Team can't unearth important details. What makes them think we'll magically do it once we're on the ground?"

"Because we're the best," Felix said. "I told you that already. Do you really think some lower-ranked team could figure this out? If we can't do it, then Commander Briar will write it off as impossible and move on to his next project."

"How are you feeling?" Arielle asked Selena once they settled into a conference room, pointing to her throat that had a light purplish tint of bruising.

"I'm fine," Selena said. "It looks way worse than it feels. In fact, I don't even feel anything."

"You ladies are such badasses," Felix said. "And you don't even know it."

Felix had substantially less combat training compared to

Arielle and Selena, and could never break up that fight the way Selena had. He always viewed people with such physical gifts in awe. Being the quiet kid in high school attracted the attention of bullies, but they only ever tried to intimidate him with words. He didn't take them seriously, so their jibes fell flat.

He supposed they left him alone *because* he had no reaction to their cheap insults. *Silence is my greatest weapon,* he reminded himself. The quiet observer rarely got into tussles, whether physical or verbal, no matter how badly he actually wanted to on the inside.

"So did you confront Commander Briar about all these changes?" Selena asked Arielle.

"No, not today. He's in his office, but I figured it's best to just worry about the mission. Did you both have time to review the details?"

Selena and Felix nodded.

"Great. If we're ready then, let's head out."

Arielle stood and shuffled to the front of the room where they had all placed their luggage for the trip into the past. Selena and Felix followed, pulling out their flasks of Juice as they joined by Arielle's side.

"First day of June in 1991, right?" Felix asked.

"Correct." Arielle unscrewed the lid from her flask and took a sip of Juice.

Within seconds all three of them had completed the same act, and sat down on the floor next to their bags.

"See you on the other side," Felix said, grinning.

Selena smacked his arm. "Don't say shit like that."

A minute later, they fell unconscious while their bodies and souls transported through time. The ground rumbled and the quaking didn't cease until they woke up in the same room, finding themselves inside a storage closet.

Felix stood up first and brushed off dust from his pants. "My goodness. The renovations that eventually happen were totally worth it. Look at this dump."

Boxes and furniture filled the dark room.

"They didn't need so much meeting space back in 1991," Arielle said.

"Apparently just storage," Selena said, a bitter countenance as she pulled a cobweb from her hair.

They grabbed their luggage and wheeled it toward the door, Arielle leading the way and opening the door to the office's bullpen. They stepped out to find a much quieter office. A handful of people sat in the bullpen, staring at boxy computers. The room smelled of freshly brewed coffee. File cabinets lined the perimeter, papers gushing out of several of the drawers. The lighting was dim, the walls bare.

"This place is miserable," Selena said under her breath.

"Relax," Arielle said. "Remember, this wasn't a headquarters yet. I think only like fifteen people total work here at the moment."

"Hello?" an older man asked, standing up from his desk in the bullpen. "When are you folks from?"

"2022," Arielle said, moving forward to shake the man's hand.

"Ah, very nice. Welcome. I'm Rich Jenkins, Lead Runner here in Denver."

"Nice to meet you, Rich. We're just on our way, not staying too far from here, actually."

"Wait a minute, are you Arielle Lucila?" Rich had a long, droopy face that perked up at this realization. He had a slight hunch in his back that he forced straight as he looked at Arielle. "I've heard of you. You do great work."

A few other heads in the bullpen looked up after hearing Rich speak, gawking at the trio.

"Thank you, Mr. Jenkins," Arielle said with a smile. "We've got a mission here in 1991."

Arielle studied Rich. He was at least in his late sixties. It was rare to see many older Road Runners. Most Runners retired from the day-to-day grind of working for the organization around the age of fifty. By then, they would have lived an extra thousand years in different eras of time.

While one could never truly quit the Road Runners, the organization allowed people to retire from their responsibilities, while still keeping tabs on them in case any needs arose.

"Well, best of luck to you folks," Rich said. "If you need anything at all, come see me. We keep a decent amount of weapons right here in the office, and have access to the system if you need to look anything up. I can also travel to different years right here from the office to meet with other Road Runners if you need to send a message. This office is the headquarters in 2022, is that right?"

"It is. I may need to send word to our commander, so I'll keep you in the loop."

"I look forward to it," Rich said with a soft grin. "Well, I'll let you get to it. Was nice meeting you all. I'll be here if you need me."

Rich smiled and returned to his desk, walking gingerly with a slight limp.

Arielle looked to the other two and nodded toward the exit.

They followed her and climbed the familiar stairwell upstairs to the marketing office. In 2022, the place bustled with at least thirty Road Runners posing as employees, phones ringing, music blaring.  Now, they found only ten people working in sheer silence.  Some wore headphones plugged into their portable CD players.

"This place is like a dungeon," Selena said as they passed through the office to step outside for the first time in 1991.

"I see why the office is the way it is," Felix said when they reached the sidewalk. "They need to blend in."

Gone were the restaurants, bars, and sleek office spaces of the time they knew as the present. Instead, they looked around at warehouses and a street lined with semi-trucks delivering goods.

"What the hell?" Selena asked. "Where *is* everything?"

"Have neither of you traveled back in time in Denver?" Arielle asked.  "This part of downtown was industrial until they opened the baseball stadium in 1995. Union Station is a few blocks away, and this entire area is a shipping dock for all the goods coming in and out of Denver. The mall is still a few blocks down, but the rest of downtown isn't developed for another few years."

"This doesn't look like a place you should be alone past dark," Felix said, looking up the sidewalk where a man leaned against the building, injecting himself with heroine.

"That's very true," Arielle said.

"I hope we're not staying around here," Selena said, face scrunched in disgust as she looked at the man.

"We're within walking distance, but we'll be at an apartment complex close to the bank.  Same building one of our suspects lives in, actually."

Arielle led the way, wheeling her suitcase behind her. Selena and Felix followed, pulling their luggage.

They had a one-mile journey to their apartment building, the arrangements set up in advance for them. On the way, they passed several more homeless people camped out on the deserted sidewalks.

"Go back where you came from!" one man yelled. "I know where you're from. Get the hell out of here!"

He had stood up from the ground, raggedy jacket and pants swaying from his body. His skin had been weathered, his facial hair scruffy. He cracked his lips into a grin, revealing yellowed teeth.

"We're just on our way," Arielle said, walking faster.

"Aren't we all?" the man replied, taking another step toward them.

Felix clutched his bag and ran past Arielle.

The homeless man grabbed his stomach and broke into hysterics. "Buncha pussies! Back when I was in the game, I never had to travel with ladies to stay safe. Good look on you, sissy boy!"

"Let it go," Felix said over his shoulder, knowing Arielle had stopped and wanted to encounter their heckler. "He's delusional."

"I was on my way once," the man said, reaching into his jacket and pulling out a flask, promptly spinning off the cap and taking a swig. He looked up and belched. "Would hate for you three to get stuck in here with me. I'll never get out! If I see you again, *you'll* never get out, either!"

Arielle shook her head and joined Felix and Selena in running away.

The man howled laughter and fell over, kicking his legs in the air while clutching his stomach.

The three Angels reached the next block within seconds,

finally out of sight from the homeless man.

"Think he was one of us?" Selena asked.

"Definitely seemed like it," Felix said. "That's why I didn't want a confrontation."

Time travelers who got stuck in the past, typically from losing their Juice and not able to get it replaced, ended up losing their sanity. Many wandered the streets, talking to themselves and anyone else who passed by. Others ended up in a padded room for the rest of their existence in the past.

Making Juice for a specific person required time, and sometimes there wasn't enough to make a new batch before a time traveler overstayed their trip. If you traveled back into the past, you had to return to your present before the past caught up with it.

Commander Briar had hoped to end this matter upon discovering many secrets in the Book of Time, but none were available. This was simply a rule that could not be broken.

"Let's just keep going," Arielle said. "We're almost there."

They had traveled five blocks and were gaining speed. "I can see the apartment building," Selena said, pointing ahead.

The building stood ten stories tall with a beige exterior and steel balconies on the corners of each unit. A crooked sign hung near the complex's front entrance, reading *Mountain View Apartments*.

"We're up on the seventh floor," Arielle said. "Peter Young is on the fifth."

With their destination in sight, the three of them hurried down the sidewalk, escaping the gloom of the suffering downtown area , and stepping into the more residential and business-focused part of town.

They stopped outside of the building, and Arielle unzipped

her suitcase and rummaged through it to pull out an envelope full of keys, one for each of them to access the apartment. She unfolded a piece of paper and read from it. "Building code is 4-5-8 to get in. We are apartment number 714."

"I haven't lived in an apartment since college," Felix said, reminiscing. He had lived in the campus dorms during his freshman year and decided it best to live alone off-campus for the rest of his college days.

They walked inside together, the main lobby housing two walls of mailboxes for the residents of the complex. Through another set of double doors was the main hallway, complete with the administrative offices, a rec room, and a swimming pool.

"Place is kind of fancy," Selena said.

"It's considered a luxury apartment in these days," Arielle added. "But really isn't priced like one. It's a hidden gem for sure."

They passed the offices and found the elevators, two shafts available for use. They rode up to the seventh floor and stepped out to a hallway with gaudy carpeting, and cheap art hanging from the walls.

"Not *too* luxurious, I guess," Arielle said with a laugh. "Looks like a hotel up here."

Their door was halfway down the hall, and they stepped into a much more appealing apartment.

The complex only had a handful of three-bedroom units, and they had lucked out being able to secure one. The apartment opened immediately to the kitchen on the right, dining area to the left. On the other side of a bartop counter above the sink was the living room. A hallway broke left, three doors belonging to two bedrooms and a bathroom. The master bedroom was adjoined to the dining area, its door ajar.

"Not bad at all," Felix said. "We own this place?"

"Not exactly," Arielle said. "Well, not right now. The Road Runners will buy the entire building in 1999, needing a central location to keep guests from out of town. Felix, I'm giving you the master bedroom so you can set up all your stuff. We'll actually be able to monitor Peter Young on a direct feed once we can get his place bugged. From my understanding, he's directly two levels below us."

Selena wheeled her suitcase to the hallway and left it there. "So Peter Young is the next likely suspect? But he didn't leave any evidence behind. He worked there, sure, but so did several other people."

Felix moved to the window overlooking the city and mountains. "He may not have left any evidence behind, but he had the perfect view."

He pulled apart the drapes and revealed the towering skyscraper that housed the bank that would be robbed in exactly sixteen days.

# Chapter 8

As much as they had complained about the Advance Team's shortcomings in preparing for the mission, the reality was they had done superb work. Not understanding who their primary target was proved a critical pain point, but they provided every other shred of information available, plus tools to make their lives easier. Typically, Felix would be the one to get Selena a job within the United Bank building. But the Advance Team had already taken care of that and provided her with a badge and keycard.

Felix reviewed their documents and slid the badge across the table. "You have a job with the cleaning crew. Nine to five, Monday through Friday."

"Wait, am I going to clean toilets?" Selena asked, appalled.

"Probably. You'll need to do whatever your supervisor asks of you. Her name is Olivia Bryant, and she's expecting you Monday for your first shift."

"I'm gonna throw up if I have to clean toilets. You guys, I've never even cleaned one, ever. How am I supposed to do this?"

Arielle laughed. "You better figure it out with all those acting skills. You pour in some cleaner, scrub with a sponge, and be done. Not much to it."

"And if you do throw up," Felix added. "At least you'll

already be next to the toilet."

Arielle and Felix broke into laughter, Selena shaking her head. "Not funny."

"Princess Selena has to clean a toilet," Felix said, gasping and placing a hand to his mouth. "Dare I say she might have to . . . mop a floor?"

Arielle slapped her leg as she threw her head back and laughed.

"I'm glad you two are getting a kick out of this. And what will you be doing while I swim in shit all day?"

They regained their composure, Arielle speaking first. "For starters, cleaning is not all you're doing. You need to study the place. Learn where everything is and the best way to access the bank and vault. Take advantage of your first few days and wander into restricted areas. See how far you can get. You'll be able to talk your way out of it. Play the card that you just started, and bat those pretty eyes. The guards won't do anything as long as you seem innocent."

"I'm not worried about that—I can get out of any situation."

"I'll be tailing Jacob Kennedy. He's still our prime target. All reports suggest he got away with it thanks to a botched trial by the prosecution. I don't know—there were a lot of things that make sense for it being him, but also a lot that oppose it."

"And I'm monitoring suspect number two," Felix said. "Peter Young. That will be rather straightforward, since I get to hang out at the apartment all day and listen to his conversations."

"Nothing is straightforward in any mission," Arielle said. "*Especially* this one. Selena, it's important you keep an ear out while you're at the building. Maybe find out where the guards hang out on breaks and try to eavesdrop. There was a suspicion that whoever committed the crime had help from the inside."

Selena nodded while jotting down notes. They each had papers spread across the table in front of them, a cluster of information on all aspects of the mission. "When will you bug Young's apartment?"

"He's off tomorrow, so Tuesday," Felix said. "He works from noon to eight, so I'll be there at about 12:30. Should be a simple place to infiltrate. He lives alone, has no pets. Small one-bedroom apartment." Felix shrugged as if he could do the job in his sleep.

"Is there a reason we didn't try following this guy in a later year?" Selena asked. "If the FBI found nothing on Kennedy, maybe Young had the money all along."

"The Advance Team already looked into it and found nothing. Young dies of a heart attack four months after the trial ended. If he ever had a plan of holding the money to use later, that chance never came."

Felix stood and crossed the room toward the window, looking out at the city. "So crazy that money was never found. If Kennedy had it, he must have buried it somewhere and never went back for it since he had a target on his back. If Young had it, that secret died with him. I know this probably hasn't been a question you've had to answer before, but who do you think did it?"

"Speculation only causes false biases," Arielle said. She took a long drink of water before putting her empty glass on the table. "But I think it was Kennedy."

"Me too," Selena said.

"Interesting. I was thinking Young. Guy gets away with it and never cashed in his prize."

"I just don't feel he was smart enough to get away with it," Arielle said. "Did you watch the clips of his questioning in the courtroom? Dude was dumb as rocks. No way he pulls it off."

"I agree," Selena said. "Kennedy was sharp. If he kept close contact with any of the guards, he could have known enough about the security changes within the building while planning the robbery."

"We have the advantage of looking at the evidence that *didn't* get presented in court," Arielle said. "Did you know they found a box full of fake ID's in Kennedy's house? And they had different names on them."

"How the hell was that not allowed in court?!" Felix asked, spinning around to meet Arielle's gaze.

She shrugged. "Because he had slick lawyers, I suppose. The judge ruled it wasn't relevant to the case because the ID's were never used—that much was confirmed."

"But that shows intent," Felix said. "Why else would he have those?"

"We don't know. And since they didn't admit them as evidence, Kennedy didn't have to answer for them. We don't know when they were created, or why. Maybe there was a legitimate reason, but we'll never know."

"Why do you keep saying we'll never know? You don't seem too hopeful about this mission."

Arielle leaned back and clasped her hands behind her head. "I'm sorry, you two. My head just isn't in this the way it should be. I feel like we're playing against the odds even more than normal. My gut feeling says this mission is a waste of time."

"Nothing we do is a waste of time," Selena said. "Even if the mission ends and we haven't changed anything, it will still be a learning experience."

"We're not paid to learn," Arielle said. "We're here to make the world a better place. Four lives were lost because of this tragedy. Four families broken, on Father's Day."

"Forgive me for maybe sounding too harsh," Felix said. "But I've never understood why it's been our problem to fix things. Life happens. Death happens all the time—tragic, sudden death. Who are we to play God and stop it from occurring?"

"Because we *can*," Arielle said. "There's a reason we never go back and stop a tornado from wiping out a small town. We can't do anything to stop the tornado. If we could, then we'd also have missions like that."

"We could warn the people and guide them out of harm's way."

Arielle shook her head. "The past doesn't allow it—that would be too easy. We could just as easily tell the four victims to call in sick on June 16th. Commander Briar once left a written letter to the principal of a high school trying to warn him about shootings that would occur three years in the future."

"And what happened?"

"The building burned to the ground."

Felix shuffled toward the table and sat back down, staring at his twirling fingers.

"The past will always fight to conserve itself," Arielle continued. "But that doesn't mean we can't change it. We just have to trick it. Remember what I mentioned about needing to block off your intent? The past knows. We play by its rules, but that doesn't mean we can't find loopholes to succeed. In fact, we *have* to. That's the only way."

"I've been practicing that," Selena said. "There are meditative practices that help train your brain to focus on something entirely different while you're doing another thing. Start simple. Paint a wall in your house, but think about cooking dinner while you do it."

"That's exactly it," Arielle said. "That's why I spend so much time learning these missions inside and out before we jump into the past. If I spent as much time studying the reports here instead of at home, it would be impossible to hide my intent while absorbing all that information. But if I do it in my present time, then the past has no way of knowing what I plan to do. A loophole, see? That way when I'm in the grind of a mission, my mind can wander elsewhere, and the knowledge I need for the mission itself is basically second nature."

"I think I'm understanding it a little better," Felix said. "Seems like it takes a lot of time to perfect."

Arielle nodded. "I've done thousands of missions. In the beginning, there were several mistakes. After a couple hundred, I got a better feel for this practice. Haven't looked back since and kept refining it. I suggest we all get a good night's rest. We'll do some light work tomorrow, but the real fun starts on Monday."

# Chapter 9

"Two weeks from today, that bank is going to be robbed," Arielle said.

They gathered at The Last Drop, a café directly across the street from the United Bank building, sitting at the outdoor patio for a clear view of the building they would all study over the next fourteen days. Notebooks sat open across the table, cups of coffee and sodas filling the spaces in between. Felix had pushed his notes to the center to make room for a towering plate of nachos.

"You know, Selena," Felix said. "Your badge will work immediately. You can head inside and have a look around."

"No," Arielle said. "That would be suspicious. She doesn't have a work uniform and doesn't even start until Monday. Let's not get ahead of ourselves."

Felix shook his head. "Who robs a bank on Father's Day?"

"Did Kennedy have kids?" Selena asked.

"Yes," Arielle said. "Two adult children. Which means if it was him, he robbed the bank, killed four guards, and returned home for lunch."

"That's absolutely absurd," Felix added. "The crazy thing is that whoever did it is probably sitting at home thinking about it right now. Hell, they could even be in this café watching the building like we are."

Arielle scanned the café, Felix's idea definitely possible. No one who resembled either Jacob Kennedy or Peter Young was in the area.

"I was only kidding," Felix said, offering a grin. "We'd obviously know if either of our targets were sitting at the next table."

"It's a small world," Arielle said. "You never know. Why don't we go have a look around the place?"

"For what?" Felix scooped some beans and chicken and shoved them into his mouth.

"Just to look. It'll be good to have a feel for the block surrounding the building."

They agreed and waited ten minutes while Felix finished his food.

Downtown Denver was deserted on Sunday morning, at least in the bank's area, which was primarily a business district. A young couple jogged past them when they stepped out of the café, and beyond that they didn't see another person within a two-block radius.

They crossed the street and looked up, unable to see the top of the skyscraper and its signature cash register shape.

"Kind of weird, isn't it?" Selena said. "It's just a building to everyone passing by. Even the people inside. But when you know something is going to happen, it has a different energy. Do you guys ever feel that way on some of these missions?"

"I used to," Arielle said. "Not so much anymore. But I still feel it at the mall where I lost my family. Just driving by. It's like I can feel the building staring at me. Watching me. Like it regrets not taking me that day."

Felix and Selena exchanged looks and squirmed.

"What's wrong?" Arielle asked, looking back and forth between them.

Felix looked to Selena, and she spoke. "Nothing's wrong. It's just . . . we never know what to say when you bring up that day."

Arielle scrunched her face. "You don't need to say anything. I never expect you to."

"It's weird for us," Felix said. "I suppose it always has been, and not just with you. Something like ninety-five percent of the current Road Runners entered this life because of some horrific tragedy they endured. Selena and myself are the rare ones who did not. It's such a common question between Road Runners, asking about those past tragedies. It's become as normal as asking someone where their hometown is. And we never know how to reply without sounding arrogant."

"Is this how you feel, too?" Arielle asked Selena.

Her teammate nodded, lips pursed.

"I guess you're right," Arielle said. "I never thought of it that way, but it is something that is discussed rather openly. It's normal to me. I don't *mean* to bring it up so much—it's just part of who I am. Something that has pushed me in life all the way to this point."

"And we get that," Selena said. "Don't take this as us telling you to stop bringing it up—that's not the issue. We just never know if we're supposed to say something back. It's impossible for us to relate. We can only sympathize."

"I appreciate that. And please don't feel pressured to reply. If you want to be silent, that's fine. I guess I talk about it just to let it out. The pain and sorrow never go away. Neither does the fear. My therapist always encouraged me to speak about it whenever the memories of that day pop into my head. Apparently, bottling it all in is no good. Who would've thought?"

"We're here for you," Felix said, extending an arm to grab Arielle's shoulder. She clasped her hand on his, tears welling in her eyes. "I mean it. Even if there isn't something that triggers the memory, and you just want to talk about it. Let us know. We're not your fan club. We're your team. Your *family*. You don't have to act like the top-ranked Angel in front of us. Let it out."

Selena joined and threw an arm around Arielle's other shoulder, the three of them now huddled in a tight group hug.

Arielle let the tears flow. "Thank you," she muttered. "I haven't developed any close relationships with anyone since the shooting. The only person I've been able to talk about it openly with is my abuela. You have no idea how much it means to me. I trust you two, and feel so blessed you've come into my life. I'm sorry if I've ever made your jobs difficult—I know I need to trust you both, but it's hard for me. I always assume something bad will happen if I'm not in control."

They released their embrace, and everyone took a step back, Arielle wiping the tears off her face. She couldn't remember the last time she'd had such an emotional moment away from her grandmother. Felix and Selena stood in front of her, watching her with eyes full of worry. For the first time since joining the Road Runners, she had met someone—in this case, two people—who expected nothing from her. They weren't concerned about discussing a mission, requesting her presence at an event, asking her to teach a course, or just wanting a moment of her time to gush about how great she was.

They were simply present. There for her. No strings

attached. It had only taken one complete mission and a couple of days into a second for their collective bond to blossom into a friendship.

Arielle grinned and looked at Felix. "You called us family. I thought we weren't even supposed to be friends."

Felix smiled back. "I guess some things are out of my control."

"Thank you. Really. I haven't had close friends in a long time. I've forgotten what it's like. I've had many roles in my life, but being a friend is one that's been pushed so far back, I don't remember how to do it anymore."

"Don't worry about all that," Selena said. "We'll help you. You know I'll call you out when you get carried away with all that top-ranked Angel crap."

She stepped forward and slapped Arielle on the arm, earning a hearty laugh.

"Thanks, you two. I already feel so much better. Should we head back to the apartment and get ready for tomorrow?"

"There she is," Felix said. "Honestly, I don't mind taking another hour and walking around downtown. When's the last time we got to explore the city? Besides, we're not even done walking around this building."

Arielle nodded. "That sounds great. And yes, we need to check out the building. The freight elevator is near the east entrance—we should start there."

# Chapter 10

Selena arrived at the Cash Register Building on Monday morning and met Olivia Bryant, her manager for the next two weeks. Every Monday morning, Olivia hosted a team meeting in the hallway outside the changing rooms for the custodial staff. At seven o'clock, Selena found herself in a huddle of fifteen others, all dressed in the same plain gray uniforms, arms crossed as they listened to Olivia.

"And please welcome our newest teammate, Ms. Selena Nicole," Olivia said, waving Selena to step forward. She did, waving a hand at the group. "Selena comes to us with plenty of experience already, so she'll spend the day with me, more to get familiar with the building. Expect to work with her over the next few months while we reconfigure the rotation. Now, everyone have a good week, and as always, let me know if you need anything."

The huddle dissolved, everyone going their separate ways while Selena remained alongside Olivia.

"You ready?" Olivia asked, placing her hands on her hips. "No break until eleven."

Selena dreaded her day ahead and had to remind herself it was all part of the process. She was inside the building that had so many questions needing an answer. But first, she had to feign interest in scrubbing the toilets and dusting rich executives' offices.

"Absolutely," she said. "How many floors are we doing today?"

"You got it lucky since you're with me. We'll do four. Everyone else pairs off and will handle eight. We budget an hour per floor. If you do well today, you'll jump into that rotation tomorrow."

"And there are how many floors in this building?"

"Fifty-two, if you include the two basement levels. Further down this hall is our break room. That's where you'll want to store any snacks or lunch. I'd say it's fifty-fifty for who eats here and who goes out downtown. You'll have a nine-hour day, with an hour for lunch at one. I tell everyone to always stay in motion. If you're not doing something, then you'll fall behind schedule.

"If that happens, someone else has to pick up your slack. They get a bonus if it comes to that. If everyone hits their allotted floors within the day, the whole team gets a bonus. An extra twenty-five dollars for every day that happens. Might not sound like much, but we get it usually four days out of the week. No one is complaining about an extra hundred bucks. That's an extra two-and-a-half days' worth of pay. Don't be surprised when people start really pushing each other around the holidays. Everyone wants the extra cash."

Selena did the math in her head to find she would make roughly five dollars per hour during her time as a custodian. She couldn't imagine having to live off such low wages, and already admired her new coworkers for their determination.

"Let's get to it," Olivia chirped, leading them down the hall and toward the elevator shaft at the end. Everyone else had already left the area, hard at work for the day ahead. They stepped in, and Olivia pressed the button to take them to twenty-first floor, explaining the building blueprints as they rode up. "We have a pretty simple layout for being such a big building. The bank takes up the first floor, at street level. They also have a vault in the subbasement level where the security office is. If you ever feel uncomfortable during the day, don't call me, call the security team. They'll move much faster. There are phones outside of every door in the stairwell throughout the entire building. They only dial to the security office."

"Why would I not feel comfortable?" Selena asked.

"Child, you are young, pretty, and a cleaner. These corporate men have all sorts of sick fantasies about sleeping with maids. Most of them will just look at you while you clean, but you never know when one might strike up a conversation, or even try to touch you. Just stay alert, and always keep your cart in the doorway so the door can't close."

"I'm sorry, is this a regular thing that happens?"

"I'm not trying to scare you. No, it's not common. We get maybe two incidents a year, but I always remind the women on the team to keep an eye out. Because when these things happen, it's usually the man's word against ours. And who do you think the authorities believe? The millionaire executive, or the minimum-wage janitor?"

"That's so wrong."

"No shit, it's wrong, but that's the world we live in, sweetie. Did things like that not happen at your old job?"

According to the fake resume the Angels had created for her, Selena had cleaned the offices for a music studio in Los Angeles before moving to Denver. "I guess not. At least, not that I realized."

"Well, that's good. I suppose there is some hope for humanity, after all. I find it best to just mind your business while you clean. Most of these people pretend we're invisible, anyway. If you don't already have one, you'll want to get one of those portable CD players. They're a real lifesaver."

The doors parted, and they stepped into a new elevator lobby, this one enclosed with glass walls and formal writing stamped onto the doors welcoming them to the Law Offices of Fields, Mercer, and Wellington.

A closet door was next to the elevators, and Olivia wiggled in a key from her pocket to open it, revealing a cleaning cart fully equipped with a mop, brooms, dustpans, chemical cleaners, rags, and long yellow rubber gloves.

"The carts are on each level of your first assigned floor. You'll start there and work your way up. Return your cart to the floor you found it, and that'll be your day."

Olivia pulled out the bright yellow cart and wheeled it toward the law office's doors, tapping her keycard against the security pad on the wall. It chimed and flashed a green light, the double doors unlocking with a forceful click.

They entered a lobby where Olivia offered a polite grin to a young blond sitting at the reception desk. The girl was on the phone, but smiled back before returning to her call. She paid no attention to Selena.

"Follow me," Olivia mumbled, turning a corner and hurrying down the hall where the restroom doors waited at the end.

Over the next twenty minutes, the two of them cleaned the men's and women's bathrooms in tandem. Selena took care of the sinks and sweeping the floors, while Olivia cleaned the toilets and followed up with a mop.

"How long have you been working here?" Selena asked.

"Twelve years now," Olivia replied. "It's crazy to think it's been that long. I guess life really can pass by in a blur."

"But do you enjoy it?"

Olivia finished mopping and leaned the mop against the wall, crossing her arms. "No one *enjoys* this work, Selena. You should know that already. I enjoy the steadiness of the job. I know exactly what needs to be done every day. No curveballs, no surprises. Just the same eight hours of work every day of the week."

"I can see the appeal."

"And what about you? You seem too young to be in this kind of job. Most kids out of college will at least attempt to do something significant first, then fall back on a job like this if things didn't work out."

"I didn't go to college," Selena said, having created a persona for the new character she had to portray for the next two weeks. "Barely graduated high school, but somehow did."

"Is your mama a cleaner? I've seen plenty of mother-daughter teams start their own business."

"She was, yes."

"Well, let me tell you this. Find something else to pursue. Especially before you have kids and need to rely on a steady paycheck. Take a chance before it's too late."

"You have kids, I take it?"

"Two boys. Eighth and fifth grade. My husband fell ill . . . twelve years ago. He was unable to work. I found this job and have had it ever since."

"What did you want to do before?"

"I was waiting tables on the weekends to pay my way

through college night courses during the week. I wanted to work as a physical therapist, but that requires a complete education and training.  Once my husband went down, I became the lone breadwinner for the family. He passed about four years into this job, so I couldn't possibly leave. Two boys require a lot of food, let me tell you."

Olivia chuckled, and Selena grinned. She understood Olivia demanded a certain level of respect from her employees. Many even seemed intimidated.  But all Selena saw was a single mother who had given up on her dreams to support her children. A modern-day angel, as her own mom referred to single mothers.

"I have four years until my oldest will start looking at colleges.  I save all the bonus money I get and put it into a savings account just for that. It might not be much, but it will help."

They continued talking, leaving the law offices and moving up to the next floor, a telemarketing firm where a bullpen full of men and women with headsets shouted into the phones.

"If you could do anything, what would you do?"  Olivia asked.

"I've always wanted to be an actress."

"Well, you moved in the wrong direction. You were already in Hollywood, weren't you? Don't tell me you left it behind for a boy."

"No, of course not.  I just had some personal matters I needed to tend to here in Denver."

"Well, you better get on the plane back to Hollywood whenever it's resolved. Chase that dream. Even if you fail, at least you tried, and you'll never regret it."

Selena sensed a decade's worth of bottled-up emotions

swimming beneath Olivia's calm and focused poise. Life had forced her away from her dreams. But Selena could read between the lines. There was a physical therapist hiding inside of Olivia Bryant. An alternate life that never came into fruition. She wondered what would happen if Olivia's husband had never gotten sick and passed away.

"It's been on my mind. I just might go back someday."

Olivia laughed. "Someday never comes, child. Someday is a myth. A lie we tell ourselves to keep going through reality. It's now or never."

She spoke with the grace of someone who had suffered plenty throughout life. It always seemed the kindest and most optimistic people were that way because they had been hardened in the past.

"I hope you get an opportunity again in the future," Selena said. "You deserve the life you want."

Olivia raised an eyebrow. "Maybe when my kids are done with college, I can revisit it. I might be too old of a lady by then to do physical therapy. This line of work definitely takes a toll on your body. We'll see."

They finished cleaning the bathrooms and returned to the elevator to go up to the next floor.

"Do we ever clean the bank? You mentioned the bank vault. I've never seen one of those in real life. Does it look like the ones in the movies?"

"It's just a big door, nothing to get excited about. But yes, we rotate the floors we cover each day. That is one thing we do to mix things up a bit. There isn't much to clean on that level besides the security office. They are nice guys in there, always friendly. Fortunately, their office space is pretty small, because they are messy men. You'll meet them soon enough."

"I look forward to it."

# Chapter 11

After an uneventful Monday where Felix wasted a day at the apartment for Peter Young's day off, Tuesday morning brought a fresh excitement.

Young left the building, dressed in his security uniform at exactly 7:45 in the morning. Felix had waited outside the complex to confirm his target was indeed out of the building.

He hurried back in to grab his backpack and promptly went down to the fifth floor, stopping outside of apartment 512 and looking around. An elderly woman moseyed down the hallway, grinning at Felix while he pretended to fumble in his backpack.

"Lost my keys," he said with a light chuckle, and the woman continued toward the elevators without a word.

Instead of keys he pulled out a lock pick and entered the apartment within twenty seconds, closing the door and locking it behind him. He stood with his back against the wall and scanned the apartment.

Young lived a messy life. A recliner faced a TV immediately to Felix's left. What looked like a bedroom nightstand stood next to the recliner, covered with nude magazines, empty beer cans, and an ashtray overflowing with cigarette butts. Behind the recliner was an open kitchen, dirty dishes toppling out of the sink, grease splattered on the wall above the stovetop, and more beer cans.

The apartment reeked of cigarette smoke, and Felix was grateful for it. Surely underneath that stench was something more nauseating, judging by the opened food containers left on the kitchen table.

"How the hell can anyone live like this?" Felix asked himself, suddenly horrified at the prospect of needing to move throughout the apartment.

He took a deep breath and started down the short hallway that branched out to the bathroom and bedroom. Felix skipped the bathroom, refusing to imagine how disgusting it would be, and stepped into a surprisingly cleaner bedroom. The bed hadn't been made, and there was a pile of clothes in front of the closet, but aside from that, he saw no beer cans or cigarettes. The pile of dirty clothes touched the low-hanging shirts inside the closet, mostly work uniforms hanging on the rack.

A nightstand stood next to the bed. Felix shuffled to it and pulled open the top drawer to find a handgun on top of a collection of wrist watches. A telephone sat atop the nightstand, so Felix pulled out his bugging kit and tapped the phone line. He hadn't seen a phone in the living room or kitchen, and assumed this was the only one in the place.

The apartment was cluttered enough to set up hidden cameras and microphones, so Felix took the next hour finding the perfect spots to place them. He stuffed a microphone in the bedroom closet, and snapped another to the clock hanging on the wall in the kitchen. He clipped a camera to the bunny-ear antenna above the TV, plugging in its thin cord to the power strip jammed behind the TV.

The cameras were slightly smaller than a tube of lipstick,

and he trusted Young wouldn't recognize them within his mess of a home.  And even if he found one, it would be impossible to know for sure what it was.

It would have been more discreet to place hidden microphones inside a lamp or a drawer, but he had the unique opportunity of being able to watch the live-feed from the apartment two floors above.

He hoped to catch Young planning the burglary. Whether it was discreet phone calls, a secret notebook of plans, or even something as full-blown as bank diagrams.

Felix still had two hours left in his allocated time in the apartment and poked around the mess to see if there were already clues left behind.

He pushed aside the dirty magazines in the living room to find a stack of bills underneath.

"Past due," Felix said, picking up the gas bill. It was two weeks late, and beneath it was the electric bill, a month overdue. "This explains the need for money."

Felix took a step back and rubbed his temples, trying to make sense of the late bills. Sure, a security job at the bank wasn't life-changing money, but it should have covered the basic bills. Just where was the man's money going, aside from the liquor store?

Felix dropped the bills back on the table and returned to the bedroom.  The robbery suspect had worn a fedora and sunglasses, and that's exactly what Felix hoped to find. The top shelf of the closet was as much of a mess as the floor. Shoe boxes piled atop each other, buried under miscellaneous clothing items like hats, ties, beanies, scarfs, and gloves.

After rummaging through at least a dozen Denver Nuggets and Broncos ballcaps, Felix found two fedoras buried against the back wall. His hands trembled as he pulled out the hats, staring at them like they were the smoking gun in this entire mission.

"Lots of people own fedoras," he reminded himself. "I'm sure Kennedy owns fedoras, too."

Felix studied the hats. Both were gray. One had faint black pinstripes, the other was solid with a black ribbon tied around the base. None of the witnesses had accurately described the fedora worn that day, only that there had been one.

If only he could get into Kennedy's house and confirm what types of hats he owned. Should he not find a fedora in Kennedy's closet, then matters became more interesting. He returned the fedoras and replaced everything how he had found it in the closet. Sunglasses were nowhere to be seen, but could have been in Peter's car, or even on his person. It was summer, after all.

A knock came from the door, and every ounce of Felix's blood froze in its tracks. He spun around from the closet and listened to make sure the doorknob wasn't being twisted or unlocked. His heart drummed in his ears, making the task that much more difficult.

A second knock banged on the door, not soft, not too hard.

Felix crouched as he tiptoed out of the bedroom, staring at the door. Sweat immediately formed on his palms. These were the situations Felix dreaded. If it had been Arielle in the apartment right now, she would have already identified every possible weapon within arm's reach, and the best places to hide from a potential intruder.

A third knock came, this time accompanied by a deep voice. "You in there, Pete? We don't have time for these games."

Felix held his breath, refusing to emit a single sound and

reveal his presence. He thought back to the gun in the nightstand and debated dashing back into the bedroom to get it.

Instead, a sheet of paper slid from under the door, and Felix listened as footsteps trailed away down the hall before stepping forward to read it.

*Two dimes by the end of the month.* The words were scribbled, barely legible.

"Two dimes?" Felix said aloud, wanting so badly to take the note, but not wanting his fingerprints left on anything. Also, he wouldn't dare remove it. The letter was clearly important and meant for Peter Young. "Holy shit."

Felix was plenty familiar with the world of sports betting, but it took him a moment to remember bookies used the term *dime.*

"Young owes a bookie two thousand dollars by the end of the month. That's where all his money has gone. He has a gambling problem."

Young needed a lump sum of money in a hurry. And what better way to get it than to rob the bank he worked at?

Felix's internal timer had gone off. It was time to leave the apartment. He had done everything he needed and could monitor the activity from the comforts of his living room two floors above.

He stepped around the note and hurried out of the apartment, pulling the door to ensure it shut all the way. As he started toward the stairwell, the man's voice from earlier called out from the opposite end of the hallway. "Who the hell are you?! Come back here!"

Felix jerked his head around, made quick eye contact with a man of at least six and a half feet, dressed in black pants and a matching leather coat, and broke into a sprint toward the stairwell.

It was all he could think of doing, and considering how long the hallways were, and how much space was between the two men, figured it was the right decision. Speed had always been Felix's best weapon, even as far back as high school. Bullies had picked on him for no apparent reason other than being a scrawny, awkward freshman. After one encounter, he simply ran away from the bullies. They could never catch him, unwilling to exert so much physical effort for something hardly worth their time.

By the time Felix reached the door to the stairwell, he looked back to see the man barreling down the hallway, but not even to Peter's door yet. Felix jumped onto the third step and dashed up the stairs until reaching the door to the seventh floor. He swung it open and hurried down the hall to their apartment, gasping for breath as he inserted the key and let himself in.

Felix slammed the door and tossed his backpack on the floor, arms spread as he slid down to the floor, smiling. His legs had once more saved him.

He had just escaped a potentially horrid situation. One thing had become immediately clear, on only their fourth day since arriving in 1991:

The past was already pushing back.

# Chapter 12

Arielle sat outside Jacob Kennedy's home on Wednesday for the third day in a row.

So far, each morning saw Kennedy's wife leave around 7:30 A.M. and return home at 4:30 P.M. She apparently hadn't reached the age of retirement like her husband.  Arielle considered this another motive for Kennedy to steal the money. Perhaps he stewed all day at home alone, guilty that he spent his days crafting model boats while his wife had to put in actual work. Maybe robbing a bank would allow her to retire.

*Get him out of your head*, Arielle had to remind herself. She had no proof that he had robbed the place, and just because he had stood trial didn't mean he had committed the crime. She hated this new type of mission. Before, she knew everything about her targets and their involvement with whatever crime had been committed. If she got too hung up on Kennedy as the suspect, she might miss opportunities that suggested otherwise. She needed to control her bias if she wanted any chance of solving this mystery.

Kennedy hadn't so much as stepped foot outside his home on Monday and Tuesday, making this mission that much more difficult. Never mind them not having the chance to bug the place, but Arielle couldn't gain any information if all he did was sit inside. After two excruciating days of boredom, Arielle spun her own theories as she saw him occasionally through the kitchen window, and other times at the dining room table where he worked on the model boats.

She hadn't even seen a clear view of him since arriving in 1991, and she wondered how many more days she could handle of the non-activity before giving up on Kennedy as a suspect. One couldn't rob a bank from their living room.

Finally, on Wednesday morning at exactly 10:41, Jacob Kennedy stepped out of his front door and trudged to his truck in the driveway. Arielle's heart nearly jumped out of her throat as she whipped out her binoculars from her duffel bag on the passenger seat and saw Kennedy live in the flesh for the first time. He had a thick mustache and wore a solid black ballcap low enough to cover his brow. Kennedy dressed in a relaxed summer outfit of jean shorts and a t-shirt decorated with a bald eagle hovering over the American flag.

He slipped behind the wheel of a beaten Ford pickup, and pulled out of the driveway in a hurry.

Arielle turned her car on and flipped it around to follow. She had rented a 1990 Honda Accord for the mission, sure to get black in case she needed to blend in at night. Felix had joined her and rented a Ford Taurus from the same year, leaving them both with transportation for the two weeks they'd spend in the past.

Kennedy drove slow through the neighborhood, and sped up significantly once on the main roads. She followed him for ten minutes and noticed he didn't once violate a traffic law. He finally pulled into a strip mall where he parked in front of a sandwich shop, The Mad Wich.

Kennedy disappeared inside for a few minutes before he reappeared empty-handed and strolled further down to a store called HobbyTown USA. Arielle killed the engine and hopped out of the car, charging toward the store and stepping in.

A bell jingled from above the door, and she looked around to make sure Kennedy hadn't noticed her. He was already down an aisle with boxes of model boat kits.

The shop wasn't too spacious, and only had three aisles, all filled with similar kits for model boats, planes, cars, and helicopters. The aisle aligned with the entrance had a glass counter display with already completed models. Behind it, where only an employee had access, were shelves filled with thumb-sized jars of paint, rubber cement, and paintbrushes in every size imaginable. No one stood at the cash register at the far end of the counter, so Arielle looked toward the back to find Kennedy disappearing behind another door with what must have been an employee.

She went down the aisle with model car kits. The first car she saw was a 1985 Audi Quattro, her father's dream car. He kept posters of the car all throughout the walls in the garage, and many evenings when she'd venture out to tell him dinner was ready, he'd pause from his workbench and nod to the pictures on the wall.

"I'm gonna build that car one day, if I have to," he'd say. "If that's the only way I can get it, I'll build it piece by piece. And I'll leave it for you and your brother when I'm gone. It might not look like much, but those suckers are *fast*."

Arielle never understood her father's obsession with the car, but she planned to one day buy it for him. She never had that chance, nor did he ever build it. Seeing the car brought a rush of memories, and her face prickled with heat as she fought away more emotions. She didn't see Kennedy step out of the back door with the store's associate, the two of them chatting about model boats and sharing a laugh.

They headed directly down the aisle where she stood, and Arielle felt her legs lock as she reached out to grab the car kit.

"Oh, hello, ma'am," the employee said. He was perhaps a decade younger than Kennedy, and offered a warm smile. "Sorry if I kept you waiting. Is there something I can help you with?"

The man stopped next to her while Kennedy walked past, brushing against her shoulder in the narrow aisle.

"I was just looking for something for my dad for Father's Day," Arielle said, glancing over her shoulder to see if Kennedy had any reaction to the mention of the holiday. He did not, and continued out of the building. "I'm really just shopping around to get ideas and prices. These models might be a little out of my budget."

The door closed, and Kennedy was out of view. Arielle shoved the kit back on the shelf and pivoted around, speaking over her shoulder. "I'm so sorry, but something just came up."

The man looked from her and back to the kit, shrugging his shoulders and rubbing his head as Arielle hurried out the door. She looked to Kennedy's truck, didn't see him, then looked to her right just in time to see him step into another business.

Arielle returned to the car and felt her mind spin as she looked up at the sign above the door Kennedy had just entered. "D&D Guns and Ammo," she whispered to herself, slipping behind the steering wheel and grabbing her binoculars. The windows were reflective glass, so she only saw herself.

"Dammit!" She punched the steering wheel and tossed the binoculars aside.

She couldn't possibly follow him into the gun shop—that would be too obvious. She had one chance to follow him and wasted it on the craft store, where she didn't learn a single thing about Kennedy or why he went in.

Arielle stewed, legs bouncing, fingers drumming on the steering wheel while she glared at the door, waiting for Kennedy to step back outside.

After five minutes he did, a brown paper bag clutched in his right hand.

"He bought ammo," Arielle said, watching as he returned to the sandwich shop further down the strip.

She couldn't bear the thought of wasting this first opportunity of Kennedy stepping foot outside his house, and reached into her duffel bag, feeling around until her fingers wrapped around a fake FBI badge.

It was a fake badge she carried with her on all missions, just in case the opportunity arose for her to use it. It was a replica of the badges used by the FBI, and rested inside a wallet with a fake FBI identification card. To an average citizen, they'd have no reason to question it. Even most police officers would take one glance at it and believe it was real.

It *was* real, by all definitions. But Arielle was not an actual FBI agent, and that would take time for any authority to figure out.

She stepped out of the car and shuffled toward The Mad Wich, peered through the glass and was pleased to find Kennedy sitting at a table by himself, unwrapping a foot-long sandwich while the brown bag sat on the table opposite him.

*Got at least fifteen minutes,* she thought, and dashed down the sidewalk, stepping into the gun shop. Rifles covered the walls around the store, while glass counters housed the smaller handguns. More racks stood in the center of the floor containing hunting rifles. Security cameras watched from every corner of the room, and Arielle made sure to keep her head cocked downward.

"Good morning, miss," the clerk said from behind the counter. He was an older man with wavy white hair and a matching goatee. A pair of sunglasses sat atop his head, and he wore a black polo shirt with the company's logo embroidered on it, two pistols overlapping each other, *D&D Guns* curved around the top of the image. "How can I help you today?"

She whipped out her badge, flashed it for two seconds, and tucked it into her back pocket. "I'm agent Lucia Ariano with the FBI. I need to ask some questions about the gentleman who just bought some ammunition from you?" She always used the alias of Lucia Ariano when impersonating an FBI agent. Something about the name felt official, and it cast no doubt when she started questioning people.

The clerk took a step back, and his eyes glanced toward the door. "I'm sorry, what is this about?"

"That man is a suspect in a major crime, and I need to know what exactly he bought."

"Do you have a warrant? And can I see that badge again?"

Arielle reached back and flashed the badge again, this time holding it open a few seconds longer to allow the gentleman to read it. "I'm afraid I don't have a warrant. Just been tailing that man for the past couple of days. Hoping you can help me as a favor."

"The hell I will," the man said, a frown taking over his face. "The government has no right to barge into my store and demand information without a warrant. Come back with a warrant signed by a judge, and *maybe* I'll share information with you."

"Sir, I don't mean any disrespect, but I am not *demanding* anything of you. I'm asking a favor. Think of it as a favor to your country."

"Bullshit! Don't try that slick-talking nonsense on me. A favor to my country is protecting the private information of my fellow citizen. I'm not telling you anything. Please leave my shop, and good luck. Don't step back in here without a warrant. If you do, I'll consider it trespassing, and I know my rights."

"Good day," Arielle said, and turned around to leave.

"Fucking bitch," the man muttered under his breath.

Arielle paused at the door, blood boiling throughout her entire body. She clenched her fists, knowing that turning back around would end horribly. She swallowed her pride and stepped outside, blowing out a long exhale from her mouth.

Few things ruffled Arielle Lucila, but sexist remarks always led to a fury she sometimes couldn't contain. If she had been a man, the clerk might have been more cooperative.

*A fucking bitch*, she thought, shaking her head. If her mission was to cleanse the world of bigots, she would have turned around and taught the clerk a lesson. But it wasn't.

Arielle gathered her emotions and started back to the sandwich shop when she noticed a pay phone at the end of the sidewalk. She ran past The Mad Wich, glancing to confirm Kennedy was still seated at the table with his sandwich.

A man stood near the pay phone, leaning against the building while smoking a cigarette.

"Excuse me, sir," Arielle said. "Do you have any spare

change so I can make a call? It's important, or else I wouldn't ask."

The man plucked the cigarette from his mouth and grinned. He looked a few years older than Arielle, and she hoped he wouldn't start hitting on her. She didn't have time for that shit right now. He pushed himself off the building.

"I work here," he said, gesturing to the building behind him, Arielle realizing it was a laundromat. "I have plenty of change, give me one second."

He nodded and turned around to enter the laundromat, Arielle watching as he moseyed toward the back and out of sight.

After two minutes, Arielle was about to start toward her car when she saw the man's head appear through the window, bobbing up and down as he made his way back outside. He held a hand out, four quarters resting in his palm. "This should be good for a few calls."

"Thank you so much," Arielle said, opening her hand so he could dump the coins.

"Not a problem at all. What's your name? Are you from around here?"

"Just passing by, sorry. I really need to make this call."

The man raised his hands in a *don't-shoot-me* manner and took two steps backward. He pulled out another cigarette and returned to his perch against the laundromat's exterior.

Arielle hurried back to the pay phone and popped in the coins, dialing their apartment phone number. It rang twice before Felix picked up.

"It's me," Arielle said. "How fast can you get to Kennedy's house?"

"Uh, I think it took me fifteen minutes last time."

"Well, drive faster, and get there in ten. I think I can buy us some time—he's not home. Get over there!"

Arielle hung up before Felix could respond, a negotiation tactic she had learned.  It created urgency and put tons of pressure on the recipient to make a move.  Felix wouldn't argue either way, but hanging up would certainly get him out of his seat faster and into the car.

The smoking man watched Arielle, but she spun around and jogged back to her car before he could say anything else. She opened the passenger door and fumbled through the duffel bag until she pulled out a screwdriver.

Arielle closed the door and shuffled across the lot toward Kennedy's truck, keeping the screwdriver pinned in her armpit, eyes stuck on the sandwich shop's only door to see if Kennedy would step outside. The man continued to smoke his cigarette, intently peering at her.

She reached the truck and decided to first take a quick look through the windows. A soda can sat in the cupholder in an otherwise clean truck. One cigarette butt lay in the ashtray, but it didn't seem he smoked too often—she had yet to see him do it over the past couple of days.

The bed of the truck held a rolled-up tarp, some rope, and a toolbox. Still nothing that suggested he might be in the midst of planning a bank robbery.

Arielle squatted down by the rear passenger tire and looked around to make sure no one could see her. Just as she reared back the screwdriver to plow it into the rubber, a voice shouted.

"Hey! What are you doing?! Get the hell away!"

Arielle looked up to see the gun shop clerk yelling from the door. He had one hand on the pistol on his waist and started toward her.

"Shit!" she cried, standing up and breaking into a sprint toward her car. She nearly dove into the driver's seat, tossed the screwdriver on the duffel bag and jammed the keys into the ignition.

The clerk had stopped at Kennedy's truck for a quick inspection and had only looked back up in Arielle's direction as she peeled out of the parking lot. Smoke flew from the back tires as she burned rubber and jerked the car onto the main road, speeding off with constant looks into the rearview.

"Will he actually follow me?" she said, shaking her head. The clerk hadn't moved with such urgency to suggest he wanted to tail her, but she couldn't show her face at that strip mall again for the rest of the mission. The clerk was already paranoid about their encounter and would surely be waiting to take a shot at the faux FBI agent if he saw her snooping around the property again.

Arielle panted for air, not having had such a close call while doing menial work on a mission. All she wanted to do was pop one of Kennedy's tires to buy Felix some time bugging the house. She had passed a tire shop one block away, and knew he'd have no problem getting it replaced. But she couldn't have slashed it after the clerk saw her. He'd definitely make a call to the police and have people alerted around the strip mall to keep an eye out for the young, suspicious woman who called herself an FBI agent. He was probably going to call the police, anyway.

*Why is this so difficult?* she wondered, staring into the rearview. The past was already gearing up for a fight, and it wasn't even the week of the crime yet. Her stomach churned at the thought of how much worse the past might push back as they drew closer to the big day.

Despite the resistance, Arielle held hope. If Kennedy hadn't committed the crime, then the past wouldn't already be pushing so hard.

# Chapter 13

Arielle had a rough night after the debacle at the strip mall. She had returned to Kennedy's house and stood watch for a couple more hours. Felix had shown up too late—Kennedy was already back home, too.

They returned to the apartment and Arielle locked herself in her bedroom for the rest of the night, citing a need to review the mission file to understand what was making the initial three days so difficult. She called for a group meeting the next morning over breakfast to discuss their findings so far.

She had never opened the mission file, instead taking a rare moment of defeat as she crawled under her sheets and stared at the ceiling for hours before eventually falling asleep. A heaviness filled her stomach. She didn't want dinner. No TV. No books.

When she woke on Thursday, the sense of dread remained, and she dressed while mentally preparing for another boring day—or perhaps chaos.

She stepped out to the smell of fresh waffles and fruit. Felix had prepared breakfast and was filling the glasses with orange juice when she entered the kitchen. "Good morning, Arielle," he said, offering a warm smile.

"Morning. Selena up yet?"

"I'm here, relax," Selena said, charging out of her room, dressed in her custodial uniform. "Everything okay, Arielle? You seemed off yesterday."

Arielle shuffled toward the table and sat down. "I'm fine. Was just a rough day. And I guess I'm not used to having those."

"Let's talk about it," Felix said, turning off the knobs on the stove before taking his seat at the table. Selena followed suit and promptly took a swig of orange juice. "So what's going on?"

She shook her head as she poked at the whipped cream topping the waffle. "I'm frustrated. I don't enjoy this kind of work—detective work, essentially. We have ten days until the crime and it feels like we've made zero progress. This time is supposed to be spent trying to figure out how to stop it from happening, not *who* did it. Everything I've explained to you about closing off your mind from the past is a lost cause on this mission. I can't close my mind from my intentions, because I don't even know what they are yet. The past is already pushing back. If things had escalated even just a little more yesterday, I would have been shot at."

Arielle balled a fist and slammed it on the table, the plates and silverware clattering.

"Whoa," Selena said. "Take it easy."

"No. I just said I could have been shot. Yesterday. *Ten days* before the crime. Ten days! Bullets! That's not supposed to happen until the day of. Just how ugly is this going to get? I don't understand all the resistance already. Do either of you have anything of substance yet?"

Felix and Selena exchanged glances. "Nothing yet from Young," Felix said. "And you know the drama I had that day.

I probably would have been shot, too, if I hung around long enough."

"My point exactly. This is dangerous. We can't do missions like this anymore. What does Young do in his free time?"

"Not much. He eats lots of microwave dinners. Smokes a ton of cigarettes. Drinks beer on his lounger while he watches *Wheel of Fortune* and *Jeopardy* all night. I've watched him for three days, and each day he falls asleep on the lounger. Two nights he woke up and moved to his bed, but the first night he just stayed there. He hasn't made a call beside the pizza he had delivered last night. Hasn't left the place outside of work hours. I don't know, Arielle, but he kind of seems like a waste of time to monitor. At least you got a little more with Kennedy. He went into a gun shop and bought ammo. That's *something*, right?"

Arielle tossed her hands up. "It's more than TV dinners, but it doesn't mean anything. What about you, Selena? Have you crossed paths yet with Young at the bank?"

"Not yet. I've seen some of the other guards, but never Young. We really only see them at the beginning and end of our shifts—we clock in and out near their offices. I won't lie, this work is killing me."

"I know. Sounds like we're all suffering. I'm afraid you have to keep doing this job. Your keycard access to the building is all we need next Sunday. Have you had any luck finding a hiding place?"

"I have a couple spots of interest. The north side of the eighteenth floor is vacant. Open floor space with conference rooms and closets. Plenty of space to hide comfortably."

Arielle wanted a tentative plan for someone on the team to hide out next Saturday night, guaranteeing they would be in the building the morning of the robbery. "Okay, that's good. We'll see how it all plays out. Felix, I might move you to that post if we're certain Young isn't involved. I'll be following Kennedy that morning."

"I don't like that," Felix said. "We're still assuming it was Kennedy. What if it's not? Then you're leaving myself and Selena alone in the building while you're following an innocent man. Seems wasteful."

"None of this is set in stone," Arielle said. "A lot can change in ten days, and it better. Is Young working today?"

Felix shrugged. "We don't know his schedule. He was up this morning, but not dressed yet. Dude sleeps naked, so I'm going to need some serious brainwashing to get that imagery out of my head. I can check back shortly."

Selena fake heaved at the mention of Young walking around naked in his apartment, and this earned light laughter from Arielle.

"Please do," Arielle said. "If he leaves for work, I want you to head straight to Kennedy's house. We can't waste another opportunity. We need the inside of that place at least bugged with mics, preferably cameras if possible. If Kennedy leaves, I'll follow him, and you need to sneak in."

Felix recoiled at the instruction.

"Is something the matter?" Arielle asked. "You've done this plenty of times."

"It's just that you're right. This mission is drastically different. Nothing feels like a normal trip. I can feel the resistance in the air. I'm not comfortable breaking into Kennedy's house, at least forcibly. If the door is unlocked, that's a different story, but if I have to pick a lock or climb through a window. . ." Felix looked into the distance and shivered like he had seen a ghost. "I just don't know, Arielle. My gut is telling me a lot can go wrong. *Horribly* wrong."

Arielle raised her hands. "Let's calm down. Everything is different about this mission, yes, but let's not get ahead of ourselves. Danger is always a risk, no matter how prepared we are. You should remain diligent. You had a close call at the last mission, but got out just fine."

"This time should be easier," Selena said. "We know the schedule for Kennedy's house. Well, his wife's. She leaves at the same time and returns at the same time every day. Once Kennedy leaves, he is the only variable. But Arielle will be on his tail and I'm sure she could buy you some time."

"Of course," Arielle said. "I'm comfortable with that, even if it means parking in front of his house and speaking with him to stall. It's risky, sure, but nothing life-threatening. In fact, the past might not even take issue with the conversation as long as I keep it neutral and boring."

"And your head clear of what we're doing," Felix said, crossing his arms. "You just admitted that hasn't been easy on this mission."

Arielle nodded. "You're right. But this is our job. Don't you remember when they warned you of this in training? They said there will be a time when you become so good at what you do, that it becomes second nature. You'll get so comfortable with your routine that you'll become blinded to the risks that are always present. Then one day, you'll face a challenge that shakes you out of that comfort zone, and you're suddenly scared to do the work you've always done. Looks like we've all arrived at that point with this mission."

"It's true," Selena said, chuckling. "Do you think I planned to clean so many damn toilets in the name of a mission? Hell no. I get high from the chemicals by ten o'clock every morning. I want this mission to end as much as you both. It's just been an awful experience all around."

"Sure, but your life isn't at risk cleaning toilets," Felix said. "I already had an encounter with someone who I'm pretty sure was a bookie. The kind with a jar of thumbs on his desk. And now, we're dealing with Kennedy, who we presume pulled off a bank robbery and *got away with it.*"

Arielle stood up. "Look, this is what we have to do. We know to not put ourselves in harm's way. Go to Kennedy's house and plant some bugs when he leaves. If something arises that prevents you from doing it, then don't do it. Same as every other mission you've ever worked on." She picked up her dishes and dropped them in the sink. "Now, I'm going to his house to do my job. Hopefully something of substance happens today. I'm not having this conversation again. Are we clear?"

Arielle rarely used an authoritative tone with her peers, but it worked when she needed. Felix nodded in silence, glaring at the crumbs left behind on his plate. Selena took her last bite as her eyes dashed back and forth from Felix to Arielle.

"Good," Arielle said. "I'll see you both tonight. Have a good day."

She turned and left the apartment, grabbing her backpack on the way out and slamming the door shut behind her. This was the type of friction she had feared upon learning they would work together permanently as a team. They hadn't encountered many issues on their prior mission, but this one was putting them all to the test. Pushing their limits.

They needed to make progress within the next couple days, or else major problems loomed on the horizon.

Arielle wouldn't dare say it aloud, but she had been thinking of a scenario that rarely happened in her career as an Angel.

*Failure.*

# Chapter 14

A couple hours later, Peter Young left for work. Felix watched the live-feed as Young scampered around the apartment dressed in his security uniform, scarfing down a bowl of cereal, lighting up a cigarette, and hurriedly shaving his face before he dashed out of the building.

Felix felt his gut tighten with dread. He had to head over to Kennedy's house, where—he hoped—his day would pass without having to do anything. He really didn't want to enter Kennedy's home. The whole matter felt off, unlike any other task he'd had to do for the Angels before. For someone who stuck to data and facts, his gut feeling was getting the best of him.

"You'll be fine," he told himself in the bathroom mirror, splashing water on his face. "You have a job to do, and you're the best at it. Go in, plant some mics, and slip out without a problem. Arielle will be nearby if he returns too soon."

Felix gulped, then nodded before leaving the bathroom to retrieve his backpack stuffed with lock picks, microphones, and other accessories needed to bug the Kennedy house.

As he took the stairs to the parking garage, Felix couldn't help but look over his shoulder. He had done just that every time he stepped outside their apartment, worried the monstrous bookie would be back, hunting for Felix now instead of Young.

He'd yet to see anyone knock on Young's door since that day and wondered if the man would stay away since an eyewitness had spotted him.

*Or maybe Young told him he's going to rob the bank he works at and will have the money next weekend.*

Felix shook the thought away. No one in their right mind would confide in someone that they planned to rob a bank.

He reached his Taurus without a problem and reluctantly pulled it out of the garage and onto the road. Traffic was light as the early morning rush hour had already passed. Business people hurried up and down the sidewalks, briefcases and purses in hand. Felix rolled down his window to let the summer air fill his lungs, drawing in a deep breath as he waited at a red light.

A convertible Mazda pulled up in the lane next to him, an attractive woman smiling as she made direct eye contact. Felix looked away and stared ahead, his face flushing as he felt heat prickle his skin.

"Where you off to, cutie?" the woman called over, and Felix felt her eyes burning into the side of his head.

He worked up the courage to return a grin. "Going to work."

"That's too bad. I'm headed to grab some coffee and would love some company."

Felix hadn't gone on a date with a woman since joining the Road Runners, and the unexpected invite sent his emotions into a whirl. He was intrigued. Not one for spontaneity, Felix supposed his interest only came because he wanted to avoid Kennedy's house. How much did they really *need* to bug the inside of the house?

"The light's about to change," the woman shouted. "You coming or not?"

"I wish I could, but I really have to get to work."

The girl shrugged and sped off as soon as the light turned green.

*Dammit,* he thought. An opportunity like that would never come again. Felix believed he was attractive, yet did little to highlight that fact. He dressed simple and preferred to blend in with the masses. As a result, women never hit on him, and it had taken him a moment to even realize that was happening at the red light.

Any time he called home, his mother always asked if he was seeing someone yet. And he always disappointed her with a negative response. He loved his work and had no time for extracurricular activities if he wanted to keep his status as the top Angel in his field. On days off, he watched sports and movies, read books, and got in a workout. All his friends were back in San Francisco, so he had virtually no social life in Denver. And he was fine with that.

But he couldn't deny the excitement he had just felt. The flutter in his stomach that came with speaking to someone of the opposite sex. Felix considered the countless possibilities that could come from following the woman to the coffee shop. Her car was still in sight, but he shook his head and continued to Kennedy's house. The fun would have to wait for another day, preferably while not on a mission.

"Was probably just the past trying to stop me."

Felix had heard plenty of stories about the past dropping random people in the middle of a mission to detract from the work. Many time travelers had fallen into the trap, guided by their own lust or overwhelming desire for love, only to find none of it was actually real. Just a thorough distraction.

He cleared his mind over the next ten minutes, and when he arrived at the Kennedy residence, he found Arielle across the street from the house and parked behind her.

She looked at him in the rearview and gave a quick nod, acknowledging his presence. Neither would step out of the car—not on this mission. On prior missions, Felix might have gone and sat with Arielle while they waited for something to happen. This trip into the past had too many unknown factors and risks. They handled every decision with kid gloves to decrease the chances of something going horribly wrong.

Felix looked at Kennedy's house and saw nothing. The two windows revealed empty rooms. Kennedy's truck sat in the driveway. A neighbor three houses down sat on their front porch and watered the lawn, sipping from a mug of coffee. Felix would forever envy people who got to enjoy such simplicity in life. His life as a Road Runner had created a sense of urgency behind every waking moment. He wondered if life would ever slow down enough to sit back and enjoy the fresh morning air without a care in the world.

Suddenly, the front door swung open and Kennedy appeared in the doorway, a backpack slung over his shoulder. He stepped out and drew a deep breath before locking the door and getting into his truck, tossing the backpack on the passenger seat.

Felix looked ahead to Arielle, seeing her strap her seatbelt on, the car rumbling to life in sync with Kennedy's truck. She looked in the rearview and nodded at Felix, instantly sending his stomach into a spiral.

"Shit," he muttered, reclining his seat to stay out of Kennedy's view.

He remained below the window for the next thirty seconds while he listened to the sounds of both vehicles drive off. When he sat back up, the block appeared deserted. The neighbor was no longer watering their lawn. Kennedy's driveway was empty.

Felix sat alone, nothing but his own fear standing between him and the house.

"This is really happening," he told himself, leaning over to grab his duffel bag full of bugging devices. He waited one more minute to make sure Kennedy wasn't returning.

Not a single car came down the block, so Felix opened his door and stepped onto the pavement on wobbly legs.

"It's the same job. Nothing is different. Get out of your head."

He looked both ways and proceeded toward Kennedy's driveway, hurrying to disappear around the side of the house.

Kennedy had clearly locked the front door, so Felix didn't bother trying it—not that he ever attempted to break in through the front. Instead, he circled around to the back, grateful no fence was present.

The backyard hadn't received nearly as much attention as the front. Weeds sprouted throughout the lawn and from the cracks of the concrete patio. A shed stood in the far corner, the door off its hinges and leaning against the exterior. Gardening tools and a lawn mower spilled out from it.

Felix returned his attention to the back door and tried the knob, finding it locked. In a swift motion, he reached into the backpack's side zipper and retrieved his lock pick, stuffing it into the keyhole and twisting until he heard the magical click of the door opening.

He twisted the knob and let the door creak open, revealing

the kitchen. He didn't step in right away, always allowing a few seconds to make sure the house was indeed empty and no one came scrambling to close the door. Silence filled the room as he entered and shut the door behind him.

"Anyone home?" he called out, ready to turn and run if a reply came.

But none did, so he stepped through the kitchen, spotting a newspaper open on the table, and clean dishes sitting on a drying rack next to the sink. Felix had been in plenty of homes thanks to his job, and this looked to be one of the cleaner ones.

"Just get in and out," he whispered to himself, taking off his backpack and unzipping it. A quick scan around the kitchen revealed no opportunities to plant a camera. He rarely had the chance to plant one inside a home since the wireless miniature cameras only had batteries with a lifespan of a few hours. The microphones lasted much longer and only activated when sound was audible. The bugs he planted sufficed for the typical two-week missions. The only thing he had to change were the tapes on the receiver he'd hide somewhere outside, preferably in a thick bush.

Felix climbed on top of the counter. His favorite place to plant a bug in the kitchen was the light structure above the sink.

Just as he felt around, the rumble of an engine turned into the driveway outside. "What the hell?" Felix gasped, and jumped down from the sink, failing to have planted the bug.

The kitchen opened to the dining room that faced the front yard, so Felix craned his neck for a view and saw a black car in the driveway. A man had stepped out and gazed at the house.

"Shit!"

Felix pulled the backpack over his shoulder and started for

the back door. The man's silhouette appeared through the blinds, and Felix spun around, lunging into the dining room. The back door's knob started turning.

He dashed out of the dining room and down the hallway, hearing the door open and shut. His heart drummed from his stomach to his head. Sweat trickled down his back as he entered the master bedroom and immediately dove under the bed.

Felix tugged on his backpack, twisting and squeezing to make it fit under the bed with him. He gasped for breath while all his senses ran in overdrive, listening attentively as shuffling footsteps approached from the hall.

"Dad?" a man's voice called out. "Are you here?"

Felix cupped his hand over his nose and mouth, his breathing still out of control. His face flushed, arms shuddering, as he scooted further under the bed to stay out of sight from whoever was wandering through the Kennedy household.

*Kennedy has a son*, Felix reminded himself. *The son was a witness in the trial.*

These thoughts made Felix dizzy. If the son spotted Felix under the bed, that would certainly provoke the past to unleash a fury of vengeance. His breathing remained irregular; he had no choice but to hold his breath once he saw two feet appear in the bedroom doorway.

"Dad?" the voice called again, this time much louder, practically on top of Felix.

He watched the feet shuffle into the room, turning left and stopping in front of the dresser. The feet turned to face the dresser and remained a few seconds while the sound of ruffling papers filled the silence.

Felix wanted desperately to poke his head out to see what

was happening, but wouldn't dare take that gamble. He tensed his entire body to stop it from shaking, horrifying thoughts running through his mind.

What if Kennedy's son planned to wait around until his father returned home? If that occurred, what would happen if Kennedy had another stretch of multiple days without leaving the house? Just how the hell was Felix supposed to get out from under the bed without being caught? He imagined the gut-wrenching prospect of somehow ending up stuck under the bed for the next week, starving and thirsty, unable to scurry for the exit.

*Don't be dramatic,* he told himself. *There will be at least one opportunity to get out of this house today.*

His heart rate had calmed down, his breathing nearly under control. The feet standing at the dresser had turned and started toward the bed, and Felix felt the weight press down on his back as Kennedy's son sat down on the edge. Had this happened even one minute earlier, Felix might have vomited because of his anxiety attack. But now, he was too focused on finding a way out.

Five minutes passed before Kennedy's son finally hopped off the bed and returned to the dresser. Felix heard buttons being pushed and presumed he was dialing a phone. This was confirmed once the man spoke.

"Hey. He's not here. I got here ten minutes ago. His truck wasn't in the driveway."

Now Felix craned his neck for a better listen. He could only hear the crackle of a voice speaking back through the receiver.

"Okay. Will do," Kennedy's son said, and hung up the phone.

Felix suspected whatever was said on the other end of the

call would determine if he'd remain under the bed for the foreseeable future, or leave.

Kennedy's son remained at the dresser for two more minutes before straggling out of the room. Felix listened while he took a piss in the bathroom next door and finally made his way out of the house.

When the back door slammed shut, relief immediately flooded over Felix. He waited five more minutes before slithering out from the bed and hurried to the dresser, where he discovered a stack of papers.

On top was an early draft of a living will document. Beneath that was a stack of bills, most of which appeared past due.

*Money problems,* he thought. *Just like Young.*

Felix had enough. He hadn't wanted to enter this house in the first place and had barely escaped getting caught breaking and entering. He planted no bugs, nor did he care at this point. Someone who didn't live in the house had just let themselves in unannounced—a major red flag for Felix's work, and something he'd never gamble with.

"That's enough of this place," Felix said, zipping up his backpack and bolting for the back door.

# Chapter 15

On Friday afternoon, Selena had waited in the bathroom until 5:10. Her shift was over, and she wanted to make sure Olivia left the premises.

She remained in her uniform and felt mentally ready to head down to the basement levels to see what information she could gather about the security office and the vault that belonged to United Bank.

Before stepping out of the restroom, she took a moment in front of the mirrors, splashing water on her face and staring at herself.

"You got this."

Selena might have over-hyped her upcoming task, mainly because she had never dealt with a bank vault before. She imagined the security similar to a Hollywood portrayal. Cameras in every corner, crisscrossed lasers daring someone to trip an alarm that would blare loud enough for everyone between Denver and Dallas to hear.

She knew this vault had nothing remotely close to that type of intense security, but the gravity of her task—and the entire mission—blew things out of proportion within her imagination.

She imagined once she approached the vault, the guards

would scream and tackle her. They'd file an official report, call Olivia at home, terminate her employment, and revoke her badge on the spot.

With a quick head shake, Selena left the bathroom on the tenth floor, where she had finished her shift, and caught an elevator to the subbasement level.

When the doors parted, she braced to see any coworkers. The cleaning crew's locker room was in the subbasement level, but she found an empty hallway once she stepped out. Her waiting game had worked, as she figured it would on a Friday afternoon. No one had interest in hanging around to chat—it was time for the weekend.

Cameras covered every floor of the building, and Selena realized she might look suspicious as she stood outside the elevator for an entire minute. She snapped out of her thoughts and started down the hall, opening the doors to a storage closet that housed their cleaning equipment.

She pulled out a cart and loaded it with paper towels, a bottle of glass cleaner, a broom, and a vacuum, figuring these options would appear standard to the security team who would soon see her outside of their office. Selena tucked her shirt back into her pants and made sure all of her buttons were in their proper places.

The subbasement level rarely had traffic outside of the cleaning crew and maintenance workers. Security never had a reason to come down since the area had restricted access. The main basement was one level up, and that's where the security team had their office a few steps away from the bank's vault.

With the cart loaded, she pushed it down the hallway to the elevators and called a car. The motor hummed, and Selena's guts tightened while she waited.

"Give your best performance," she whispered to herself. "That's all you can do. You're a seasoned cleaner just doing her job."

The elevator doors parted, and she stepped in, a musty smell filling the small space. She rode it up one level and stepped out to another empty hallway.

The area mirrored the subbasement level. Concrete floors and walls. No attempt at a single decoration. The lighting, however, was much brighter. A couple of doors stood closed along the walls, presumably more storage space.

Selena started forward, making a concentrated effort to move at a normal pace down the hall. Her eyes stayed ahead, waiting for someone to step out of the security office and send her back.

But no one did, and within a quick minute, she stood directly outside the security office.

The door was solid, but the walls were glass, giving Selena a clear view inside. From the door, she tipped her head enough to look inside and saw two guards sitting behind a desk, monitors glowing on their faces, showing multiple angles from around the entire building.

Selena pulled her cart into the middle of the hallway and grabbed the broom to sweep the floor. She kept her head cocked low, but high enough to see inside the security office.

From what she could gather, more than half of the monitors showed the bank. She saw the bank lobby, the teller windows, the nearby vault, and a short hallway that led to different bankers' offices. The other views showed different areas of the building, office workers heading out for the day, others getting started for a night shift.

*If their focus is the bank, how the hell did it get robbed so quickly and easily?* she wondered. *And with the vault right in front of them?!*

Selena swept the broom further down the hall, now in plain sight of the security guards if they simply looked out their windows. She looked ahead toward the vault at the end of the hallway, its circular door closed, containing hoards of cash within its impenetrable steel walls.

She hesitated to get any closer, instead studying the area from afar. There was no barrier between herself and the vault, and she found this peculiar. If a robber were to get on this specific floor—not something that proved too difficult of a task for someone smart enough to rob a bank—they would face no further resistance beyond the security office. The vault had its complex locking devices installed, but the ease of being able to walk right up to it seemed an irresponsible move on the bank designer's behalf.

This bank had a mantrap to the side of the vault, presumably as a second access point. But the main entrance stood unimpeded.

*Whoever designed this bank and its vault must have been asleep at the wheel,* Selena thought. On the day of the robbery, the vault had been open because employees were inside. If the robber knew the vault would be open—which Selena didn't believe was a coincidence—then that removed the only true barrier between the robber and a vault full of cash. All the robber needed to do was get past the security team.

Selena placed her broom on the cart and grabbed the glass cleaner and paper towels. She shuffled right up to the security office windows and sprayed the liquid, promptly wiping it clean.

This caught the guards' attention, and one of them stood up, waving to Selena. He made his way to the door, and Selena's heart drummed while he pulled it open.

"Evening," the man said, poking his head out. "I think somebody already came by this morning to clean our office."

Selena saw the name badge clipped to his shirt. *McDowell.* She recognized the name from the mission reports. Bill McDowell was the guard who would end up being shot in the elevator that the robber used to enter the building. A heavyset man with lots of stubble on his face, McDowell watched Selena curiously.

"Oh?" she said. "I wasn't aware of that. My supervisor asked me to come down here to sweep, mop, and clean the windows. I can go back to make sure."

"Don't worry about it," McDowell said. "Just thought I'd save you time, but if that's what they asked you to do, carry on. Did you need to clean inside of our office?"

Selena nearly started drooling at the invitation to step inside the security office and promptly nodded. "Yes, if that's okay."

"Of course. It's the end of our shift—not a lot going on."

McDowell pulled the door open all the way and stepped aside to allow Selena room to enter.

"Do you mind if I put my cart in the doorway?" Selena asked. "Would make it easier for me to not have to go in and out."

"Be my guest," McDowell said with a warm smile. Selena guessed the man was in his late fifties thanks to the streaks of gray in his hair and stubble. He had a soothing gentleness when he spoke, and this immediately put Selena at ease as she wheeled in her cart.

Another guard sat behind the desk, digging into a bag of potato chips.

"That's Dawkins," McDowell said. "And I'm Bill McDowell.

Are you new here? I don't think I've seen you before."

Bill returned to his seat next to Dawkins and leaned back, arms crossed over his chest. Dawkins was closer to Selena's age and struggling to keep his eyes off of her.

"I am," Selena said.

Selena grabbed the broom again and started sweeping around the office, glancing up every few seconds to absorb the views and surroundings within the room. A macabre sense of destiny filled the air, as if the past had made its presence known, daring Selena to try something that would change the course of the murders set to occur in just nine days.

Below the highest monitors hanging on the wall opposite their desk, Selena saw the direct, clear view they had of the vault. Anyone in the security office would have no problem seeing any activity or motion that took place in the vault area. She studied the two dozen screens. They cut to different angles every few seconds, but she found it odd that over an entire minute, not once did she see outside the building.

She had so many questions she wanted to ask about their processes, but knew it would only raise suspicions if the new custodian took a sudden interest in the building's security.

Selena swept closer to the desk, her eyes falling on the log sheet that appeared to track each guard's shifts, duties, and incidents that arose. The log separated two smaller monitors that stood on the desk, each connected to a keyboard the guards could control, presumably to choose which camera they wanted to view.

"How are you liking it here?" McDowell asked, breaking the awkward silence. Dawkins remained involved with his potato chips, his eyes peering out from the mop of messy black hair tousled over his forehead.

"It's been good so far," Selena said. "Can't complain. Everyone on the team has been really nice."

"You let us know if you need help. All the phones in the stairwells call right down here. Sometimes new hires have their keycards set up wrong and can't get into every room they need. If you come across that, just give us a buzz and we'll get you in. Right, Dawkins?"

McDowell let out a hearty chuckle as he leaned over and clapped a hand on his young colleague's back.

"Yes, sir," Dawkins mumbled, face flushing red as he avoided eye contact with Selena.

"Well, I appreciate that," Selena said, putting the broom back onto her cart. "It looks pretty clean in here already. I'll get out of your way."

She offered a wide grin before pushing the cart back into the hallway and letting the door close behind her. Selena tried to avoid getting emotionally vested in her missions, but once she was free from the security office, she knew one thing.

*I don't want Bill McDowell to die.*

# Chapter 16

"Let's discuss our findings from the week," Arielle said on Saturday morning as they gathered around the breakfast table. Felix had whipped up some pancakes and sliced bananas for them to enjoy.

They had Young under surveillance, and Arielle would drive to Kennedy's house later in the morning.

"For starters," Felix said. "I don't think Peter Young is involved. The guy does *nothing*. We're a week in, and all he does is watch TV, eat, and sleep. He's like a house cat."

Selena giggled at this.

"We can't rule him out, though," Arielle said. "There's a chance he's planning everything while at work. Why not? Everything he needs to know is right in front of him there. The bankers' routines, the security schedule, building access, and knowing all of the escape routes. He can literally walk the different routes he might want to take on his way out. He's still a prime suspect for us. Have you seen him at work yet, Selena?"

Selena shook her head, drawing a circle on the table with her finger. "Yesterday was the first time I got to venture down to the security office. There were only two guards in there. He could have been off already, or doing his rounds somewhere else in the building."

"And what about Kennedy?" Felix asked Arielle. "It doesn't seem like we're gaining traction with him, either."

"Because we're not," she replied. "He at least does things, and has occasionally left the house. That day I followed him was to the shooting range. Naturally, I thought that was some big revelation. He wanted to practice shooting, right? When I followed him inside, though, he was shooting with a hunting rifle—not at all the gun that was used in the robbery. Hunting season isn't for another five months, so he must just be staying sharp. No signs of him preparing for a robbery."

"Forgive me for not knowing this," Selena said. "But what exactly would that preparation look like?"

"Well, visits to the site ahead of time. Which hasn't happened. Trips to the shooting range—if he was using the appropriate guns. That's probably the extent of what we'd be able to see from outside his home. As far as within, he could study blueprints of the building, maps of the surrounding area, suspicious conversations with his wife—assuming it's a secret from her."

"There's so much that can go on inside that house," Felix said. "Every step of preparation, in fact. The guy is home alone all day. He can literally spend eight hours plotting this robbery, all to have his notes and plans packed away before his wife gets home."

"But you didn't see anything like that, right?" Arielle asked.

"No. But I wasn't exactly on the hunt for that sort of thing. I was in the kitchen and the master bedroom. Didn't see anything in either spot. But there were stairs to the basement. A whole other world I didn't get to explore."

"We need to get back into that house."

Felix shook his head vehemently. "Don't count on it. After that last encounter—I refuse to step back inside."

"That reminds me. Did we ever hear about Kennedy's son? I still wonder what he was doing there."

"They found nothing of substance. Completely clean background from now until the end of his life. Was never mentioned in the trial outside of his testimony that Kennedy had lunch with his kids on that Sunday. Never had a sudden spike of money."

Arielle crossed her arms, staring to the ceiling in deep thought and frustration. "I just don't get it. He goes there, calling for Kennedy. No answer. Calls someone from the house phone and tells them Kennedy's not home. Why would he need to call someone to tell them that? It sounds so suspicious—I can't wrap my head around it."

"There can be a lot of moving parts to a robbery. Young could have the security aspect under wraps. Kennedy's son could have been involved in the preparation or aftermath of the robbery. They could have paid off the next-door neighbor to serve as an alibi."

"Sure, but for $200,000? The more people involved, the less money Kennedy would get to keep."

"Don't look too deep into the amount that was robbed. I highly doubt they planned to only steal $200,000. I'm betting they got cold feet and bailed sooner than they wanted. There was how much in the vault? Something like three million dollars?"

Arielle nodded. "You're right. And this feels like it's becoming a mission where we will find nothing out until the morning of. And it fucking disturbs me—this is not how I work."

She felt the rage steaming within, but refused to show her frustration through any emotion. If her team sensed the doom she was experiencing, the wheels would fall off this mission within hours. They looked to her for confidence, and she needed to exude that at all times. It was her burden to shoulder—part of the territory as the top-ranked Angel.

They must have sensed something, however, as both Felix and Selena sat in silence, poking at their food, looking down at their plates to avoid eye contact.

"Look, Arielle," Selena said. "Don't think you're alone in this. We've never dealt with a mission like this, either. We're all reacting to whatever each day brings us."

Arielle clenched her teeth behind sealed lips. While she appreciated Selena's attempt to ease her concerns, she hated that someone else had to step in to console her. That was supposed to be her job.

She gulped before replying. "What did you see in the security office last night?"

Selena looked across the table to Felix, who nodded silently in response.

"Not much to speak of. I met one of the victims. He's a really nice guy. Their office overlooks the vault. They have monitors that cover every inch of the building. However, I didn't see any that showed views from outside the building. They might exist, but I didn't see them while I was in there."

Arielle stood from her seat and circled the table to lean against the counter. Her frustration was reaching its limits with this mission, and she could no longer sit still while they lost at every turn. "I'm going to sleep on this decision over the weekend. But I think we need to attack this mission with more intensity. Nothing is going to just fall into our lap on this one—we need to force the past to reveal at least one of the cards it's playing in this game."

"Won't that be dangerous?" Felix asked, leaning forward. Arielle had grabbed his attention, and she knew she would. Felix liked to play things safe, and the mere mention of potential danger usually spun his worries out of control.

"I don't think dangerous is the right word," Arielle said. "Our lives won't be at risk—I'd never do that. But there may be risks. Some gambles. For one, I want Selena to encounter Young while at work. We have to force the issue. Try to get close to him. Talk to him while he's in the security office. See what sort of papers he has nearby that might suggest he's involved. Like I said, this won't pose a threat to your life, but it could result in losing your job."

"Do we know for sure what shifts he works?" Selena asked. "I'd be able to plan my day better to make this happen."

"We have one week of data," Felix said. "We can use it to guess, but security jobs like this can vary from week to week. It's actually quite rare for a guard to have a set schedule. They'll rotate who is working on weekends and graveyard shifts."

"I might be able to find out," Selena said. "There was another guard in there when I stopped by. Someone our age. Wouldn't stop checking me out."

"Use that," Arielle said in a serious tone. "We need to pull out all the stops we can. Felix, I think you should go back into Young's apartment one more time. This time to look for clues."

"Yeah, but the last time I was in there the mob came knocking at the door."

"That wasn't the mob. You'll be fine. Once you know he's

gone for the workday, you can take your time. No need to answer the door if someone comes knocking. Just go about your business."

"And does this mean you're going to knock on Kennedy's door to have a chat?" Selena asked.

Arielle scrunched her brow in thought. "I might. I've been thinking of what I can possibly do to get in there. Pose as a salesperson? A maintenance worker?"

"But why?" Felix asked. "It's not like you'd be able to just snoop around the house while he's home. If he thought you were up to something, this guy might shoot you."

"Maybe I can distract while you rummage through his things."

"Excuse me?!" Felix gasped, standing up to meet Arielle's eye level. "I already told you, I'm not going back in there."

"Well, I might need you to. But I'd be there too."

Felix sat back down, shaking his head. "You're being reckless, Arielle."

"Reckless? They gave us a mission to play detective. We are *not* detectives. The commander is being reckless by giving us this mission."

"That doesn't mean we have to play with fire. You do know that it's okay to fail sometimes, right? We can treat this mission like we would any other, and if it doesn't work out, then we tell the commander our work style doesn't fit this type of mission. And guess what? We won't get missions like these again."

They sat in silence for a few seconds, staring at each other.

Selena spoke next. "He's right, Arielle. If we succeed on this mission, we'll just keep getting assigned more like it."

"I'm afraid I'm just not wired that way," Arielle said. "We

were given a mission to complete, and that's what we're going to do. I'm not going to give up on it because it's too hard, or to avoid future ones. I have a standard of work to uphold, and I hope you'll join me in completing this."

Now Selena stood and circled the table to stand directly in front of Arielle. She reached out and grabbed both of her shoulders. "We will always have your back. But we need you to run your ideas by us. You're flustered. We see it. We won't tell anyone. But this means you might not make the best decisions. Lean on us. Trust us to help you complete a mission."

Tears welled in Arielle's eyes, and she looked at Selena through blurred vision. This was only their second mission working together, and she already saw the growth in both Selena and Felix. They were confident in themselves and their small team. They were holding Arielle accountable while also taking a weight off her shoulders.

She didn't wipe the tears away, instead letting them streak down her face. "I'm scared. I'm worried we're going to fail. I've never felt so lost since I've become an Angel."

Felix stood and joined them to make a huddle around Arielle. "You're losing sight of yourself. You've put too much pressure to live up to your reputation. Yes, this mission is hard and has so many unique challenges." Felix pointed his index finger and jammed it into Arielle's chest. "You're Arielle fucking Lucila. You don't live up to your reputation. Your reputation lives up to you. Stop overthinking everything, and do what comes naturally. *That's* what makes you the best."

Selena wiped away Arielle's tears. "Clear your mind. Hit the reset button. And we can all discuss how next week will look. We have eight more days to figure this out. We will succeed."

"Thank you," Arielle whispered, stretching her back to

stand up tall, her confidence slowly returning.  She knew exactly what needed to happen next.

# Chapter 17

Selena insisted on joining Arielle outside Kennedy's house on Sunday morning. She had originally proposed they all take the day off and spend it downtown. There was a chalk art festival just south of the Sixteenth Street Mall, with vendors selling food, clothes, and random goods.

Arielle, unsurprisingly, refused to blow off a whole day while on a mission. She claimed that if nothing of significance was happening at Kennedy's house by two o'clock, they could head back downtown for the festivities.

Selena didn't believe her. She had already come to know Arielle well enough to see through the thinly veiled lie. It was no different than a parent telling their nagging child "we'll see" to mollify them.

Felix remained at the apartment, another slow day of watching Peter Young lounge around in his underwear. At least he wore that much.

It was ten o'clock when they turned onto Kennedy's block and parked across the street from his house.

"Well, what do you know?" Selena said. "They're sitting in the dining room having breakfast. A late breakfast, at that. Riveting stuff."

Arielle shook her head. "If you only knew. This is maybe the most action I've seen all week. Mostly it has only been dinner when I've seen them together. I sat out here yesterday for eight hours, all while Kennedy was nowhere to be seen, and Mrs. Kennedy cleaned every nook and cranny of the house."

"So another day of wasted time? Got it."

Arielle laughed, a bit of lunacy swimming beneath its surface. "You don't get it. This is the work I do. It's not anything new. Sure, this mission might move slower than normal, but if you really break down all the missions I've worked on in the past, it's probably sixty to seventy percent just sitting around. Everyone thinks my job is to break into buildings and shoot the bad guys—which it is—but it's just not that way all the time. There's a certain buildup to get to that point."

"Then what separates you from the pack?" Selena asked. "I'm sure your counterparts face the same struggles."

"They do. The difference is I fill that downtime with knowledge. A lot of the others will just sit there all day. Maybe knit a blanket, or something to pass the time. I learn everything I can about the mission. The file is my bible, and I study it until I know every little detail inside. There is always something overlooked that can change the entire trajectory for a mission."

"Then why haven't you been doing that for this one?"

Selena saw those words sting Arielle. She knew their leader was dealing with plenty of doubt—and confidence issues—regarding this mission. She didn't mean for her words to sound so cold, and could only brace for Arielle's response.

Arielle looked forward through the windshield, gazing into the distance. The Kennedys could have been on the moon right now, for all she knew. After thirty seconds of silence, all she did was shrug. "I don't know. I've tried. Don't get me wrong. But when I read this file, it's like the words just run together. The images all look both familiar and foreign."

"Do you think it's the past?"

"It could be. But this mission . . . it just hasn't been simple. We don't even know who pulls the trigger. There's a chance it's neither Kennedy nor Young. We have no idea."

"But why does it matter? We can still show up ready to stop the crime from happening. We don't *need* to know who it is."

"But we do. We can't take gambles. There could be multiple people involved. Decoys. I know it sounds absurd, but things like that really happen. We could end up killing a—somewhat—innocent person. And besides, the mission instructions are to find out who committed the crime. It doesn't actually say to stop it from happening. Legally, we're not bound to do anything the Commander says, but rather what's in writing on our official mission reports. And it's plain as day on the second line of the document. 'Objective: To identify the persons responsible for the acts of violence at the United Bank Robbery on June 16, 1991, also known as the Father's Day Massacre.' And that's it. Nothing about stopping it."

Arielle held her gaze out the windshield, despite Selena whipping her head around toward her. "Are you saying what I think you're saying?"

"What? That we only need to observe who does it and not worry about stepping into the line of danger?" Arielle paused, leaving Selena in unnecessary suspense. "Sure I've thought about it, but can I actually just sit by while a crook murders four innocent people? Can any of us justify doing that if we're already here?"

Selena hadn't yet considered that angle.

Did they have a moral obligation to prevent the murders from happening, simply because they knew they would occur? The Road Runners had authorized hundreds of missions deemed 'observational' in the past, strictly to watch and learn what had happened at critical historical events. They knew what would happen while in the moment, yet never made moves to interfere. And these were crimes much more horrific than the one they were dealing with.

"Do you think there's something bigger at play?" Selena asked.

Arielle finally broke her long-distance gaze and met Selena's eyes. "I've thought about it. It's possible. Commander Briar could be seeing how we act under these circumstances, but that doesn't seem like him. He's very transparent about everything we do. He's not one to play mind games. Which is why I think this just slipped through the cracks. It's either a miscommunication or a misunderstanding. The commander reviews dozens of mission reports each day. Did this small detail just slip by him?"

"That seems more likely. Especially with everything else he has going on."

Silence fell over the car while they both looked to the Kennedy house, surprised to see Jacob standing in the open front door, giving his wife a kiss, keys in hand.

"What?!" Selena gasped. "Where's he going?"

Arielle fired up the engine. "This is why I come on the weekends. He's off to somewhere by himself."

After a minute, they had followed Kennedy onto the main road. All Arielle could do was pray that he was going to do something related to the robbery. She couldn't bear the thought of another wasted day.

"Any idea where he might be headed?" Selena asked as they stopped two cars behind him at a red light.

"So far, it's the same direction he went that day I followed him to the gun shop and sandwich place. But he could be going anywhere. It's almost eleven o'clock."

They followed him through the light Sunday traffic for another ten minutes before he turned into the parking lot belonging to Mad Shot Sports Bar. The bar had a sign hanging over its entrance portraying an angry, cartoonish dog shooting a basketball. Arielle giggled at the sight.

"A *sports bar*?" Selena questioned, looking around to make sure there wasn't any other business. "Seems strange for a man who never leaves the house. And on a Sunday morning in June? There aren't even sports on yet."

"Guess we need to follow him in to see what he's doing here. Keep in mind, liquor stores are closed on Sundays. That law wasn't changed until much later. He could just be getting his fix for the day."

Kennedy parked in the front row, only three other cars in the lot. Arielle took her time turning in and parking on the side of the building, out of sight from Kennedy.

The bar had a brick exterior and only one window on the side, in which hung a Denver Broncos Budweiser neon light. A dumpster stood next to a side door that presumably led to the bar's kitchen.

Arielle and Selena stepped out, and Arielle looked through the window, but couldn't see much through the neon light.

"Do we need disguises?" Selena asked.

"For what? He doesn't know who we are."

"I always use disguises. Just in case. You never know when he might recognize you elsewhere."

Selena's approach on missions was to never be spotted. And if she was, to look as bland as possible. They were both dressed in jeans and t-shirts, a fortunate happening that would help them blend in inside the bar. She retreated to the car and leaned in to open her backpack on the floor. She returned with two pairs of sunglasses, handing one to Arielle.

"Wear sunglasses inside a bar?" Arielle asked. "I feel like that will make us stand out more."

"Oh, we're already going to stand out. I guarantee you the only men inside there are like Kennedy. Middle-aged and boring. We're young and hot. They're going to be looking at us. Might as well hide our faces best we can."

Selena rarely had trouble understanding how to best adapt to her settings, given the location and year, and this time proved no different. Morning trips to the sports bar, outside of football season, never garnered attention from the younger, college crowd.

"If you say so," Arielle said, slipping the sunglasses over her eyes, tossing her hair back.

"Let's go," Selena said, rounding the corner toward the entrance. She paused before opening the door, turning to Arielle. "We need to go to the opposite side of the room. If he's to the left, we go right. If he's at the front, we hang back."

Arielle nodded, and Selena pulled open the door, the scent of beer and fried chicken immediately rushing them. The bar was practically empty. Several men sat at a table along the left side of the room, next to a pair of pool tables. And Kennedy sat at the bar toward the front, minding his business while the bartender filled a couple of steins full of beer. Four TVs were mounted above the bar, two showing a golf tournament, while the other two showed the pre-game talk for the Yankees and Orioles game about to begin.

Classic rock played through the speakers, not too loud to drown out conversation, but not subtle, either. Selena led them to a table in the corner to their right, giving a direct view of Kennedy's back. He'd have no reason to turn all the way around to look at them. As Selena predicted, the two men, who had just received their beers from the bartender, stopped their conversation to admire the two women who had just entered the building.

The bartender, an older gentleman with wavy gray hair, approached them and placed two menus on the table. "Good morning, ladies. Can I get you anything to drink?"

"Tequila sunrise," Selena said without hesitation, immediately grinning at Arielle, as she knew the alcohol order would bother her.

Arielle looked down to the menu. "I'll just have water. . . while I think about it."

"You got it," the bartender said, nodding before returning to his post to make their drinks.

Arielle said nothing about Selena's order, too focused on Kennedy. She held up her menu to glance over the top in his direction.

They sat across from each other, both able to see Kennedy through the sides of their vision. "What's he doing?" Selena asked.

"He's watching baseball. Doesn't even have a drink or food in front of him."

"Do you think he really came here just to watch baseball?"

Arielle shrugged, putting the menu down. "So far it seems

like it.  But we'll stay to see.  I can't say I'm interested in spending all day in this bar watching sports."

They spent the next fifteen minutes watching Kennedy watch baseball. Selena sipped her drink and ordered a round of hot wings, claiming it would help them blend in more.

That's when another man stepped into the building and made his way straight to the bar. He wore raggedy jeans and had a cigarette stuck between his lips.

"Is that who I think it is?" Arielle asked, unable to look away.

Selena had tracked the man from the moment he stepped in. She knew exactly who it was. "Yes. It's Peter Young."

# Chapter 18

They never went to the downtown festival on Sunday. Instead, they had spent the rest of the afternoon at Mad Shot Sports Bar, conversing with Felix, who had shown up just after Young.

This surprise meeting between the two suspects injected fresh energy into the stalled mission. They spent Sunday evening reviewing all the potential crossover between Young and Kennedy.

On Monday morning, Selena rolled out of bed ready to attack the day. She had every intent on bumping into Young at the office. She still wasn't sure what she wanted to get out of the encounter, but knew initiating the contact would at least open up fresh possibilities with six days until the robbery.

As the day progressed, anxiety mounted.

Olivia had a strict rule about the cleaning crew not interacting with anyone else in the building. They were to move in the background unnoticed. If she were to find out Selena was stopping by the security office, it would result in a reprimand. And that the security office wasn't part of her cleaning schedule, which just might lead to more suspicions. Ones she couldn't currently afford.

Selena arrived at seven o'clock on Monday morning, an hour before her scheduled start time. Not even Young had left for the office yet. She took her time changing in the locker room, and browsing the day's schedule, pinpointing exactly where Olivia would be at certain times of the day.

Olivia worked the lower floors, including the basement, but would be done with those before lunchtime. The highest she went in the building was the sixth floor, where she'd be around three in the afternoon. That's when Selena planned to head down to the basement and pretend to clean around the security office again. She gave herself a twenty-minute window to meet Young and then return to the twenty-third floor where she was assigned.

Cleaning office after office helped the day pass. She had bought a portable CD player from the thrift store and chose Mariah Carey's self-titled debut album to listen to on repeat. After lunch, she couldn't take any more, and ditched the music.

When the clock struck 2:50, she rolled her cart into a storage closet on the twenty-third floor and took the long elevator ride down to the basement level.

She had no nerves this time, confidence shooting through her veins as the elevator doors parted. Selena wasted no time marching down the hall, swinging open the storage closet doors, pulling out the cart, and continuing down the hallway toward the vault and security office.

No sign of Olivia or any coworkers. She was home free.

She grabbed the broom first and started sweeping the area outside of the security door. She leaned over to peek in and saw Young sitting behind the desk next to McDowell and Dawkins, the two she had met during her last venture to the basement.

"I'm in," she whispered, cracking a wide grin as she knocked on the door.

McDowell was sitting nearest the door, and opened it. "Selena? Good to see you again. What brings you down this way?"

"Oh," Selena said, cocking an eyebrow. "Was someone already down here? My schedule says to clean the security room at three."

"Someone was in earlier in the morning," McDowell said. "But there's no harm in having it extra clean, I suppose."

He chuckled and stepped aside.

"Thank you."

Selena entered the office and saw Dawkins look at her before jerking his head away. Young stared ahead at the monitors like a mindless zombie. McDowell returned to his seat and shoved an elbow into Dawkins's side.

"You guys having a good day?" Selena asked, pulling out a duster and running it over the front of their desk.

"No complaints here to start the week," McDowell said. "But I'm sure that will change by Friday."

"Dawkins, right?" Selena asked the young guard, his face flushing immediately.

He nodded. "You can call me Brian."

"Good to see you again." She turned her attention to Young, who had finally broken his gaze from the monitors thanks to Selena impeding his view. "I don't believe we've met. I'm Selena. New to the cleaning crew."

Young stood up and stuck out a lazy hand. "Peter. Nice to meet you."

His hand was clammy, Selena glad for a quick handshake. Seeing him up close for the first time completed the puzzle of the man they had been watching on the live-feed. He had a scraggly mustache, fuzz on his cheeks, and a slightly lazy eye.

He had a toothpick in his mouth that kept moving from side to side.

"We were talking about going out for drinks after work today," Dawkins said. "Would you be interested?"

Selena looked around to make sure he was talking to her. "Today?"

"I know it's a Monday, but we work such weird schedules. We hardly know what day it is anymore."

"You're all going?" Selena asked, looking around the room to McDowell and Young.

Both men nodded, McDowell grinning. "Us old-timers don't go out too often. Ain't that right, Pete?"

Young cracked a faint smile, finally plucking out the toothpick. "No, we don't. But what the hell? I don't mind having a good time."

"Count me in," Selena said. This trip to the basement couldn't have gone any better. "I get off at five."

"So do we," Dawkins said. "Well, more like 5:15. Gotta wait for the next crew to show up and get settled. We're just going across the street to The Last Drop. Do you know it?"

"I do. I thought it was just a café , though."

"They have a full bar. Quiet evening crowds. Just how these old guys like."

Dawkins winked at McDowell who returned a chuckle.

"Sounds like a good time. I'll see you there at 5:15."

Selena gave a quick sweep over the floor, not forgetting she needed it to look like she really needed to clean their office. Within two minutes, she bid them farewell and left their office.

Her mind flooded with the possibilities of what this evening out with the security team could mean for the mission. She'd even have time to run back to the apartment after work and let Felix know what was going on.

She was on the cusp of discovering just how much Young was involved in the robbery.

# Chapter 19

Selena had wasted no time when the clock struck five o'clock. She had already packed up and stored her cart before heading down to clock out for the day. Olivia had commented on her quick and impressive work, but more importantly, had no idea about Selena's brief meeting with the security team.

Olivia had tried to strike up a conversation, but with the clock reading 5:05, she had less than ten minutes to get out of the building before the security team left from their shift to head across the street.

Feeling somewhat rude, she had bolted out of the locker room and building and ran to their apartment where she changed into a fresh pair of jeans and a new blouse. As long as she could keep Dawkins interested, she'd have more opportunities to get close to Young, even if only for the rest of the week.

She let Felix know her plans, and he vowed to head down to the café as soon as Arielle arrived home, typically around 5:30.

Selena left a frazzled Felix without another word. She hurried back toward the office and stopped in front of the café at exactly 5:28.

The front exterior was all glass, decorated with markings

advertising their morning happy hour for coffee and their evening happy hour at the bar—a detail she hadn't noticed the day they first came. Through it, she saw a group of men huddled around a standing table in the back corner.

"Play it cool and be natural." She always offered a few words of encouragement to herself.

She headed straight back to the table where Dawkins and McDowell conversed over a couple mugs of beer. They had changed out of their security uniforms, both men wearing jeans and button-up shirts. She found Dawkins rather handsome now that she saw him in the real world, and he must have felt the same, as he couldn't look away.

"Selena!" McDowell greeted. Two other men had stood at the table on the opposite side of her friends, and they spun around. "Let me introduce you. These are a couple other guys from the team. You might see them around. This is Harvey and Sid."

"You can call me Wilson," the one called Harvey explained. "Bill here refuses to call anyone by their first name."

McDowell shrugged. "It's a military thing, I guess."

"Wilson Harvey," Selena said, more to herself. The name was another one of the victims in the robbery.

"I know. Two first names. Or two last names. Whichever you prefer. My parents must have been drunk when they named me."

"That explains so much," McDowell said, and the entire table howled in laughter.

Wilson looked to be in his early forties. He pushed six feet, and seemed to keep in good shape judging by the muscles bulging beneath his skin-tight t-shirt.

"And I'm Hassan Siddiqui," the one called Sid said, stepping forward to shake Selena's hand. He was close to Selena's age. "Sid for short. I guess my Pakistani name is too much for Bill to say."

This earned another round of laughter as the men all took drinks from tall beer steins.

"Well, it's nice to meet you both. Thank you for having me. I haven't had much of a social life since I moved to Denver."

"We're happy to have you," McDowell said. "Aren't we, Dawkins?"

Dawkins immediately turned red and started shaking his head. McDowell couldn't have made it any more obvious. This was all some sort of setup for Dawkins to spend time with the new cleaning girl outside of work.

"Wasn't that other guy I met today coming?" Selena asked, taking the spotlight off Dawkins. "I think his name was Peter."

"Pete? Yeah, he'll be here. He was still wrapping some things up. Might even head home for a second—he doesn't live too far from here, actually."

*Oh, I know,* Selena thought, the anticipation brewing.

"He's probably pre-gaming at his apartment so he doesn't have to spend any money here," Wilson said. "Pete is a bit of a cheap-ass."

They all howled again, clearly growing more tipsy with each passing moment.

"And to think it's only two-dollar beers. He'll still bitch about it being watered down or something."

"Stop it," McDowell said, nodding toward the entrance. "He's coming."

Peter Young entered the café and shuffled to the back corner where his colleagues waited. He had a cigarette pinched between his lips as he walked up with a crooked smile. Selena made a mental to note to ask Felix if Young was a chain-smoker.

"How's it going?" Young asked, squeezing in at the table between McDowell and Harvey.

"We're doing just fine," McDowell said. "Get yourself a beer—it's happy hour."

"Oh? How much?" Young raised an eyebrow as he reached into his jeans pocket for his wallet.

"Two bucks until six o'clock. Still have a half hour."

Young nodded, satisfied, and pulled out a five-dollar bill before strolling over to the bar.

Everyone else at the table stared around at each other, holding their laughs in.

Selena saw the door swing open from the corner of her eye, Felix appearing in the entryway for a moment before scurrying to the opposite corner of the room, grabbing a corner booth with way too much space for himself.

A minute later, Young returned with two beers, handing one to Selena. "Saw you didn't have anything yet."

"Oh," Selena said, surprised. "Thank you, Peter. That's very nice of you."

He killed his cigarette on the table's ashtray and nodded, expressionless.

Young looked toward the entrance and waved, causing everyone else to look.

"Well, I'll be damned," McDowell said, a wide grin consuming his face. "Is that who I think it is?"

Selena froze in place while Jacob Kennedy made his way toward their table, her heart pounding against her chest like a vicious thunderstorm.

"Gave him a call," Young said. "Told him we'd be here for a bit."

McDowell opened his arms and threw an embrace around Kennedy. "It's so good to see you, Kennedy. How's the retired life treating you?"

McDowell hung back to allow Kennedy space at the table while he shook hands with everyone, pausing at Selena. "And who might you be?" Kennedy asked her, his voice deep and somewhat lazy.

"Hello. I'm Selena. Started working at the building with these guys—cleaning crew."

"Well, nice to meet you," Kennedy said, his push-broom mustache hiding a faint grin. He took a step back to speak to the table more easily. "And retirement has been everything I could have hoped for."

"You still making those model boats?" McDowell asked.

"Every day," Kennedy said, sticking his thumbs into his belt loops, a small gut protruding over his waistband. "If I didn't have those boats, I might go crazy. Not sure what else I'd do."

"Still refuse to take up golf?"

"Eh, not for me. I go to the shooting range now and again, but outside of that, I clean around the house, work on my boats, and read some books."

"Reading, huh? You hated doing that when you worked with us."

Kennedy shrugged. "Had good company, I guess. The wife still goes to work—she'll retire at the end of the year—so it's pretty quiet at home all day."

"Let me grab you a beer," McDowell said.

Kennedy raised a hand, shaking his head. "Not drinking much these days. Tried it a few times at the start of retirement, and realized how shitty it makes me feel. Tell me what you guys have been up to, huh?"

The group of guards started discussing and griping about their jobs. The noise drowned into the background for Selena as she looked around the circle, completely out of her element.

That's when she looked toward the corner booth for Felix, and instead saw Arielle stepping through the entrance.

Arielle scanned the café , spotting Kennedy and Young together, then bulged her eyes upon seeing Selena in the middle of the gathering. They locked eyes, Arielle speaking through their stare as if saying, *What the hell are you doing?!*

Selena looked away, grinning and nodding to blend in with the conversation she knew nothing about, then looked back at Arielle to nod toward the restrooms behind the rowdy group of men.

"Excuse me, gentlemen," Selena said, putting her beer on the table. McDowell smiled at her, and no one else seemed to notice her slip away and head into the ladies' room. Before she stepped in, she looked over her shoulder to confirm Arielle was on her way.

Selena made her way to the sink and checked herself in the mirror, brushing back a couple of frizzy hairs that had come undone from her ponytail during the workday. A few seconds later, Arielle entered the restroom, closing the door shut behind her.

"Selena?" she asked in a loud whisper. "What the hell is going on?" She joined Selena at the sink, leaning against the counter as they locked eyes.

"Things escalated quickly today," Selena replied. "I went down to the security office to meet Young—which I did. But then the other guys invited me out for drinks. Young apparently invited Kennedy, and here we are."

Arielle bit her bottom lip, something Selena noticed she did when she became flustered, assuming she didn't have any gum to chomp on. "This is so dangerous. Do you understand that?"

"Of course. It's not like I planned for this to happen. The only reason I accepted the invitation was because Young said he was coming. Thought I'd get to know him a little better. Never expected Kennedy to just show up like this."

Arielle drew in a deep breath. "Tread carefully. Normally I'd say you need to bail right now, but both me and Felix are here, and we'll keep a close eye in case anything goes wrong."

"I can handle this," Selena said with complete confidence. "I won't speak to Kennedy unless spoken to. I'll blend in and just try to listen."

"Be aware of everything. If you stand in the wrong spot, it can prevent a conversation from happening, and the past could start pushing back. If you say the wrong thing and change the subject—the same thing can happen."

"I got it. I'll be a fly on the wall. Did something happen today at Kennedy's house?"

"Of course not. Just another slow day. Until he left. Imagine my surprise when I followed him all the way here, right across from the bank. We should keep a close eye on him once he leaves here."

"That will need to be you or Felix. I can't just leave whenever Kennedy decides—that will look suspicious."

"You could leave early. I honestly doubt Kennedy is going to say anything about his plans to rob the bank where all these men work."

Selena shook her head. "I'm going out there and will be

totally natural. I trust my instincts to guide me. If I need to leave, then I will. If not, I'm staying."

"Just don't get drunk."

Selena rolled her eyes. "Did that really need to be said? You still don't trust me, do you?"

"I trust you fine. Just reminding you what the focus is on tonight. No mistakes."

"I'm going back out there. See you at home, *Mother*."

Selena stormed away from the sink and left the bathroom before Arielle could say anything else. She really was sick of Arielle's assumptions that she lacked self-control.

When she returned to the table, the group of guards seemed to have a more focused discussion. Selena stepped up next to McDowell, who stood behind the small huddle, but was still involved in the conversation.

"I heard they took your guns away," Kennedy said. "Seems wild to do that for a security team guarding a bank. Do they just expect you to fight off people with your fists?"

McDowell laughed as he shook his head. "Don't even get me started. We still have batons, but that's about it. I'm not sure what they expect us to do if someone holds up the bank? Throw the baton at them?"

Everyone laughed. Except for Kennedy. His eyes narrowed on McDowell. "Why did they change that?" he asked. His tone didn't have a hint of the amusement as his peers.

McDowell shrugged. "No idea. Policy change is all they told us. Probably some dirty liberal who thinks guns are the devil."

This earned more laughter. Still nothing from Kennedy.

Selena took a step sideways to get out of Kennedy's line of vision. The amount of concentration she could see in his eyes was alarming, especially considering the conversation. She couldn't risk him getting distracted by seeing her. His dials were clearly in motion, and that realization wrapped a fist of dread around her soul.

Gone was the joy Kennedy had when he stepped into the café and saw all of his old friends. Instead, Selena saw the same blank expression that she had become familiar with from the mission report. The same distant stare as Kennedy's mugshot and candid photos from his trial.

"Well, that's too bad," Kennedy said, breaking out of his trance and standing tall. "You boys stay safe over there. Glad I left before they changed that policy—probably would have pushed me to quit."

"We'll be fine," McDowell said. "It's nothing I'm worried about. Police are only five minutes away. Now that I think about it, maybe it's just a liability thing. Don't wanna pay extra insurance if one of us gets shot, so they want us to hide with everyone else."

"Defeats the purpose of having security, I suppose," Kennedy said. "I should get going, though. Said I'd make it home for a late dinner. Can't piss off the missus."

"Wouldn't dream of it," McDowell said. "Take care of yourself."

They all slapped Kennedy on the back as he made his rounds to say goodbye. He shook hands with Young and appeared to whisper something to his friend before they parted and Kennedy exited the café . He said nothing to Selena, or even acknowledged her on the way out. She was completely fine with it.

Selena looked up to see Arielle trailing behind Kennedy, Felix remaining in the booth as he kept a close eye on Young.

*It has to be Kennedy.*

# Chapter 20

They all convened at home by nine o'clock on Monday night. Selena had been the last to arrive, caught up in a conversation with Dawkins about their lives and childhoods. She had no pressure to follow either Kennedy or Young, and they both left once the bartender told them they were getting ready to close. Dawkins gave Selena his phone number, so for the rest of the week, she had an insider on the security team.

Arielle urged Selena to take advantage. Perhaps call Dawkins one night and see what he knew about Kennedy and Young.

Selena didn't plan to stop by the security offices anymore, deeming it too risky. Eventually, she'd get found out, and still needed to ensure access to the building over the weekend.

All the doubt that had hung over their mission like a dark cloud had given way to hope. Arielle moved and spoke with purpose, as she had always done while leading a mission. On Tuesday morning, before her and Selena headed out for the day, they gathered in the kitchen for a quick cup of coffee.

"We have five days between us and the robbery," Arielle said. "What are your thoughts?"

Selena spoke first. "I think they're both involved. Young is in the building every day. He knows exactly what's going on with the bankers, their schedules and routines, and same with security. The robbery was pulled off too cleanly for the robber to not have known all the little details. He's relaying the information. Kennedy already knew about the guns being taken away from the security team. Who else would he have heard that from?"

"I'm not sure," Felix said. "I feel like they would see each other more often. And he's yet to make a call to Kennedy from his apartment phone. In fact, he still hasn't called anyone besides takeout from restaurants. I don't exactly see him as the brightest bulb. The times he's left the apartment has been to the liquor stores and grocery store. Twice a week, he heads down to the gas stations and buys lottery tickets. He's never used a pay phone. So he's calling Kennedy from the office—which would be even dumber than calling him from home—or they set plans for their next meeting each time they're together."

Arielle paced circles, the coffee no longer appealing as her mind had drifted. "It's impossible to say. Kennedy is definitely the brains behind the operation. I'm sure he's told Young to not make any calls to his house. He's a retired cop—he knows what sort of evidence can come up later in a trial."

"She's right," Selena said. "There's no way he just went in to this based on memory of the building."

"He has a map of the building's interior layout," Felix said. "That is something they give to each security guard upon hiring them. He was familiar with the layout after working there and had a map to study during all this time. I've read all the details about the trial. He has the map, a box of various bullets, and even fake ID cards with different aliases—the judge blocked these from being shared during the trial. But it seems like he was planning to run away and start a new life. Why else would someone need all that?"

"And what was revealed about Young during the trial?" Arielle asked.

"Young testified as a witness in the trial. The defense even tried to position him as a possible suspect. Well, he *was* a suspect in the beginning of the investigation before they arrested Kennedy."

Arielle sat down at the table, planted her elbows on the surface, and rubbed her temples. "I can see both sides of the argument. My gut tells me Young is involved in some capacity. We've never seen him mingle with anyone else, but he's gone out with Kennedy twice in the two weeks leading up to the robbery. I can't discount that as a coincidence. At the same time, the two of them never stepped aside for a private conversation at the café. They hung out with the group the whole time."

"You didn't see the look in Kennedy's eyes," Selena said. "When he started asking about the change in gun policy within the security department, his mood completely changed. I could feel it. Almost wondered if I was feeling the past brewing its sick plans right along with him. I trust my gut feeling."

"We should've gone to that trial," Felix said. "I'm not sure anyone on the Advance Team considered it. I think they just gathered newspaper reports that covered it. We should have had someone in that courtroom for the duration. We'd know a lot more."

"We can't dwell on that," Arielle said. "Besides, I think I'm understanding this mission a little better, and why it's been so difficult. I haven't been able to block my mind from the past because we don't know all the facts. And this isn't a mission where we're trying to stop something from happening. Instead, it's grounded in knowledge. We want to learn the truth, and the past knows that. It's blocking us from knowing the truth. This case becomes cold after Kennedy walks, and the identity of the killer is never known. Young dies four months after the verdict, and Kennedy lives shrouded in privacy for the rest of his life. Knowledge of who is responsible can change the lives for dozens of people involved. The detectives, the judges, the jury, the families of the victims and Kennedy. This has a wider reach than we initially realized. Young could have done it and taken the secret to his grave. Same with Kennedy."

Arielle stood up rummaged a drawer for a pack of gum, promptly popping two pieces into her mouth. "There's something we need to do this week," she said, shifting her focus to Felix. "You're going back into Kennedy's house."

# Chapter 21

Felix woke up Wednesday morning after a rough night of sleep and immediately ran to the toilet. He thought he was going to vomit, but nothing came up. Arielle allowed him all of Tuesday to process and plan for a day inside Kennedy's home on Wednesday.

He protested the decision, but Arielle assured him his safety. She had plans to lure Kennedy out of the house and make it a seamless process for Felix.

That didn't matter, as he couldn't shake the overwhelming feeling that the past would push back and something would go horribly wrong.

After ten minutes of hugging the toilet with no action, he pulled himself to his bedroom to get dressed, slipping into his all-black attire reserved for when he had to break into a stranger's home.

He had insisted on returning to Young's apartment to poke around more—he'd feel safer being in the same building. But Arielle had only crossed her arms and shook her head. "You'll be doing that later this week. Tomorrow is about Kennedy."

She then went into a rant about growing as an Angel. How taking chances was the only way to expand one's abilities and horizons. She was once a timid Angel, playing it safe and taking every caution in the book. It wasn't until she started taking chances that she saw her rank climb the charts.

Her intended motivational speech fell upon deaf ears, however. Felix had no interest in climbing the charts, content with his present role and ranking. He was the best at what he did. And while entering a target's home to plant bugs was part of his job, he felt this upcoming task was far out of the realm of his day-to-day.

Once ready for his assignment, he headed downstairs where Arielle had started the coffeepot and had a box of doughnuts on the table. Selena sat, crumbs already sprinkled across the napkin she had laid out.

"Good morning, Felix," Selena said, looking up from her food. "How are you feeling?"

"I've been a lot better. I rarely have trouble sleeping, but last night was a disaster."

"You have no reason to be nervous," Arielle said. "I know this is intimidating, but I think you're making it out to be something bigger than it is. I will keep Kennedy away. Trust me."

"Kennedy wasn't the problem last time, remember? His son just let himself into the house. So we know for sure his wife and son have access to the house. Who else? Doesn't he have a daughter, too?"

"You're thinking too much. We're running out of time, and we need answers. The closer we get to the day of the robbery—which is only four more days, by the way—the harder it will be to get anything done. You hid just fine last time, so be ready to do the same if someone shows up again."

Felix shook his head and bit his lip. He already knew he wasn't going to change the situation. He was going into

Kennedy's house today, and could only hope he'd come back out alive. He had debated traveling back to his present time to call Commander Briar, but already knew he would side with Arielle.

"Do I still really have to drive myself?" Felix asked. "I don't exactly feel in the best mental state to drive a car."

Arielle's lips parted, and she let her jaw hang for about ten seconds before replying. "We need to speak in private. Right now." She looked to Selena, who glared back before standing and retreating to her bedroom. The walls were thin in this apartment, and she'd likely still be able to hear whatever Arielle had to say.

Arielle waited until Selena closed her door, then spoke. "Look, Felix. I know you don't want to do this—it's clear. But we need this. I think entering Kennedy's home while he's gone is a less dangerous task than following him, as I've been doing. Not because Kennedy has been a threat to anyone, but being closer to a subject while in the past can lead to more opportunities for push back. There may be some resistance getting into his house, but I consider it low risk."

"Bull," Felix said. "You just said yesterday how us seeking information is what the past will push against. How is me going into Kennedy's house not that?"

"Yes, that's still true. But it's still nowhere near as high of a risk as if we were trying to stop this robbery from happening. I'm still going back and forth on if we should try that or not."

"Well, it won't be me or Selena stopping this robbery. That's *your* job." Felix felt his heart drumming. He never raised his voice toward authority figures.

"Of course that's my job. And so is deciding how to best use our team to solve this mission. That includes you going into Kennedy's house to poke around. I'm not going to let anything bad happen to you."

Felix tossed his hands in the air. "Fine. I'll go pretend I'm a spy and do a job that is way over my head."

"Dammit, Felix, it isn't." Arielle balled a fist and slammed it on the kitchen table. "Do you know what your problem is? You have no faith in yourself. You are by far one of the smartest people in our entire organization, but you'd never know it from speaking with you. We don't have time to dive into why you have so much self-doubt at this moment, but you need to kick all those negative voices in your head to the curb.

"Honestly, with some combat training, you'd be right up there on the charts with me. I consider you smarter than me. You think fast on your feet and can adapt to any situation. You've proven it repeatedly through all your work with the Road Runners. So stop feeding me your nonsense about how badly this part of the mission will go. I'm not even asking you to take anything from Kennedy's house. Just walk around, see what clues there might be, and report back to me. That's it."

Arielle panted for breath after her rant, her face having turned a soft shade of red.

"Okay," Felix said after a minute. "I'll do this. Let's go."

He didn't wait for a response or reaction from Arielle, grabbing his keys and leaving. Felix had battled self-doubt for most of his life, never believing he was good enough, despite what the rest of the world had to say. He had discussed this matter with a Road Runner therapist during his climb to the highest-ranked Angel on the technology side.

A belief that he wasn't deserving of such an accolade plagued him to the point of his quality of work suffering. Felix had a difficult time getting out of his own head and trusting his natural skills to lead the way. He had an education like no one else in the Road Runners, and an understanding of technologies from all eras of time unmatched by anyone.

Yet he still never felt good enough. His therapist had once suggested he inflicted this doubt upon himself, because of guilt from leaving his parents behind to run the fashion boutique in San Francisco. They had done so much for Felix's education, and he fled right after graduating college. His parents had never brought up the matter, either, claiming to be fine with his decision to start a life of his own, wherever that should be. He manifested the shame on his own and supposed that was why it seemed impossible to shake free from his psyche.

Once Felix reached his car parked in the underground garage, Arielle bolted out of the stairwell door and hurried toward him.

"Wait!" she shouted.

He stopped before pulling open his car door.

Arielle needed a moment and leaned against Felix's car to catch her breath. "What's going on? You can't just leave like that."

"Sorry. But I'm ready to get this over with. You're right, Arielle. I can do this, and I apologize for acting like a frightened child. There's just a lot on my mind, I guess, and it was clouding my vision. Let's knock the rest of this mission out so we can go back home. I'm gonna need a few days off before the next one."

"Is everything okay?"

Felix shrugged. "I honestly don't know, and that's the problem. I call my parents and chat with them between missions, but I don't know the last time I've gone out to see them in person. I need to go to San Fran when we get back."

He shook his head, letting it hang low. Arielle reached out and placed a hand on his shoulder.

"Look, Felix, I get it. I visit my grandmother when I can. Our lifestyle makes it hard to maintain relationships outside of the Road Runners. But if you need time away, then take it. I wish you would have just come and talked to me. I assumed you were just being difficult about all of this."

"I would have if I had known what was bothering me. I think I'm a little homesick."

"Well, you know what's wrong, which means we can help you. I'll fly you to San Fran on my jet right when we get back, that way you don't have to deal with booking a flight or any of that hassle."

"Thanks . . . That's really kind of you."

"It's the least I can do."

"Let's get out of here before I change my mind," Felix said with a crooked grin.

The two hugged before getting into their separate cars and leaving the for Kennedys' house.

# Chapter 22

Felix stood on the back porch of Kennedy's house, hand shaking as he stuck the lock pick into the doorknob, letting himself in.

Arielle had driven ahead to Kennedy's favorite shooting range and paid for a one-hour time slot. She then called him from a gas station pay phone, posing as the shooting range to remind him of his scheduled appointment, something he quickly disputed, then agreed to go after learning it was already paid for. She had no idea if the plan would work, but Felix had waited in his car across the street and watched as Kennedy pulled out and left, Arielle appearing from around the corner to follow him, shooting Felix a thumbs up before they disappeared from the block.

Felix had no idea what she had done and only watched in amazement. She had told him he'd have at least ninety minutes in the house alone. He planned to use exactly one hour to snoop around and then get the hell out.

When he let himself into the house, Felix found the place even more disorganized than last time, perhaps because Kennedy had left in a hurry. Dirty dishes filled the sink, the scent of toast filled the air, and a jug of orange juice sat on the counter.

Felix wanted to take no chances this time, bolting the back door's lock to ensure he'd hear someone fidgeting with it should they show up again. He checked the front door to find it already bolted and felt more at ease knowing he'd have some warning before someone barged in, unannounced.

He wanted to spend a majority of his time in the basement, where they suspected Kennedy was planning the robbery in private, away from his wife. But first, he strolled into the master bedroom and slipped on a pair of rubber gloves before touching anything.

The bedroom had been picked up, the bed tidy, dirty clothes out of sight. Felix shuffled toward the dresser where Kennedy's son had stood during the suspicious phone call.

Last time, he had only seen a handful of utility bills, but rummaging through the pile, he found a stack of past due bills for water, cable, phone, and electricity. The Kennedys were at least three months behind on their bills, totaling around seven hundred dollars. Felix didn't think too much of it—that certainly wasn't enough to justify robbing a bank—until he found the next bill underneath. It was for a Visa credit card and had an outstanding balance of twenty-one thousand dollars, also three months past due, which meant it had likely accrued more interest since the bill had been delivered.

"Jackpot," Felix muttered under his breath.

He placed the bills back how he had found them and continued down the dresser, finding loose jewelry, receipts, books, and a few CD cases scattered in a mess. Felix crossed the room and opened Kennedy's nightstand drawer, which he assumed was his thanks to the magazine on top with model boats on the cover. Inside the drawer was a couple of hundred dollars in cash—and a handgun.

Felix picked up and examined the Colt .45. He put it back and pulled out a notepad from his back pocket to jot down his findings in the bedroom. He couldn't remember the gun used in the robbery, and would cross-reference that fact when he got back to the apartment.

Out of due diligence, he checked Mrs. Kennedy's nightstand drawer and found nothing of significance, then proceeded out of the bedroom and down the hall toward the stairwell leading to the basement. From the main level's landing he could see out the front window, and confirmed he was still alone.

Felix started down the dim stairs, refusing to turn on any lights. When he reached the bottom, the musty smell of rarely used basements filled his nose. A quick glance around suggested the place was mainly used for storage. Boxes and bins piled from the floor to the ceiling all around the perimeter. It was an open floor space, no walls or partitions. The only spot along the perimeter that didn't have boxes was the washing machine and dryer. A box of detergent stood atop the dryer, its lid flipped open, a pile of clothes stacked next to it.

A square table was on the other side of the basement, directly below a hanging light, covered in newspaper and miniature bottles of paint.

"This is where you do your boats," Felix said, shuffling toward the table. Only the tools were present on the table: paint bottles, brushes, tweezers. No boat, however.

Felix found this peculiar and rummaged through the box on the floor underneath the table. He saw two unopened boat kits, and more paint bottles. If Kennedy spent all of his time in the house, shouldn't he have at least been in the middle of a new boat project? It was possible he had just finished one and was taking a break.

"Or he's been too busy planning something else," Felix whispered. He looked around and saw no finished boats, either. That wasn't as odd—they were likely elsewhere in the house to be displayed, considering no one came down to the basement.

As much as Felix wanted to believe there were clues tying Kennedy to the robbery, he'd yet to find anything of true substance.

He checked his watch to find only twenty-five minutes had passed. He had plenty of time left to raid the basement, and intended on using every second.

"Okay. If I were planning a bank robbery in this basement, how would I do it?" Felix asked himself, pulling out the chair at the table and sitting down. He propped his elbows and looked around the room from Kennedy's angle. He had a clear view of the stairs and could easily see if someone was coming down. The table had likely been set up that way if Kennedy wanted to keep his secret under wraps from his wife. The box of boat materials was under the table so he could quickly pull it out and give the appearance of working on a model.

"If I had papers scattered on the table and needed to put them away in a hurry, I would just dump them into the box. . . but they can't stay there."

Felix looked straight ahead, where two boxes stared back at him. They were unmarked, despite all the other surrounding boxes having labels on them like *photo albums, kids' trophies, memorabilia.*

The boxes were on the opposite side of the laundry machines, sandwiched between others. Dust covered everything except for these two boxes. From the seated position, if someone were to come down and talk to Kennedy at the table, the boxes would be to that person's back, out of sight.

"Easy to get to while still hidden," Felix muttered, feeling his stomach tighten as he stood up, unable to break his stare from the two boxes.

He shuffled to the wall and pulled the box on the left, flipping open the flaps that served as a lid. "What the hell?"

The box was heavier than he expected, and now he saw why. Filled from the bottom to top were pornographic magazines and VHS tapes. Felix, suddenly feeling the urge to take a shower, shoved the box back into its place. Judging by the lack of dust on that box, Felix concluded Kennedy enjoyed pleasuring himself during his trips to the basement.

"Ooookay," he said, turning his attention to the box on the right, quickly accepting he might not find the smoking gun they were all hoping for.

The next box felt even heavier, so Felix braced himself for more dirty magazines as he opened the top.

What he found froze his heart mid-beat.

Felix crouched to sift through the contents. There was a smaller box inside, about the size of a shoebox, filled with an assortment of ammunition of all different colors, shapes, and sizes. He found a gun, another Colt, but one he presumed carried .38 caliber rounds, most of which were in the ammunition box.

A manila folder was pinned against the box by the ammunition, and Felix plucked it out, finding the word *PLANS* scribbled on one side. He flipped open the folder and floor plans of the United Bank building spilled out. They showed the layout of the basement, subbasement, and main levels. The page on top showed the vault area and its proximity to the security office.

What Felix found most odd was nothing drawn on the floorplans. If Kennedy were truly planning to rob the place, wouldn't he have at the very least drawn a preferred route in and out of the building? Or did he know the place well enough to not feel the need to do that?

Felix placed everything back into the folder before returning it to its proper place in the box. Below the gun was a stack of plastic cards all tied together with a rubber band. He pulled these out and flipped the stack over, finding the top card as a Colorado driver's license with Kennedy's portrait, but a name of Lucas Reynolds.

"Here they are."

He snapped off the rubber band to see the other cards, finding four more driver's licenses: two more from Colorado, one from Texas, one from California. They all had Kennedy's same portrait, but different names. The man was also Kenny Pearson, Joshua Wilson, Charles Wallace, and Ethan Miller.

Felix wrote these names down in his notepad and would research them later. These were the pieces of evidence the judge ruled to keep out of the trial.

"He's planning on running and hiding. That's the only explanation for this many fake IDs."

Felix wrapped them all back in the rubber band and dropped them into the box. He pushed everything around. He found nothing else and closed the box back up.

When he picked it up off the table and spun around to put it back in its place, a booming knock came from the front door upstairs. Felix dropped the box out of shock. His heart jumped all the way to his throat, limbs stiffening as he found it nearly impossible to move.

*This is the moment you knew was coming,* he thought.

A second knock followed, just as loud and aggressive as the first. He felt better knowing it was someone who couldn't let themselves into the house, or else they wouldn't have knocked again.

Felix debated taking the gun out of the box and going upstairs, but didn't want to risk something happening to the potential murder weapon—that would surely throw a wrench in the past's plans to carry out the attack.

Instead, he remained frozen in the basement, grateful it had no windows to the world outside. If needed, the basement was probably the best place to hide in the entire house. He could move a stack of boxes and hide behind them. The room was such a mess; he doubted Kennedy noticed if anything was out of place—beside his own boxes that he seemed to frequently access.

Felix waited five minutes before finally grabbing the box and putting it back, and starting up the stairs. He had wanted to poke around more of the house, but the loud knocking had thrown out all of those desires. It was time to get out.

When he reached the top landing, adrenaline blasting through his body like a broken water pipe, he scanned the area to make sure no one had discreetly slipped into the house. Besides his heart drumming in his ears, the house was silent. He tiptoed toward the dining-room window and craned his neck for an angle at the front door.

No one was there. Whoever had knocked had already given up and left.

He dashed through the house, stopping at the back door to peer out the window that stood inches above his line of sight. Once he saw no one, he stepped out and sprinted alongside the house toward the front.

His car sat across the street and he blazed directly toward it, jumping in and closing the door as he panted for air.

*I made it.*

Felix let out a nervous laugh as he turned on the car and sped away.

# Chapter 23

Later that night, the team gathered for dinner a few minutes past seven. Felix ordered a pizza, citing he was too eager to share his findings to cook a meal.

"Our guy can shoot," Arielle said, starting the conversation once they were all seated and had grabbed a slice. "I booked his time at the shooting range and grabbed a bay for myself four spots down. After seeing the clinic he put on, I'm convinced it's him. Keep in mind, the robber fired eighteen rounds that day, and all but one found their target."

Felix nodded, shifting forward in his seat and pushing back his plate he had yet to touch. "It's gotta be him. For starters, him and his wife are over twenty-thousand dollars in debt. So there's a motive. He had a gun in his nightstand drawer—probably for protection—but he had another in a box in their basement. And I'm pretty sure that box is dedicated to his robbery plans."

"Why do you say that?" Selena asked.

"Well, there was the gun, a box of bullets, five fake IDs. But the biggest giveaway of all . . . he has the floorplans to the bank, including the vault. Combine all of that. What do you get? Someone looking to rob a bank. Case closed—you can thank me later."

Felix chuckled, clearly satisfied with himself.

Arielle shook her head, promptly wiping away Felix's cheesy grin. "I'm afraid it's not that straightforward. A gun and bullets mean nothing. He goes to the shooting range often. What type of gun was it? Because according to the notes from the trial, a .38 Colt Trooper was used during the robbery. Silver revolver with a wooden handle."

Felix nodded. "That was it."

"And the fake IDs are definitely suspicious, but they don't guarantee anything. He never used them, according to the court documents. I'm not dismissing Kennedy as the main suspect, but we still have nothing definitive. These findings make things lean toward Kennedy, but we have one more suspect to check. Felix, you're going into Young's apartment tomorrow for another look around."

"I expected as much," he replied, crossing his arms.

Arielle waited for another outburst, but none came. Felix must have gained some serious confidence after his venture into Kennedy's house. "By the end of tomorrow, we should have a good idea who we want to narrow our focus on. There's still a chance—likely, perhaps—that we'll have to tail both Kennedy and Young on Sunday morning. But if we find nothing of importance in Young's house tomorrow, then we're moving all-in on Kennedy."

"And we're positive it can't be anyone else besides those two?" Selena asked.

Arielle scrunched her face. "There isn't anyone else of interest. Why do you ask?"

Selena shrugged. "There are many people who work in that building. Even just the security team. I'm not saying anyone specifically, but I feel like there can be more moving parts to this than we realized. This could be a coordinated effort involving multiple people wanting to split the heist."

"What, you think your boyfriend is involved?" Felix asked, his grin returning.

Selena rolled her eyes. "You're hilarious. No, I don't think Dawkins is, but he might have information that can help. I'm debating if I should call him tomorrow night to talk on the phone, or invite him to go out somewhere. Just him and I."

"Definitely on the phone," Arielle said. "If you go out, he's going to think it's a date, and that adds a whole other dynamic."

"Right, but if he thinks it's a date, he might be more willing to talk about anything, including his coworkers. That topic might be of no interest if we're on the phone."

Felix chimed in. "I think the phone is better, too. It reduces the risks. The past will still try to fight back as we get this information. Worst-case scenario, if you're home on the phone, the call will drop. Who knows what might happen if you're out and about."

"Very good point," Arielle said. "Just because today ran smoothly doesn't mean that will hold up. Every day closer to the robbery is more opportunity for chaos. You should make the call from right here."

Selena finished the crust from her first slice, nodding as she brushed the crumbs off her fingertips.

"Okay. Phone call it is."

"It'll be like high school," Felix said. "You can talk on the phone for five hours until someone falls asleep. No one wants to hang up first."

Selena crumbled up her napkin and chucked it across the table to drill Felix in the face. Everyone burst out in laughter.

Arielle was glad to see such free flowing conversation from her team. They were comfortable. They trusted each other. And that would only pay dividends in the long run.

"Did you see any guns in Young's apartment?" Arielle asked, bringing the focus back to the group.

"He had one in his nightstand—that seems to be a thing with these security guards. It wasn't a Colt, though, so no match to the gun used in the robbery."

"But he is a gun owner—that's what I was more curious to know. I wonder why he's never gone shooting with Kennedy. It's clear they have a solid friendship."

"Can't be seen together in that type of setting," Felix said. "Kennedy knows how to cover his bases—you keep forgetting that. He's too smart to get caught, and that's why he never was, even after being arrested and put on trial."

"Do you think we'll have to stay afterwards to find out who did it?" Selena asked. "Like you said, the mission isn't to stop this robbery from happening, it's strictly to find out who did it."

"I've been mulling that over," Arielle said. "There's a chance we'll stay until Monday. It's hard to say how Sunday will play out. We know the route the robber will use when running out of the building, but after that we don't know where he goes. Does he get in a car and drive away? Is someone else waiting for him in a car? There could be some sort of handoff—maybe Kennedy gives the money to Young and they go their separate ways.

"Let's keep in mind, Kennedy isn't arrested until three weeks after the robbery. By Sunday night, no one has a clue he might be a suspect. I'd love to find out where the money is hidden. Assuming Kennedy did it, he has a three-week window to hide the cash, dispose of the gun and everything else he took from the security office. That's a long time."

"Are you saying we stay even longer than Monday?" Felix asked, raising an eyebrow.

Arielle shifted in her seat, crossing one leg over the other as she looked to the ceiling. "Are you not curious? We're already here. Why not plan on seeing where the money is? Who knows, we might find that out on Sunday and can leave then. I just want to go back with all the information we can get. Most importantly, who did it and where that money is stashed."

Felix raised his hands defensively. "I'm all for staying. I guess we're just a little surprised about your change of heart. Just last week you were ready to bail on this mission. Now you want to stay beyond the robbery."

Selena nodded to support Felix's statement.

"Well," Arielle said. "I let the logistics of the mission cloud not only my vision, but my passion. I put too much stress on myself trying to make this mission fit the mold of prior ones. I might have been a little offended that we received a mission that didn't require us to disrupt the robbery. A slap in the face is how I first took it. Usually new Angels get missions where they go back in time just to learn something and report the findings. But I've since seen why they chose us for this one. It's complex and messy, and I'm still not sure how clear of an answer we'll get once it's all over. So thank you both."

"What did we do?" Selena asked, shooting a puzzled look to Felix.

"You both kept your head down and worked, despite my feelings. It would have been easy for you to agree with me and lose interest in the mission. I wouldn't have been able to blame you if it came to that, since I was the one spewing the disgust. But you ignored me and kept at it. We wouldn't be anywhere close to where we are today without that. So I thank you. And I owe you."

"You don't owe us anything," Felix said. "But you *could* buy that first round of margaritas when we get back home."

Selena nodded, a wide grin taking over her face at the mention of a margarita.

"Margaritas, huh?" Arielle asked. "Do we have a new tradition now, after missions?"

"I suppose we do," Selena said. "D'Corazon after each mission sounds just fine to me."

"Consider it done," Arielle said. "Now let's get some rest. Tomorrow should be another fun day."

# Chapter 24

Felix was awake first on Thursday morning. They had three more days until the robbery, and two candidates: one a clear front runner, the second not as obvious. The goal for today was to cross Young off the list so they could narrow their focus strictly on Kennedy. At least, that was Felix's goal.

He had woken at six-thirty, a half hour before Young typically got out of bed to start his workday. Today was no different, so Felix used the extra time to prepare a full breakfast for himself and the ladies. Eggs, bacon, toast, sliced fruit. He didn't care how loud the bacon sizzled in the stillness of the early morning; the smell was the perfect jump-start for the day.

By seven-thirty, everyone had eaten, dressed, and left the apartment building, including Peter Young. Felix hung around until eight, just to make sure Young didn't return for any reason. Once deciding it was safe, he left the apartment and took the stairs down to the fifth floor.

The hallway was abandoned, minus a mother dragging a whiny child from their apartment, a baseball bag slung over the kid's shoulder.

Once they cleared out, Felix marched up to apartment 512, reached into his pocket for his trusty lock pick, jamming it into the keyhole and twisting until he heard the satisfactory *click* of success.  He had this part of the process down to a basic instinct after having done it so many times.  He spent less than three seconds in front of the apartment door before disappearing inside and closing it behind him.

Young's living quarters didn't look too different compared to last time, but Felix could also take his time on this trip.

The aroma of coffee filled the small apartment, the abandoned coffeepot sitting on the counter next to the sink, still filled with dishes to the brim. Felix had watched Young enough to know the man only washed a dish when he needed to use it. He'd even used a dirty plate on various occasions, something that made Felix gag each time he saw it.

He went to the bedroom first.  Again, nothing looked different from last time.  Clothes remained on the floor in front of the closet, its doors wide open. Felix shuffled to the nightstand, slipped on a pair of rubber gloves, and opened the drawer, seeing the pistol still in place.

"A Ruger P89 or 90," Felix said, pulling out his notebook to write the model. It was not the gun used in the robbery, and this satisfied Felix. One more piece of evidence that suggested Young hadn't carried out the attacks.

He closed the drawer and turned his attention to the dresser near the bedroom's doorway. On top was scattered change, old receipts, pens, blank notepads, and three pairs of sunglasses.

The robber had worn sunglasses, and one pair looked like the same style seen in all the pictures and sketches that would show up during the trial.  Felix noted this finding in his notepad, discouraged by the potential clue. Nearly everyone in town owned a pair of sunglasses, so it wasn't exactly a smoking gun, either.

He then started going through the dresser's three drawers, each filled to the brim with unfolded clothes, underwear, and socks. Nothing of significance.

Felix spent the next fifteen minutes doing the same thing in the closet, with much more of a mess to sift through. He found a shoebox filled with old pictures of Young and a blond woman of around the same age, presumably an old girlfriend, judging by the obvious signs of affection. Besides that, he found nothing.

Relieved all signs still pointed to Kennedy, Felix returned to the living room. His gaze fell on the closet doors near the apartment's entrance, and that's when his gut wrenched, a sense of dread drenching him like a bucket of ice water.

The closet had a pair of bi-fold doors with a grab handle on each. A set of handcuffs clasped around each handle to prevent the doors from opening. Felix had no idea if those handcuffs had been hanging there on his last visit—it seemed like a detail he wouldn't have missed, but he hadn't exactly been scanning the room for such things.

The cuffs gleamed in the dim light coming through the shaded window overlooking downtown. Felix approached, fishing out his lock pick that would work easily on a pair of handcuffs.

He had them unlocked within seconds, leaving them hanging from one handle.

When he pulled the doors open, the dread kicked into a higher gear. He had found a hidden treasure of incriminating evidence all piled up within the closet.

Unlike Kennedy's organized box of goods, Young had stuff all over the place, scattered about the floor and on top of boxes. The first things he found were three sandwich bags full of ammunition. Upon closer examination, he deemed them as .38 and .357 caliber. On the closet's top shelf lay a revolver, and he pulled it down to find it fully loaded.

"Shit," Felix muttered. After twenty minutes of hope and optimism, Young remained a primary suspect, perhaps even more so than Kennedy, once Felix continued digging through the closet.

He flipped open the top box's lid and found a police scanner and two speedloaders that fit the revolver above. This discovery was perhaps the most alarming, seeing as the robber had fired eighteen rounds from a revolver in fairly rapid succession. One loaded revolver plus two speedloaders equaled eighteen rounds and allowed the shooter to reload in seconds. Sprawled on the bottom of the box were five different police badges, each for a different department from around the state.

They looked and felt real, but Felix wasn't versed enough in police badges to know an obvious fake. He took a moment to write his findings in the notebook before closing the box and opening a second.

In the next one, he discovered two batons and four grenades, prompting him to close the box and leave it untouched. The last thing he needed to tempt the past with was an opportunity to blow the entire apartment complex to the moon.

A small notebook, roughly four by six inches, lay on the floor between the tower of boxes. Felix squatted down to pick it up, a title scrawled in sloppy handwriting: *Confidential need to know only.*

The first few pages had disturbing drawings of gravestones, including one for Young himself. After flipping a couple of pages, it became clear Young meant the drawing to be a cemetery. There were dozens of names, none of which Felix recognized aside from Young. Certainly no names that had any ties to the robbery.

Chickenscratch began on page six, and with it, a new thread of evidence Felix couldn't deny, including a disclaimer at the top of the page:

*Warning—these entries are blunt and brutal. Sensitive psyches are advised to stop now. If you are emotionally unstable, close this journal immediately. There is one caveat—my deepest secrets are not revealed here. You'll never know a damn thing. I trust no one.*

Reading this caused gooseflesh to overtake all of Felix. He shook his head and continued on:

*If you're reading this, then I'm already rotting underground. A fitting end to a lame attempt at life. However, it was not as lame as you detectives and police officers. I have a question for you all. How can you be so pathetic? Your investigative abilities—if you can call them that—are at best guesswork and pure luck. How does the old saying go? You have done too little too late!*

*To wrongfully accuse a man is a level of cowardice I can't begin to comprehend. How low must one go to simply pin fault on another human being without having all the facts? I'm not saying I lived a perfect life. Far from it. I've done both good and bad in this world. But I never committed the crime you supposedly believe I did. That reminds me of my mortal flaw—I never forget who screwed me over. And guess what? I have another flaw! I am patient to a fault. I believe in getting even. I have the patience to do just that. Even if I have to wait 50 years, I will get even. That's a promise.*

*The last time I stole money was when I was eight years old. I wanted a Superman comic so bad from our neighbor's yard sale. My mom said no, but I snuck into her bedroom and took the two dollars anyway. And guess what? I felt guilty. So much that after a week, I confessed what I did. I got quite the ass-whooping that night, but that doesn't upset me. It was deserved.*

*What isn't deserved, however, is having to go through a bullshit trial for being accused of robbing an ATM. How stupid do you take me for? You actually think I would openly rob an ATM at my place of employment? With all of the cameras around? None of which showed me doing anything even remotely close to robbing a machine.*

*This may all be a part of your lame job, but that one accusation has ruined my life. Even after being found INNOCENT, do you know how the public treats someone who had to stand trial for such a crime? Like a fucking PARASITE.*

*And it's funny, because there are TWO actual parasites, and they both work for United Bank: Tom Trawinski and Alvin Lasch. If you open the dictionary to the word 'asshole', you'll find a picture of these two scumbags. These are by far the worst employers I have ever worked for, and I've worked for some shady people. They tried to lock me up for something I didn't do.*

*Lying Tom can burn in hell. It WILL happen. The Lord will have his way with men like Tom. He's the one who should be in the federal pen raking rocks with a 16-pound hammer. Not me. Alvin, too. These men are a disgrace to humanity and society.*

Felix snapped the notebook shut and looked around the apartment. He felt like he had fallen into a trap by reading the lunacy penned by Young. There were plenty more pages to read, and Young seemed nowhere close to finished with his rantings.

One notebook had just swerved this entire mission into a different direction. A shift was underway, and Felix couldn't help but wonder if the past had placed that notebook in the closet to distract them from Kennedy.

"Or this is real, and Young did it. We have the rest of today, all of tomorrow, and all of Saturday. Two and a half days until the morning of the robbery."

He stood in the closet for five more minutes, playing through all scenarios, trying to think about what Arielle might have done if she was standing in the closet right now.

"I'm going for it," he said, and stuck the notebook in his pocket before leaving the apartment.

# Chapter 25

Felix had fought off an excessively trembling body for the two hours after he returned home with Young's notebook. He felt like he had just committed a major felony, one that could lock him up for years. He could only hope the past didn't have that sort of appetite for justice.

During the first hour in the safety of his apartment, Felix had put the notebook on the kitchen table and sat there staring at it. He never opened it or touched it, treating it like a lethal bug that could end his life with one drop of venom.

He didn't understand the past on the complex level that Arielle did, so he wasn't sure what to expect as far as a time range for something to happen. Would someone come knocking on his door, accusing him of being inside an apartment that wasn't his? Or perhaps nothing would happen until Young returned home and discovered his notebook missing.

Felix took a gamble and believed Young wouldn't seek the notebook over the next two and a half days. By now he had over ten days of live and recorded footage of Young in his apartment, and he hadn't once seen him open those closet doors. In fact, he pulled up a recording from last week, curious to see if the handcuffs had always been clasped around the closet's door handles. Sure enough, they were, and he beat himself up for missing such a detail. Felix prided himself on his keen observation skills, and this felt like a blunder that should have never happened.

He didn't dwell on it for too long. The handcuffs would have become obvious had Young actually used the closet. Instead, they blended into the backdrop, no different from the black-and-white poster of Marilyn Monroe hanging in the living room.

After that first hour had passed, Felix worked up the courage to open the notebook and resume reading. By five-thirty in the evening, the notebook was stuffed with different colored sticky notes on what seemed like every page. He had paced circles around their living room, and continued doing just that while he waited for Selena and Arielle to arrive.

At 5:50, Arielle finally stepped through the door. She looked to the kitchen, saw nothing cooking, then to Felix, who had beads of sweat forming on his forehead, and finally down to the notebook clutched in his grip.

"Is everything okay?" she asked. "Where's Selena?"

Felix shrugged. As much as he had been watching the clock, it hadn't occurred to him that Selena should have been home already. His stomach dropped to his knees as he couldn't help wonder if his stealing of the notebook had led to something bad happening to Selena. He wanted to spew out hundreds of words at a time, but didn't know where to start.

"Felix?" Arielle said, dropping her backpack by the door and crossing into the living room. "You don't look too well. What happened today?"

Felix nodded, a lump suddenly forming in his throat. He had no idea why he had become so nervous to speak to Arielle about his findings. He supposed part of it was knowing drastic changes might need to be implemented with less than three days remaining.

"Sorry," he finally managed. "I don't know where Selena is. Did she maybe go out with that guy, after all?"

This drew a look of concern from Arielle, her eyes glancing to Selena's open bedroom door, as if she were in there and no one knew it. She checked her watch and shook her head. "If she's not here by six, we'll need to go for a walk and see if we can find her."

"Oh my God!" Felix gasped, causing Arielle to take a cautious step backwards. "Young should be home, and I haven't even thought to check."

He smacked a hand on his forehead and dashed into his bedroom where he kept his laptop on the bed. He had become so convinced that Young was the robber, that he forgot his main job was to watch the angry, isolated man.

When he flipped open his laptop, the feed showed Young in his typical position on the recliner, a microwave dinner on his lap while he flipped mindlessly through the TV channels. The handcuffs remained on the closet doors.

"Okay," Felix said. "We're okay."

Arielle came into his bedroom and tossed her hands in the air. "What's going on? Seriously—tell me right now."

Felix jumped off his bed and pushed past Arielle back out to the living room where he had tossed the notebook on the couch. He held it up like an all-powerful relic. A book from the heavens that contained every answer to life's greatest questions. "Before I start, did you find anything on Kennedy today?"

Arielle shook her head. "Wish I could call it a productive day, but he did nothing. Never once stepped out of the house."

"Can't say I'm surprised." Felix could feel the words coming out faster than normal, and attempted to slow himself down. "I have in my hands a journal belonging to Peter Young. It is loaded with the thoughts of a madman who wants *revenge* on United Bank!"

Arielle's jaw dropped as she stared at the journal. "Felix, do you know how dangerous having that in your possession is? You need to put it back."

"I thought this through. I think we'll be okay for the night. I can take it back in the morning—I can't in this instant, obviously. But at least we'll have it for the entire night to pick it apart and see what else we can find. Young has one twisted mind. The guy is a nutjob!"

Felix recapped what he had read, getting Arielle caught up with what he referred to as the "heavy details."

"Do we know if those two guys still work there?" Arielle asked. "Trawinski and Lasch."

"No clue. We'll have to see what Selena can find about those names. But it gets more interesting." Felix thumbed the journal open and ran a finger down the page, reading the entry aloud. "'This whole process has been bad enough, but the most humiliating part was having to ask my dad for money to pay for the lawyers. Ten thousand dollars. I barely make that in a year, and now my dad resents me for having to borrow it. On top of that, my dad actually believes I robbed that ATM.

"'He worked at a bank his entire life, and insists I'm guilty. My dad was my best friend in this world, and I've lost that relationship because of this false accusation. My life has been completely ruined, and that leaves me only one option. My accusers will be judged by a higher authority, and I hope He has mercy on them. I will not.'"

Felix closed the journal, keeping a thumb between the pages to save his spot. "This paints a pretty obvious picture, don't you think?"

Arielle nodded. "It's hard to argue his motive."

"It sounds like he had a pretty up-and-down relationship with his dad. Says he was his best friend, but also goes on about how it all soured after this accusation. I can't help but wonder if Father's Day was chosen on purpose because of that, as some sort of sick way to prove something to his father."

"What was the timing of all this?"

"It sounds like Young was arrested for this ATM robbery in May 1990, was acquitted by the fall, and his father passed away in January 1991. It really was a rough stretch for him."

Arielle sat down at the kitchen table, pale. "Great work, Felix. I think we were all ready to dismiss Young, but now we can't. Even if he isn't the one who directly robs the place, he *has* to be involved somehow, right?"

"I believe so. Between the handful of meetings with Kennedy, and learning about all of this pent-up hatred for the exact bank that will be robbed . . . how can we believe otherwise?"

Arielle checked her watch and stood up. "It's 6:10. We need to go make sure Selena is okay. We're going to have a long night digging through this journal." She chuckled as she shook her head. "Good call on taking it. I probably would've done the same thing."

"Thanks. Let's go. I want to come back as soon as possible to finish going through this notebook."

# Chapter 26

Selena changed her plans in the middle of the day, opting to ask Dawkins out to drinks and dinner after work.  Just the two of them, she had emphasized during a quick trip down to the security office during her lunch break. Dawkins eagerly agreed.

At 5:15, Selena changed into a pair of jeans and a crop top. She figured that would distract Dawkins just enough to let his guard down and speak openly about his colleagues.

It worked immediately. When she stepped out of the locker room, Dawkins was already waiting in the hallway, having changed into jeans and a button-up. His eyes immediately fell to her exposed abdomen as he did a double take.

"You look incredible," he said, unable to keep a grin off his face.

"Oh, this old thing?" Selena teased, putting her hands on her hips and batting her eyebrows.

Dawkins cackled. "Shall we head over?"

"Please. I'm starving."

They shared the details of their day with each other as they walked down the hallway, took the elevator up to the street level, and strolled across the street toward the café .

A few people hustled up and down the streets of downtown

Denver, most clearly leaving work. It was a warm summer evening, and the heat seemed to radiate off the concrete. Selena's mouth watered at the thought of a cold drink.

Once they entered the café , the bartender waved them over to sit in a booth along the window. They looked out and had a clear view of their office building immediately across Seventeenth Street.

"Always a good feeling to get out of that place," Selena said. "Don't you agree?"

"It's not that bad. You don't like your job?"

Selena shrugged. She'd never had a regular nine-to-five type of job, and only knew how people talked about them from what she had seen on TV. "It pays the bills, but it's not exactly what I want to do."

Dawkins laughed. "Well, I don't suppose too many people are doing what they *truly* want to do. I don't see myself being a security guard for the rest of my life."

"You want to become a cop?"

Dawkins shook his head. "Nah. I know that's the stereotype with guards, especially in our building. Everyone is a former cop, wants to be a cop, or failed in the police academy. If I can be honest, I'm not entirely sure what I want to do for a career. What about you?"

"Acting has always been my passion. It's something I've done since I was a little girl. I *wanted* to be in school plays and all that stuff. I know I just moved here, but I want to go to Hollywood and take my shot."

Dawkins nodded, clearly impressed. A server came over and Dawkins ordered a couple of appetizers for them to munch on. Selena was sure to order a frozen margarita.

"That's impressive," he said. "Why not go for it, right?

What do you have to lose? You can always find different jobs to the pay the bills, but you don't get a second chance at life. Chase your dreams while you can."

Selena smiled. A genuine smile. Brian Dawkins sat across from her in the booth, oblivious that she had come from the year 2022. She had planned on toying with him to get new information about his colleagues, but she suddenly found herself drawn into his natural charm.

He had a true interest in her, paying full attention while he spoke, gazing at her with welcoming eyes.

Selena had to shake herself out of the trance and remember what she came to do. "That's a nice thought. So you don't like your job too much, either?"

"I actually enjoy it. It keeps me in shape and has lots of downtime. Being such a massive building, I must walk at least five miles a day during sweeps. But there's also three hours of just hanging out. I can read books, do a crossword. Hell, might even bring in an actual jigsaw puzzle one day." He laughed while the server returned with a basket of French fries and a plate of chicken wings. "Please, help yourself."

Selena grabbed a fistful of fries. "How are your coworkers? You all seemed like a pretty tight bunch that day we were here for drinks."

"They're good guys. I don't really see any of us staying friends beyond this job, but I suppose we keep each other company while we're there." He gave a subconscious nod toward the building.

Selena could tell he wasn't going to elaborate anymore, so she needed to force the matter. "Well, they seemed like a fun group to me. What was the younger guy's name? Sid?"

Dawkins nodded after taking a bite of chicken. "Sid. He's

a really cool dude. Probably my closest friend at work since we're both younger."

"And I know all about Bill. He's probably the nicest person I've met since I started working there."

"Bill is the man. He looks out for everyone. He's not a supervisor, but he acts like one. Which is good for us. He keeps everything running smoothly, so the higher-ups never come down to check on us. They just see the work getting done every day and don't question it. But it's all Bill's doing."

"Who was that other guy? Kind of chubby, wears those big glasses?"

"Peter Young. He's . . . interesting."

Selena sat forward. "How so?"

"How much time do you have?" Dawkins asked, letting out a chuckle.

*To hear about Young, I have all the time in the world.*

"That bad?" Selena asked. "We haven't even ordered dinner yet, so why don't you tell me about him. He's seemed really distant in the couple times I've encountered him."

Dawkins waved over their server so they could order their entrées. He asked for a steak, medium-rare. And Selena ordered a chicken sandwich with extra tater tots on the side.

"Distant?" Dawkins asked when they resumed their conversation. "That would be a compliment. That guy gives me the fucking creeps."

Selena placed her hand on her bouncing knee to keep it under control. She couldn't help but sense something valuable coming her way. "The creeps? I don't know if I'd go that far."

"That's because you don't have to sit in a room with him all day. He speaks to no one. He might say hello at the beginning of a shift, and goodbye at the end. But that's a big maybe.

Outside of that, he just sits there all day in silence. He can clearly hear the conversations we have in the office, but he never chimes in. He'll occasionally read a book, but most the time it's like he's staring into space. Like no one is home inside."

"Do you think he's okay? Does he need mental help?"

"Hard to say. Bill has told us he wasn't always this way. I guess last year one of the ATMs was robbed. Something like $30,000 was stolen. The guards used to refill the machines on the weekends—we don't anymore, because of this. But Peter was arrested and had to stand trial. They blamed him for it, even though there was no actual proof. The video footage was spotty—the lights had been turned off in the room—and all they could make out was the general body outline of the robber. They felt Peter was the closest fit, but it honestly could have been anyone. There were four guards on duty at the time of the robbery, and since it was a Sunday, it clearly had to be an inside job since the building was closed and locked to the public. There was no evidence of breaking and entering. Nothing even reported on the security log that entire day."

Dawkins leaned back and raised his eyebrows, proud of himself for having remembered so many details about Young's story.

"And he still works there?" Selena asked. "How is that even possible?"

"He was suspended during the trial, obviously. But after they found him not guilty, he returned to work. Because of the verdict, the bank had no grounds for terminating his employment—he was an innocent man in the eyes of the law. Everyone thought he would quit, anyway. Who would want to work for a company that falsely accused you of robbing them?"

"But he didn't."

"Exactly. And no one knows why. It's not like security jobs are hard to find. You can get one almost anywhere. Everyone knows he hates upper management. But he comes in, does his job, and goes home without saying a word. We've speculated he does this to keep his job. It's fair to think the company would jump at the slightest of opportunities to fire him, so he makes it impossible by being a virtual robot."

"Were you working there when this all happened?" Selena asked. The server had brought their dinner, but she didn't even notice, too enthralled by the story involving one of their main suspects.

"I wasn't," Dawkins said. He noticed his sizzling steak and wasted no time grabbing his utensils to dig in. "I started maybe a month after Peter's trial had ended, but it was still such a hot story around the security office that I heard all about it."

"Why do you think he stayed?" What Selena really wanted to ask was if Dawkins thought Young was planning some sort of revenge. Whether that was by robbing the bank or murdering everyone who falsely accused him. But that seemed too specific of a question, and she didn't want to seem *too* interested in this story.

"Hard to say, but I think it's because of the location. He lives walking distance from here, and I know he has some medical conditions where he shouldn't drive long distances. Even though he drives all the way out to Flagler to visit his mom."

Selena was taking mental notes and filed this tidbit away to revisit later. "Okay, so this is all really interesting, but if he's such a closed-off person, why did he come out with you guys?"

After washing a bite of steak down with a swig of beer, Dawkins asked, "Why are you so curious about Peter Young? Shouldn't we be talking about you and me?"

Dawkins raised a fair point, and Selena had to remind herself that she was on a date with this handsome source of information. She cracked a soft grin, hoping it appeared seductive. "I'm sorry, but this is something I've always done. It's part of my desire to act, I guess. I've always tried to get inside the mind of interesting people. *Different* people. What makes them tick, you know? There will be plenty of time for us, but I want to hear how this all ends."

Dawkins let out a chuckle. "Well, if you insist. I mean the story itself is over, but sure, let's keep talking about Peter Young. It's romantic."

Selena laughed and nodded for him to continue.

"Okay, so the only reason Peter came out with us is because his friend showed up. Jake Kennedy. He used to work on the security team—also before I had started. I don't know much about Jake besides that. I've only met him a couple of times, but he seems like a nice enough guy. Rumor has it that he helped Young rob that ATM, but Jake wasn't even working there at that point—he had retired. So unless he came to work with Peter that morning, that story makes no sense. Someone would have definitely mentioned a non-employee being in the building at the time of a robbery."

"Hmm, that is strange, but I guess everyone has friends, right? Even someone like Young."

"I suppose they do."

"It's crazy to think a guard on the inside robbed the ATM.

Or do things like that happen more often than I realize?"

Dawkins looked around before leaning forward over his plate, speaking in a hushed tone. "We talk about it all the time. How easy it would be to rob a bank, especially ours. Wouldn't take a genius to figure it out." He leaned back and spoke in a normal tone again. "We're not exactly known for having the best security detail at our bank. Quite the opposite, in fact. We have access to the vault, know the coverage from the cameras, the schedules of when the vault will be open. We don't have guns, so I'm not sure how they honestly expect us to stop anyone if they were to come in with a gun. I mean, if Peter robbed that ATM, he got away with it! In the middle of a Sunday afternoon. No clear footage, no fingerprints. Nothing. A quick five-minute job that had no chance of being traced to anyone. It's a joke."

Selena took a bite and chewed on it excessively. She had learned this trick from Felix, who never hesitated shoving food in into his mouth to buy himself a few more seconds to think and process information before replying.

"Well, I'm sorry to hear you can't do your job well," she said. "Sounds like if they asked us to clean the floors and leave us with no mops."

Dawkins laughed. "That would be quite the task."

"Do they not think your bank has a high risk of being robbed? I just don't understand why they would disarm security guards who protect a vault full of cash."

"I wish I knew their logic behind that decision. They must suppose the vault is safe since it's two levels below the actual bank. Even if a robber were to hold up the tellers, it's pretty much impossible for them to get down to the vault. And if they did, they wouldn't have enough time to take the money and escape before the police arrive. And this is all assuming the vault is even open. So, no, I don't particularly consider our bank at a high risk to get robbed."

This confirmed essentially everyone's belief that it had to be an inside job. But who was the insider? Kennedy didn't work there. Young did. The two seemed to still have a tight bond, and both had a motive: revenge for Young, and clearing a mountain of debt for Kennedy.

They had spent their time trying to pin the robbery on one of the two, when it was clearly becoming obvious that they were working together.

Selena had heard enough, satisfied with the evening's findings. "That's all fascinating to me. I just hope you never get robbed."

When Arielle and Felix arrived at the Last Drop, they spotted Selena and Dawkins sitting in a window booth and had to stop to turn around, instead crossing the street to watch them from a distance.

Arielle figured Selena was fine, but they wanted to keep a close eye, just in case. She assumed Selena was trying to prod information from Dawkins, and didn't want the past to unleash its fury.

That it had thrown no obstacles their way yet made Arielle uneasy. Even with all the facts and evidence they had accumulated, something still felt off. With only two full days before the robbery, they had officially entered the home stretch.

"Doesn't this seem like a waste of time?" Felix asked after they sat on a sidewalk bench just out of sight from the café. "We have a notebook we can examine together that has everything but a confession in it."

"We'll head back soon. Who knows how long Selena will be? This guy doesn't seem to pose a threat. I'm sure Selena is playing him like a fiddle."

"How do you trust your instincts so easily? You've taken, what, two looks at that guy and can already tell he's harmless?"

"Instincts develop the more you do something. Do you know how many people I've had to watch from a distance?  For *weeks* on end.  Trying to analyze and figure out their next moves. Besides, we have research on everyone involved. This Dawkins guy comes from a loving family, private education, and the worst thing on his record is a speeding ticket for driving ten miles over the limit.  I know that doesn't mean anything definitive, but it's not exactly a recipe for concern, either."

"I guess that makes sense."

"Let's head back.  I don't think there's anything here for us."

Arielle stood up, then Felix, who turned around to look at the bank building behind him. "Don't you want to go in there?"

Arielle grinned. "Of course, but it's too risky now. Selena gets to have all the fun inside."

"We should at least plan what we're trying to do on Sunday morning, no?"

Arielle crossed her arms and turned around to face the bank. "We can make a tentative plan, I suppose. Follow me."

Arielle led them toward the intersection of Seventeenth Avenue and Lincoln Street, breaking right to walk along the west side of the Cash Register Building on Lincoln.

A bridge connected the skyscraper to a small parking garage across the street. They passed under it and walked the rest of the block until reaching another parking garage for employees of the building.  Next to that was an entrance for freight deliveries and armored vehicles that delivered cash to the bank.

The security gates had been lowered to block entry after hours, but Arielle reached out and grasped the gate, peering through the slots for a look inside the garage. "It's kind of dark, but you can barely see the silver of the elevator doors along the back wall."

Felix stepped next to Arielle and squinted as he looked. "I see it."

"So, all we know is the robber entered the building through that elevator. He called security posing as the vice president of the bank, asking to be let in."

"Wait, these gates were open on a Sunday?"

Arielle nodded. "Cash delivery day for the bank. That's why the vault was open and there were employees working. So the robber would have strolled in through the open gate, pretended to be the VP, and everything spiraled from there."

Felix looked around and pointed to a security camera mounted high on the column next to them. "No footage of the robber walking in that morning?"

Arielle shook her head. "Tapes were swiped from the security room, remember? All the tapes that would have shown the robber's path throughout the attack. A clear inside job—it was done with too much attention to the little details." Arielle stepped back and looked around, brushing her chin with a finger. "What we still don't know is which way the robber escaped. We can assume he left the same way he came in, but if he had someone else driving a getaway car, it could have been any of the exits, even on the other side of the building."

"I've studied the layout and I don't think that makes sense. He would have covered a ton of ground to run to the other side of the building, and I'm thinking he wanted to get out as fast as possible. I think he took the stairs. There were no logs of a keycard being used during the robber's departure, and those are the only doors that don't require one since they can't open from the outside."

"Excellent point." Arielle stepped even further back, wanting to absorb the building and its surroundings. "I've had similar suspicions, but that makes sense, especially if you've examined the security and layout."

Felix stepped back to join her, looking up toward the top of the skyscraper, which was out of sight. "I don't have any proof of this, but it's my best educated guess. There might be another possibility we're not even aware of. Selena might know better, having been in there."

Footsteps approached from their right, and Arielle saw Felix's eyes bulge. She looked over to see Selena and Dawkins within twenty feet of them, continuing to stroll closer.

Selena had been laughing and abruptly stopped when she realized who was standing on the sidewalk in front of her. She locked eyes with Arielle first, pursing her lips and narrowing her eyes. Arielle interpreted it as *Don't say a word, everything is fine.*

Arielle grabbed Felix by the shoulder and pulled him away to walk back toward the café .

"What are you doing?" he muttered under his breath, looking over his shoulder to see Selena and Dawkins disappear into the parking garage.

"Relax. She's fine. I think he's giving her a ride home."

Arielle sped up, nearly in a power-walk, and Felix had to jog to keep up. "So, we're just going home?" he asked.

"Yes, it might be a stretch, but let's try to beat them there."

Arielle debated seeking a cab, but figured it would take too long to track one down. It was roughly a fifteen-minute walk back to the apartment complex from the café , and she figured they could make it in ten minutes if they jogged.

She didn't ask Felix, knowing an argument would ensue, so she started running.

"Wait!" he shouted, and she only looked over her shoulder with a wide grin.

"Keep up!"

Felix tossed his hands in the air before gathering the courage to jog as well. Arielle knew he'd be fine. Felix kept in good enough shape to handle a simple run through downtown on a warm night.

After two blocks, they didn't have to deal with any traffic lights and pedestrian crossings. Each block had stop signs instead, which they promptly ran straight through. She knew driving from the bank to their apartment would take less than five minutes, but she was counting on added time for Selena and Dawkins to find his car and drive out of the garage. If they were lucky, he might have even needed to run inside the building to grab something before leaving. In that case, they would definitely beat them back.

That wasn't the case, however, as they found Dawkins and Selena already parked in front of the complex when they rounded the corner. Felix gasped for air, placing both hands behind his head as he stared at the sky.

Arielle had seen Selena's silhouette through the car window and ducked behind another car two spaces back. Felix crouched next to her. "What are we doing?"

"They're right there," she whispered, cocking her head in their direction. Arielle stood taller, but not completely straight. They had the advantage of the rapidly growing darkness with each passing minute. The sun would be completely gone within the next half hour. She saw their heads bobbing in conversation for the next three minutes before Selena finally stepped out of the car and closed the door behind her, waving to Dawkins, who turned his car around and drove away.

"Selena!" Arielle shouted, stepping back onto the sidewalk.

Selena spun around, startled. Once she saw Arielle and Felix approaching, she grinned while shaking her head.

"What the hell? Were you guys following me all night?" Selena asked, tossing her hands in the air.

"Actually, no," Arielle said. "We were worried when you didn't come home, but figured you might have gone out with Dawkins. Thanks for telling us about the change in plans."

"Sorry. It just sort of happened. I had every intent on making the phone call tonight, but trust me, this turned out even better than I imagined. I learned so much tonight, my head is spinning."

"Well?" Felix asked.

Selena frowned and looked around. "Well, nothing. We're not talking about it out here. Let's go inside."

She didn't wait for the other two and pivoted around to walk back inside the complex. Arielle and Felix followed her all the way up to their apartment, no one speaking a word as they clung to the thick anticipation.

Once they stepped in and closed the door, Selena let the words fly like air out of a popped balloon. "I think Young and Kennedy are in cahoots. Dawkins said all the guards joke about how easy it would be to rob the place. Young stood trial for robbing an ATM *in the same bank*! There wasn't enough proof to find him guilty, but Dawkins said he changed after that trial. Speaks to no one, and only went out that other night because Kennedy was there. I'm convinced it's both of them."

"That lines up with what I found in his notebook," Felix

said, hurrying to the table where he had left it, and holding it up for Selena like a prized possession.

"I'm not quite there yet," Arielle said. "I can see the obvious connections, but let's remember Young testified at Kennedy's trial. Young wasn't working when the robbery happened. He had no alibi, but his keycard never registered on Sunday morning, either. If he truly has a role in all of this, then he either did the robbery—which eliminates Kennedy from the picture, because Kennedy had no way of working things from the inside—or all of his work is happening right now."

"Not entirely true," Felix said. "Kennedy could still be the brains behind all of this. He could make the exact plans for Young to follow without having to get his hands dirty. In fact, that could explain why he eventually gets off—because there was no physical evidence tying Kennedy to the crime."

"This is tricky, and I don't know that we'll get our answers before Sunday morning. All we can do at this point is keep this knowledge in the back of our minds while we work through these next couple of days. Buckle up—it's going to be a bumpy ride to Sunday."

# Chapter 28

On Friday morning, Selena left for work an hour earlier than scheduled. Over the past week she had scouted potential areas where she could hide Saturday night.

With fifty floors in the skyscraper, she had plenty of options, but wanted to position herself to minimize potential roadblocks that might spring up on Sunday morning. She had discovered multiple vacant office spaces throughout the building, simply by learning which floors were skipped on her cleaning route.

The only problem she faced was the distance from these floors to the basement level where the robbery would occur. She couldn't risk being spotted on security footage on the morning of the robbery, running through the halls at hours when no cleaning crew was present. Especially if they had to stay beyond Sunday to solve this crime. Selena's idea of a good time was the end-of-mission margaritas waiting back in 2022. Not running from the authorities because they spotted her on camera hours before the bank was held up.

"What if I stay in the basement?" she asked the empty locker room. She had initially dismissed this idea as lunacy. While she wanted to be close for the moment of the robbery, she didn't want to risk the chance of being seen by any of the guards roaming the basement and subbasement levels. That was a recipe for the past to unleash the wrath of hell to protect the robbery.

The locker room wouldn't suffice, however. Aside from the lockers—which she could squeeze into if absolutely forced—there was a shower in one corner, and nothing else beside the benches in between.

The restrooms were further down the hall, and while she could guarantee privacy over Saturday night—none of the guards were women—she couldn't quite wrap her mind around the idea of sitting in a stall for fifteen hours.

Selena had changed into her uniform for the workday, and still had fifty minutes to spare before the start of her shift, so she stepped out into the hallway and strolled down to the storage room.

She inserted her key and pushed the door open. *No keycard needed for this door,* she thought, already giving the room an advantage. No keycard meant no trail of her movement throughout the building. The door closed behind her and she bolted it locked.

Selena flicked on the light switch to reveal a space that would certainly work. The room was approximately fifteen by fifteen feet. Filing cabinets lined the back wall, covered in dust. Boxes lay scattered across the floor, but could easily be moved to create a makeshift hiding spot. Old signage that once belonged to the businesses in the building leaned stacked against the wall to Selena's right, not taking up too much space.

Upon first examination, the room was crowded, but with time to spare, she could set it up in a reasonable manner to hang out for several hours on Saturday night.

The only problem was the concrete floor.

It was cold, and a draft seeped from somewhere she couldn't locate. It wouldn't be the most comfortable place to hang out for an extended time, but it beat sitting in a bathroom stall.

"This will have to do," Selena said to the empty room, already imagining how she wanted to arrange everything for her stay.

She planned to arrive at the building on Saturday around five o'clock in the evening. From there, she'd head to the locker room to change into her work uniform, to at least give the appearance she was there for her job. The cleaning crew didn't work Saturdays regularly, but sometimes were asked to come in. This hadn't happened in her brief time with the company, but it gave her an excuse if she needed to make up a lie on the spot.

Once dressed, she'd go straight into the storage room where she'd remain behind the locked door until Sunday morning. She could only hope whoever was working security at the time wouldn't pay attention, and leave her in peace.

Selena had a lot of factors to juggle without worrying about how the past might respond to her presence. She had to plan her meals for all of Saturday, timing them so she could use the restroom before leaving for the office. She wouldn't be able to step out of the storage room to use the building's facilities.

A big breakfast on Saturday morning would have to hold her over for twenty-four hours until she could slip out of the office on Sunday morning. Her stomach churned just thinking of the starvation she'd face by Saturday night, alone in a dusty room with nothing to eat.

"I can handle a one-day fast. People do it all the time." She spoke the words into existence, hoping to fuel her confidence in the matter.

She'd bring a backpack filled with a small pillow and sheets. There was no reason for her to stay awake the entire time, and she could even sleep overnight if she wanted. That would help pass the time—and hopefully some of the hunger pangs.

Selena studied the room once more, trying to figure out the best place to sleep, when a knock boomed from the door. Her muscles tensed as adrenaline kicked in. She had seen no one since arriving this morning.

The room fell silent, and she glared at the door. A second knock came. Louder and heavier, dust puffing from the hinges.

*Just open it. It's Friday morning. You're working today. It's not like you're doing anything wrong.*

Selena shuffled toward the door, confidence building with each step. A knock boomed one more time as she reached for the handle and pulled open the door.

"Dawkins?"

Her date from last night stood in the hallway, grinning from ear to ear with a cup of coffee in each hand.

"I really wish you'd start calling me Brian," he said. "This whole Dawkins thing makes it feel like you're one of the guys."

Dawkins extended one coffee to Selena, who quickly grabbed it and took a sip.

"What are you doing? Why were you knocking on the door like the police? I thought you didn't have work today."

He threw his head back to laugh. "Happy to see you too, Selena. I was supposed to be off today, but was asked to come in. There was a message waiting on my machine after I got home last night. Someone called out, and apparently that's my problem. So here I am, working overtime."

Dawkins drank his coffee and moved back to allow Selena to step out of the storage room. "And I could ask you the same question. What are you doing in this room?" He peered over her shoulder.

Selena stepped out and closed the door behind her. "Was looking for some extra bottles of glass cleaner. Olivia asked me to grab them yesterday, and I forgot. Thought I'd sneak in early to get them."

Dawkins looked Selena up and down. "Well, where are they?"

Selena shrugged. "She told me they were in this storage closet, but I couldn't find them. She must have meant another one. I'll have to look around."

"That makes sense why you were in there so long."

"I'm sorry, were you watching me?"

Dawkins smiled. "Well, I saw you and watched you go in there. Got a little worried—wasn't sure why you'd be in there so long. And what if I was watching you? Can you blame me? I sort of like you."

Selena didn't need to act. Her cheeks really flushed. "Well," she said, grinning. "You shouldn't abuse your power to stalk me. I'm just here for work."

"Of course. My apologies, Ms. Nicole. I won't let it happen again."

Tension filled the airwaves between them, and part of Selena wanted to pull Dawkins into that storage room and rip his shirt off. She couldn't deny he possessed a certain charm, and wondered how a long-distance relationship might work through time.

Selena shook her head, still unable to wipe the smile off her face. She knew this was probably just the past playing tricks with her—likely, in fact. Fortunately, she knew better and took another drink of coffee. If Dawkins still treated her this way once the mission was over, then she'd reconsider. For now, she had to take everything that happened over the next three days with a grain of salt.

"I want to see you again," Dawkins said, his smile fading to a more serious expression. "I really like spending time with you."

*Time,* Selena thought. *The one thing in my life that has no real way of being measured.*

"I had a great night, too. I'm pretty busy this weekend, though. Might not be free until next weekend."

"You didn't like the weeknight date after work? We can even go further from this place. Maybe catch a movie or something. That new Robin Hood movie with Kevin Costner comes out this weekend—looks pretty kick-ass."

"That could be fun. I'll have to let you know. What do you have going on this weekend?"

"Well, I've already been told I might have to work tomorrow morning for a few hours, so we'll see. If not, I'll probably head up to the mountains and hike. Sunday I'll probably go golfing. It's Father's Day, you know. My dad and I used to golf together, but he lives in California and wasn't able to make it out here. And I certainly can't fly there on this minimum wage job. So I'll call him in the morning and head out to the course to commemorate the day."

"That's really sweet of you." Everything Dawkins said made Selena like him a little more. "We should probably get back to work—I still have to find this glass cleaner before Olivia gets here."

Dawkins tugged his sleeve to check his watch. "I guess we should. Don't be a stranger if you're down here in the basement again. I'll be here until four."

They stood in silence, and Selena sensed his urge to hug her, possibly even kiss her. She wanted to give in, but gave a quick nod before taking another sip.

Dawkins offered an awkward grin before turning down the hall toward the security office. "I'll see you later."

"Have a good day."

Selena finished her coffee before returning to the locker room to kill a few minutes before her shift officially started. If everything played out smoothly this weekend, she planned to ask Dawkins out on that date for next weekend. She could figure out the logistics later.

# Chapter 29

Across town, Arielle sat in her car, witnessing a typical Friday morning for Jacob Kennedy. He had breakfast with his wife and saw her out the door by 7:45. As usual, Kennedy spent the next half hour getting dressed and ready for the day.

Today, however, he didn't retreat to his model boats. He grabbed his keys and bolted out of the front door. He peeked into the bed of his truck and vanished to his backyard for a couple of minutes before returning with a three-foot gardening shovel, tossing it into the back, and getting behind the wheel.

Arielle snapped her hand to the ignition and turned on her car, not expecting to be leaving so soon. She felt a distant flutter in her stomach, as part of her believed Kennedy was about to do something directly related to the robbery.

She followed him out of the neighborhood as he made his way toward westbound Sixth Avenue, a state highway that ran from Denver to the mountains west of Golden. In her few trips following Kennedy, he had yet to get on the highway.

They drove for fifteen minutes while Arielle remained five car-lengths behind, entering the foothills of the Rocky Mountains. Arielle studied what she could of Kennedy from such a distance. He maintained a speed five miles over the limit, not once looking around as he sped down the highway that eventually merged into I-70.

He knew exactly where he was going.

Engulfed with dark green trees to the left, and an elevated view over a valley to the right, Kennedy took Exit 253, the sign identifying it as Moss Rock Road. No vehicles were between Arielle and Kennedy when they got on the ramp, so she had to lower her speed to keep a safe distance.

Kennedy reached a stop sign and took a right onto Stapleton Road, a hairpin curve that headed back west on a dirt road. Because of the change in direction, Kennedy and Arielle momentarily faced each other from opposite sides of a median. He had apparently slipped on a ballcap, keeping it cocked low to cover his eyes. She could only see his thick mustache protruding from beneath it.

She followed him for another half-mile as the road wound deeper into the foothills, before he pulled off to a parking lot with a sign welcoming them to Beaver Brook Trailhead.

"He's going on a hike?" Arielle asked herself, trying to remember what type of shoes she had seen Kennedy wearing when he stepped out. She was fairly sure they were the usual mud-caked tennis shoes he had worn most of the time, but now had her doubts.

The parking lot was a single row of thirty spaces. There were already twelve other cars parked from the early risers looking to beat the heat for their morning hikes.

Kennedy parked in the very first spot, directly in front of a shed-like structure that housed the restrooms. Arielle saw the lot had two entrances, and drove around to the other side, parking in a middle spot where she could see the tail end of Kennedy's truck sticking out.

She killed her engine and rolled down her driver's side window, the fresh air coating her lungs and hitting her with nostalgia that brought her back to the many times her family would spend weekends camping in the mountains.

She could smell the succulent scent of meat sizzling on the grill while her dad tended to it, tongs in one hand, a beer in the other. Her mom would be inside their camper, preparing side dishes while she danced and hummed along to Vicente Fernández pouring out of their old stereo. Arielle and her brother would spend this time chasing butterflies or skipping rocks across the lake.

Tears welled in Arielle's eyes, the memories growing to a near unbearable level.

The slam of a door snapped Arielle out of her trance, bringing her back to the present—well, 1991 present—and she spun around to see Kennedy trudging from the parking lot toward the thick clump of trees in the opposite direction of the hiking trail.

"Where the hell are you going?" she whispered, opening her car door and staying crouched low. She looked around and saw no one else in the immediate vicinity.

Kennedy had reached Stapleton Road, the shovel clutched in his grip as he looked both ways before crossing.

Arielle ran toward where his truck was parked and had a clear view of Kennedy as he jogged into the thick evergreens. The trees essentially served as a wall, blocking out all views from anyone driving by or hiking the trail.

Kennedy was out of sight in a matter of seconds, and Arielle broke into a sprint to cross Stapleton Road, looking back over her shoulder once more to make sure no one was watching her.

Hundreds of evergreens towered over her, creating a maze-like sensation to search for Kennedy. She tried using her ears, but a gentle breeze mixed with chirping birds made it impossible to hear anything else.

Arielle zigged and zagged through the woods, careful to not step on any sticks that might snap and draw attention. She moved from one tree to the next, making her way deeper into the mountain, praying she'd be able to find her way out.

Fortunately, the space started clearing after fifty yards, and that's when she spotted Kennedy in an open clearing, strolling toward a lone evergreen, not another of its tree brethren within a hundred feet.

"Oh my God," Arielle said, placing her fingers to her lips as she watched Kennedy. "This is where he hides the money."

She couldn't move. She didn't *want* to move. This was history in the making.

Kennedy circled the tree twice, patting the earth with his shovel before deciding on a spot where he began digging. Arielle stayed within the trees, watching like a distant eagle.

The accused robber had found the perfect hiding spot out of sight from society. It was his own private corner of the world. The amount of people who pushed their way through the patch of woods to come out on this other side were certainly less than a handful. People driving by probably assumed the evergreens stretched for miles along the mountainside. Why would they ever stop and venture into it? And the hikers who climbed the trail across the road? Why would they wander into the woods when they had the safety of a footpath, a restroom, and even a couple of picnic tables at their disposal?

Arielle wondered how Kennedy stumbled across this site, and how many times he had been up here already. This was his first visit since she had arrived in 1991, and this meant the robbery had definitely been planned for an extended time.

She sat down between two trees, their sprawling pines concealing her from Kennedy should he look back. He dug for a half hour before stopping, tossing the shovel to the ground, and throwing his hands behind his head while he gasped for air. Kennedy didn't exercise, from what Arielle had witnessed, and this task was surely putting a strain on his body. Five minutes passed while he caught his breath, then he picked up the shovel and dug for another thirty minutes.

A mound of dirt stood about two feet high, and Arielle assumed the hole Kennedy had dug was around three feet deep. He huffed and puffed as he circled his finished product, examining the hole from every angle.

Kennedy never once looked over his shoulder. He had complete confidence in the privacy of this location. If someone wandered back in this direction, he was already a quarter of the way to having a full grave dug and had a weapon in hand.

This intrigued Arielle, slipping a dark thought into her mind.

She could make Kennedy disappear right now. She had her throwing knives in the car, and could get close enough to use them before Kennedy realized what was happening. Even with her bare hands, she was confident she could take him down despite his shovel. And in the middle of nowhere, with no people in sight, how could the past push back and cause resistance?

The mission could end today, and they wouldn't even have to worry about burying his body. They had a crew that would come clean up the mess and make it look like no one had ever set foot on the other side of the woods.

She watched him, mentally calculating how long it would

take her to run up from behind him and end his life.

"But I can't," she told herself.

And she wouldn't.

Even with the obvious evidence standing right in front of her, none of this confirmed Kennedy was the actual robber. It still could have been Young who carried out the murders, and maybe Kennedy had dug this hole to play his role in the cause.

At this moment, Arielle was ninety-eight percent sure Kennedy was the one responsible, just as the FBI had been when it originally happened. But ninety-eight was not one hundred, and that lingering two percent was filled with possibilities they could only hope to eliminate by Sunday morning.

At the very least, they could plan to have someone monitor this location on Sunday. She presumed the robber would head straight here to hide the money and get it off the grid, with plans to dig it out later.

Once Kennedy had recovered his breath, and spent a couple minutes massaging his legs, he clutched the shovel and started back toward the trees. Arielle debated running to the hole to see exactly how deep it was, even potentially filling it back in to throw a wrench into the plans.

As tempting as it was, she opted to follow Kennedy. He moved with too much purpose to ignore, and she wondered if he might head somewhere else in relation to the robbery.

Kennedy bolted into the woods, and Arielle made her way to trail his path, sure to keep a safe distance. Once they broke free on the other side of the evergreens, Arielle went right to cross the street, not wanting to be directly behind Kennedy while he tossed the shovel into the bed of his truck. She crouched as she crossed Stapleton Road, lurking behind the parked cars as she spied on Kennedy.

He wasted no time getting behind the wheel and backing his truck out of the parking spot. Arielle had to dash to her car to keep up, panic settling in as she thought he might get away.

Fortunately, Kennedy had to stop at the exit to wait for a car to pass before turning onto the road. This bought Arielle just enough time to gain ground.

Kennedy sped away. Arielle's engine roared as she tried to keep up, not putting too much pressure on herself, as Kennedy would have two stop signs before getting back onto the highway.

When he reached the first, he stopped for an excessive amount of time. No other vehicles were present to prevent him from driving forward, yet he remained.

Arielle started slowing down well before reaching him, but couldn't come to a complete stop at such a far distance. That would look suspicious if Kennedy was paying attention to what was happening behind him.

Once she was within three car lengths of his truck, he turned left without using a turn signal—the first time she had witnessed him violate a traffic law—and sped toward the next stop sign only one hundred feet away.

He again waited at the stop sign, and Arielle's entire body tensed when she pulled up behind his truck waiting to turn onto the highway.

Kennedy wasn't looking around for other cars. His eyes were glued to his rearview mirror, locked into a stare-down with Arielle.

This standoff felt like an eternity for Arielle, her heart drumming up to her throat. But it was only five seconds before Kennedy looked away, turned left, and floored his accelerator as he got on the highway.

Arielle remained frozen in her car, fingers squeezing the steering wheel as her knuckles turned white. Kennedy was gone, out of sight, but his presence lingered.

A horn honked from behind, making Arielle gasp as she snapped back into reality. A car had pulled up behind her. They drove around, flipping Arielle the bird as they passed and skidded onto the on-ramp.

"Did that really just happen?" Arielle asked her empty car. She hardly noticed the rude driver, still trying to process her encounter with Jacob Kennedy.

She drove ahead, not turning onto the highway, instead pulling to the side of the parallel frontage road that had hardly any traffic. Thoughts tumbled throughout her mind, and she felt helpless trying to grasp one to focus on.

*Was he really looking at me? Was it just a coincidence that he looked up and we locked eyes? Did he recognize me? Do I need to stop following him? What will happen if he sees me again?*

Arielle fought to slow down her mind, making a checklist of all the points she had just mulled over.

"He *was* looking at me. That wasn't a mistake."

Arielle's mouth grew incredibly dry, and she rummaged through her backpack for an emergency water bottle she kept stashed. She unscrewed the cap and nearly chugged the entire bottle.

"He *knew* I was following him. That's the only explanation for why he stopped and waited *twice*. He wanted to look me in the eye to tell me he knew I was there. I wonder if he saw me hiding in the woods."

The possibility made her queasy. If that was the case, Kennedy might already have plans for a backup location to hide the money.

She shook her head, disgusted with herself for somehow getting caught. She didn't even understand how it had happened. Five cars were between them during the entire drive over on the highway.

*Could he have noticed the same car parked across the street every day? It was never even directly in front of his house, and he never looked out the window.*

"Fuck!" Arielle shouted, balling up a fist and punching the steering wheel. The car's horn let out a subtle squeak. "Friday morning and this mission is *fucked*."

She put her car back into drive and turned around to get on the highway, fuming.

*One thing's for sure,* she thought. *I can't go anywhere near Jacob Kennedy for the rest of this mission.*

# Chapter 30

Felix spent his Friday morning reading through the rest of Peter Young's disturbing diary. The man was a lunatic—there was no way around that fact. He had a dark obsession with revenge, not just on the bank that had wronged him, but toward everyone who had ever maltreated him throughout his life.

He even mentioned elementary school bullies he hoped would "have maggots crawling over their skeletons as they rotted in the soil."

Mentally, Felix had gone through such a dark tunnel from reading these sinister rantings that he needed a break after a couple hours. So he went outside for a walk around the neighborhood before the heat became too unbearable. It was only eleven o'clock when he stepped outside and saw Arielle shuffling down the sidewalk with her head hung low.

Felix paused for a moment, at first not sure that it was actually Arielle, then once realizing it was, debating if he should approach her. For all he knew, she was working the mission and wouldn't welcome his interruption. She also never returned to the apartment during the day.

Judging by her slouched shoulders and lethargic pace, he figured something had gone wrong.

"Arielle?" he called out, startling her into a more upright position. She frowned as puzzlement mixed with her apparent anguish.

"Felix? What are you doing out here?"

"Well, I spend my days here. What are *you* doing here?" Once they met in front of the apartment building's entrance, Felix saw Arielle's eyes were red and puffy. "What's wrong?!"

Traffic passed on the road while a group of middle schoolers started skipping down the sidewalk. Arielle looked over her shoulder to them before returning a depressing gaze to Felix.

"I messed up," she said, an octave above a whisper. She bobbed her head up and down in a subtle nod. "We're screwed."

"We're not," Felix said. "I just came out to walk around the block. Join me."

He turned around to face the same direction as Arielle and started walking. After a couple of steps, she finally joined him. He allowed the tension to linger, waiting for Arielle to speak first. Once they reached the corner of the block, she did.

"Kennedy saw me," she said. "I've played it over a hundred times already, and he definitely looked right at me. He knew I was following him, so he stared me down so that I'd stop. And it worked. Here I am."

Arielle tossed her hands in the air before sharing with Felix the full story of what had just happened in the foothills.

"I can follow him," Felix said.

"No. That's not the point. None of us can follow him anymore. This all proves he's been suspicious. We shouldn't even drive down his block anymore. Tomorrow might be the most crucial day in figuring out how this all plays out, and now we have to sit here and hope we catch something on

Young. Speaking of, he's off work today, right? Has he done anything?"

"Not yet. He didn't get out of bed until 9:30. Took a shower and made some bacon and eggs. Ate in front of the TV as he always does. Had no vibes of someone preparing to rob a bank in two days."

Arielle shook her head. "It doesn't make sense. Young's involved. I have a hard time believing otherwise. Do we know if he works tomorrow?"

"We don't know."

Arielle rubbed her temples as they continued their lap around the neighborhood block. "I just can't believe we're in this situation. Kennedy can be doing *anything* related to the robbery today, and we have no way of finding out."

"Swap cars with me," Felix said.

"Kennedy's still going to be paranoid. Especially now. I'm worried he'll recognize my face. What if he tells Young about me following him? What if he knows more about us than we want to believe is possible. He could know we're living in the same building as Young."

"Remember, he's in his Original Time. Why would he have any reason to suspect someone is following him for a crime that hasn't happened yet? That's just not how any of it works. And he knows that, being a retired cop and all. Honestly, Arielle, *you* sound a little paranoid."

Felix watched as Arielle chewed on this thought.

"I'm not going to say it's impossible that it was all a coincidence. But I also trust my gut. He was looking *at* me. Intentionally. Was it because he recognized me, or was he just having some fun with the car driving behind him? Both seem like logical explanations, but also illogical. I don't know."

"I'm telling you—go back. Take my car. Hide further down the block. Ten houses down if you need to. And if he leaves and you need to tail him again, stay even further back. You might lose him because of it, but at least you're trying. Because sitting here with me all day will guarantee you find nothing of use."

"I'm afraid, Felix. Just . . . don't tell anyone I said that."

"Afraid of failing this mission? Since when? This mission is a joke. We could have just as easily showed up on the day of and chased whoever comes running out of the bank with the bag of money. All we need to know is who did it—we don't need to stop it. Did you forget that?"

"Of course not. I've done this long enough to know it wouldn't be that simple. I don't know if this incident with Kennedy is part of the past pushing back—I think it is, but we can't truly know for sure. Sunday morning won't be easy. I suggest you come to terms with that now."

"It's all about spacing. You need to have more faith in our team. I've been studying the map of the bank, the layout of the street blocks, and all possible escape routes. There are three of us to cover the perimeter—"

"Plan for just you and I. Selena will be inside, and we can't guarantee she'll be able to get out before the robbery happens."

"Fine. Two of us is still enough to cover the west side of the building. All common sense points to the robber exiting the same way he entered. Besides, we're going to know early Sunday morning how involved Young is. The first timestamp, according to the old police reports, shows that the robber called the security team from the freight elevator at 9:14 A.M. If Young is still sitting in his underwear by nine o'clock, then we can rule him out."

"I have to go to Kennedy's house that morning, no matter how risky it is. We have to have a visual on him."

"I've already mapped out your morning," Felix said as they rounded the complex's northwest corner and started back toward the main entrance. "It takes eighteen minutes to drive from Kennedy's house to the bank. The latest Kennedy can leave his house is 8:55 to fall into the timeline of events. I'd say you should plan to leave there by 8:50 if it doesn't appear he's leaving. That will give you five minutes to spare."

"I'll need more than five minutes if the past is going to push back."

"I can be down at the bank, so don't worry. If Young isn't showing any signs of movement by nine o'clock, I'm zooming over there."

Arielle shook her head, and Felix was relieved to see her mental dials cranking once again. "We're close enough to ditch the car. Walk—that's gonna be your best bet. I'll be there with the car to chase down whoever drives off."

"Walk? That doesn't seem like the right call at all. You know I'm one of the top drivers in the Road Runners, right?"

"That's not the point. Just trust me, okay?" Arielle paused and looked up at the sky for wisdom. "I'll be there. You can hop into my car and we'll be ready for anything."

Felix nodded. They reached the entrance. "Okay, that's reasonable."

"Thank you. Let's go inside and figure out the rest of the day."

# Chapter 31

After much debate, Arielle agreed to let Felix go to Kennedy's house on Friday evening. He vowed to park at the far end of the block, opposite the house, and watch from a distance with a pair of binoculars.

Felix stopped at a McDonald's on his way to grab a couple of burgers for his stakeout. He was surprised to have kept his nerves at bay, but that was mostly thanks to his strong belief that Young was responsible for everything about to unfold. He expected the night at Kennedy's house to pass without excitement.

And that's exactly what happened for the first four hours of excruciating boredom. When Felix had turned onto Juniper Street at 4:15, Kennedy's truck wasn't even parked in the driveway. No one was home, and the temptation to go back in and properly bug the house swelled to an uncomfortable level, but he had strict orders from Arielle to not so much as approach the house.

While her decisions didn't always make sense, he trusted them. Arielle never made an order for the sake of making one. There was guaranteed to be a long, thought-out reason behind it with factors Felix had yet to experience during his time with the Road Runners. Arielle had amassed wisdom from thousands of missions, and had no reason to lead them astray. .

Felix had settled into his spot at the far end of the block, an open grassy field to his left as he faced the house. He had killed the engine and sat in silence, eating his burgers while he waited for something to happen.

Some kids had come to the field and tossed a baseball around. Couples went out for evening walks with their dogs on long leashes, holding hands as they strolled down the sidewalk to enjoy the first night of the weekend.

It was absurd to think a potential bank robber and murderer lived among such regular people.

When the sun started setting, the kids who had played baseball earlier ran their equipment home and returned with even more kids, nearly all dressed in black. It wasn't long until a very intense game of hide-and-seek kicked off across the neighborhood.

Kennedy still wasn't home, and not so much as a light was turned on inside or outside the house.

"Where's his wife?" Felix asked aloud.

She could have met him wherever he was once she got off work. Or Kennedy could be out with friends—or accomplices—while his wife went to a happy hour with coworkers that was stretching well past dinnertime.

By 8:30 the sun had set, the hide-and-seek game in full swing with kids scattered all about the neighborhood. None of them paid Felix any attention, assuming they even noticed him. Although, one kid hid behind his rear bumper for a couple of minutes before making a mad dash to the lone tree standing in the center of the grass field.

Headlights appeared at the far end of the block, snapping

Felix out of the lull he had fallen into. The lights seemed to glare into his soul before they turned into Kennedy's driveway.

The sounds of the screaming, energetic kids drowned into background noise as Felix pulled out his binoculars. The street lamps cast an orange glow up and down the block, and provided just enough light for the binoculars to pick up Kennedy's moving silhouette as he moved from the truck toward his front door. He had what looked like a plastic grocery bag clutched in his grip.

Two kids were down near his house, and Kennedy waved at them. They appeared to stop and say something in return, but Felix didn't have a clear enough view to be sure.

Kennedy disappeared into his home, and Felix stepped out of the car.

There were at least twenty kids scattered about the block, and it provided him enough cover as he crossed the street and started toward Kennedy's house. The porch light had been turned on, as was the dining room, where he saw Kennedy sitting at the table, head planted in his hands.

"Long day of planning the robbery?" Felix whispered under his breath, taking cautious steps as he stood in front of Kennedy's house. His truck was within range, so he hurried along the sidewalk until planting himself behind the bed of the truck, out of sight from Kennedy in the dining room.

Felix looked around to confirm none of the kids were paying him any attention. He stood on his tiptoes to get a better view and looked into the truck bed, finding a mud-caked shovel, a five-gallon container of water, and a pair of dirty boots.

He reached in, briefly wanting to steal the boots for further examination, when a woman's voice called out from behind.

"Hey! Get the hell out of my truck!"

Felix spun around, stomach already leaping into his throat, and saw Kennedy's wife parked in the middle of the street, window rolled down, jaw hanging open. They locked eyes for a millisecond before Felix pivoted and sprinted away.

"Get back here!"

Felix had already passed four houses when he looked over his shoulder and saw the car creeping down the block to follow him.

"Shit!" he gasped between breaths, lungs burning with each heave of air he took in.

He had no chance of outrunning a car and needed to get crafty. He didn't want to risk Mrs. Kennedy finding out what kind of car he drove, either, so getting back into his vehicle and speeding away wasn't an option.

A Rottweiler rushed the chain-link fence of one house Felix ran past, snarling and barking to cause all the attention in the neighborhood to shift to the man running through the night. Even the kids fell silent and turned their attention to the unfolding scene.

Felix approached the end of the block where the road curved left to exit the neighborhood. He'd have no chance of escaping that way, and couldn't risk hiding in someone's backyard. There were already too many eyes on him.

Mrs. Kennedy was still about five houses down, likely afraid to speed because of all the kids running around, so Felix took the chance to bolt to his right and cross the street, running right by his car as he stepped onto the grassy field.

A handful of kids stood frozen at the tree serving as their "home base" and gawked as the grown man ran in their direction.

"Get out of here, mister!" one kid shouted, a boy who

couldn't have been older than ten years old.

Felix sprinted past the tree, paying the kids no attention, a decision he believed was the reason he didn't end up with a mob chasing him. From where he had parked his car earlier, Felix wasn't able to see where the field ended. Now, he saw its outer perimeter still fifty yards ahead, where it backed up to a ditch filled with tall, yellow weeds. On the other side of the ditch was a paved pathway that wove into another neighborhood.

Felix reached the ditch and stopped to turn around. The ground had sloped just enough where he could still see the top of the tree, but none of the kids under it. He tried to listen for their voices, to see if they were following him, but he couldn't hear anything over his heavy pants for breath. He had just sprinted the length of nearly three soccer fields, his legs and lungs happy to punish him for it.

Seeing how tall the weeds were, Felix stepped into the ditch to let them conceal him even more. He crouched, breathing in heavy amounts of pollen and whatever particles were floating in the air, burning his nose and throat.

He crouched lower, knowing he only needed to pass five minutes before he could safely step out. The kids might still be outside playing late into the night—it was a Friday night, after all—but he presumed Mrs. Kennedy wouldn't expel too much effort chasing down someone who hadn't even taken anything from the truck.

*Unless she gets Jacob, and he comes searching with his gun.*

The thought made Felix dizzy. The four and a half hours of boredom had caused him to get greedy. He hadn't planned on approaching Kennedy's house at all. But once he saw Kennedy arrive home, all that boredom swirling around in his mind made him want to make his wasted time worthwhile. What would it hurt by just walking by the house? The neighborhood was plenty busy and Kennedy wouldn't have noticed.

Felix didn't know how good of a look Mrs. Kennedy had gotten of him. It was dark, sure, but there was enough light to make out a face—he had seen hers just fine, even if for a quick second. He hadn't worn a disguise. Even a pair of sunglasses, or a hat, would have made him difficult to identify.

Something slithered against Felix's ankle, prompting him to look down, his blood instantly freezing in his veins. He had long suffered from a severe case of ophidiophobia, and seeing the garter snake swirl in a circular motion around his ankle instantly made his head spin while a heaviness pressed down on his back.

"My God," he whispered, unable to look away from the snake that was at least twenty inches long. "The only poisonous snakes in Colorado are rattlesnakes. This is a Garter snake. No poison—hardly any venom."

Part of a therapy to overcome his fear of snakes was familiarizing himself with all the snakes he might encounter in his line of work across North America. Garter snakes posed no threats, their venom causing redness around a bite mark, at worst. Knowing this still didn't help, Felix growing more nauseous with each passing second.

His body broke into chills as beads of sweat formed on his forehead. He focused on taking deep breaths and swallowing large pools of saliva to keep his dinner down. The snake refused to leave him alone, satisfied to keep circling his ankle as the world spun.

Felix ran out of spit to swallow, his lips and tongue turning dry as dirt. His balance wavered, and he started flailing his arms. "I'm not gonna make it. Dear God, please don't let me die in this ditch."

The snake opened its mouth and sunk its fangs into Felix's calf in one swift motion. Felix couldn't shriek, his jaw locking into place as his entire body tensed at the sharp pain exploding up his leg.

He felt the warm stream of blood oozing toward his ankle, soaking into his sock. That's when he took three drunken steps backward to get out of the ditch, and fainted on the grass.

# Chapter 32

Arielle and Selena were already on their way by 8:15.

Selena had arrived home shortly after six, having taken an hour after her shift to head back to the storage room to move some boxes around. She created a fort that would conceal her presence if someone wandered into the storage room on Saturday, an event she considered unlikely.

They discussed dinner plans for when Felix arrived, but when they hadn't heard from him by 7:30, Arielle grew concerned. They spent the next half hour debating what to do. Selena argued Felix had likely found something of interest and didn't want to leave.

Arielle knew the games the past liked to play. If Felix had found something crucial to the mission, the more reason for the past to resist him from gaining and sharing that knowledge.

Arielle had moved Felix's laptop onto the dining room table, where they watched Young devour an entire pizza by himself, something Selena had deemed "both disgusting and impressive."

At eight o'clock, Selena surrendered her position. Felix wasn't one to stay out past dark, and she acknowledged the possibility that something indeed could have gone wrong.

They took the next fifteen minutes changing into all-black attire, loading their pistols, and slipping into bulletproof vests. Just in case.

Selena told Arielle to stop overreacting, but she refused to cave. You could never be too cautious when dealing with a stubborn past.

"Young's not doing anything," Arielle said before they left the apartment. "The guy is a total bum. I'm thinking it's impossible for him to be involved in any capacity with this robbery. He just sits there all day and night, drinking beer and eating junk food. No wonder he dies from a heart attack next year."

They checked the monitor to find Young passed out in his recliner, jaw hanging open while he held a beer can in one hand and a cigarette spewed tiny streams of smoke from the ashtray on his side table.

"I have to agree," Selena said, nodding to the screen. "Does anyone really believe that man had such a major impact on the world?" She chuckled as they turned away and left the apartment.

They took Arielle's car and sped across town to Golden. Selena outlined her plans for tomorrow during the twenty-minute drive, and Arielle grew impressed with how thoroughly Selena had plotted out her part of the mission.

Not only did the young actress have a solid plan in place for a seamless execution, she had also pinpointed potential vulnerabilities and had backup plans around those. Hearing it all, Arielle wouldn't have planned it any differently.

They reached Juniper Street by 8:40.

Arielle turned onto the block from the west, the opposite end of Kennedy's house.

"Look!" Selena shouted, pointing across Arielle's body. "It's Felix's car."

"Shit," Arielle muttered under her breath, slowing down and swerving across the road to park right behind it. "He's not in it."

Silence filled the car once Arielle killed the engine. Neither of them knew what to do or say, looking around for any signs that might provide a clue.

"Think those kids saw him?" Selena finally asked, nodding toward the group of kids huddled near the lone tree standing in the grass field.

There were only eight kids remaining from the big game of hide-and-seek that had just ended minutes ago when Mrs. Kennedy chased down the man running from her house.

"There's a good chance," Arielle said. "We might need to ask them, but let's get out and look around first. Don't want to seem too suspicious if we don't have to."

Selena reached out and pressed her arm against Arielle to pin her back in her seat. "You're not suggesting we go down to Kennedy's house, are you? Which one is it?"

Arielle nodded in the direction. "That one with the pickup truck in the driveway."

They stared at it, seeing the glow of lights through the house's windows.

"They're home," Selena said. "You don't think Felix went over there and tried to sneak in or something?"

"I highly doubt that, but he may have drifted that direction, and who knows what might have happened. I could see him wanting a closer look. He might be in their backyard hiding. Hopefully that's all it is."

Arielle opened her door, and Selena followed suit. The kids

were watching, studying them from a distance.

"I think they saw Felix," Selena said. "Why would they be staring at us like that?"

"Don't think too much into it. We're strangers in their neighborhood—they're probably just being nosy."

It was natural for people to gawk at an unknown person, but they usually returned to their own business after a few seconds. A minute passed, and the kids were still gazing at them.

"What do we do?" Selena whispered as she came around to meet Arielle on the sidewalk.

"Act natural. Let's stay on this side of the street and walk down a few houses. Keep an eye on these kids. If they follow us, then something is definitely going on and we might need to bail."

"We can't just leave Felix."

"That's not what I said. We just might need to leave this neighborhood. We can drive around to the next block and try to sneak our way back. I'd never leave an Angel behind—you should know that by now."

Arielle started forward, taking long, confident steps. She knew plenty well how to act like she belonged. Any sign of doubt, even from a distance, would only further raise suspicions from the attentive kids.

After fifty feet, they reached the edge of the field that gave way to houses and yards for the rest of the block. Once they passed the first house, Arielle stopped and turned around. Selena was only several paces behind and nearly crashed into her.

"Are they following?" Selena asked, refusing to look back at the same time.

Arielle shook her head. "I don't see any of them. Let's keep going—we might be in the clear."

Arielle didn't know what to think. Something in the air felt off, and she had no way of knowing if it was her instincts or the past trying to interfere. After passing two more houses, she continued down the sidewalk with an occasional glance over the shoulder. Still no kids visible. They remained in the field, minding their business.

"I think we're clear," she said to Selena. "Let's stop across from Kennedy's house and see what's going on. Do *not* cross the street and step onto his property."

"Don't worry about me—I have no interest in that."

They arrived after a minute. The living room and dining room lights were both on, but no one was visible through the windows. For the first time that Arielle could recall since observing the house every day, the curtains were drawn shut. Her first thought was that Kennedy was planning the robbery at the dining room table. Why would he have the sudden desire for privacy?

"Arielle, get down!" Selena gasped, pulling Arielle's arm as she crouched behind a car parked along the sidewalk.

A police cruiser had just turned onto the block from the end they had come. It crept at a painfully slow pace, and didn't stop until it parked right in front of Kennedy's house.

"What's going on?" Selena whispered, but Arielle didn't respond. She held her gaze to the police car and watched two officers step out and trudge up the pathway, knocking on the front door. The car's emergency signals remained off and the two officers didn't appear in any hurry. Arielle assumed their visit wasn't for anything too serious.

Mrs. Kennedy opened the door, dressed in a flowing nightgown. Jacob appeared in the doorway next to her a few seconds later.

Despite the near silence that had fallen over the neighborhood, they were too far to pick up on any of the words being spoken. Mrs. Kennedy did most of the talking, at first pointing to the truck in the driveway, then swinging her arm around to point all the way to the end of the block. Where they had parked. Where the kids were loitering in the field.

"Don't move," Arielle muttered. "Not 'til they're completely gone."

They waited another couple of minutes for the conversation to end. Kennedy shook the hands of both officers, and Arielle presumed he had shared his ex-profession with the two gentlemen standing on his front step.

"Let's see where they go," Arielle said in a hushed tone. "They might give us an idea what happened."

The cops returned to their vehicle and immediately flipped it around, driving back the same way they had come. Arielle saw Mrs. Kennedy watching from the window, holding the curtains apart for a clear view of the far end of the block.

As tempting as it was to drift back that direction for a better look, Arielle and Selena remained grounded in their positions. If Mrs. Kennedy saw two women lurking across the street, there was no saying what might happen. For now, they had the concealment of the dark, out of range from the street lamps.

The officers stopped their car directly next to Arielle's, prompting her heart to race. Would they snoop around the vehicles parked along the street? Did Mrs. Kennedy identify Felix's car as one she hadn't seen before? This could lead to complications, and might even leave them stranded in the neighborhood.

But they never gave a second look toward any of the vehicles. Instead, the two officers whipped out their flashlights and shone them at the kids, sauntering over to them with the continued carelessness of a walk through the park.

The kids huddled around the cops, and the group chatted for three minutes.

The tallest kid in the group kept pointing a lanky finger to the distance behind them. The officers looked in that direction multiple times, shining their flashlights.

"This has to involve Felix, right?" Selena asked.

"It definitely *feels* like it. The good news is I don't think he's hurt. There would probably be more urgency if that was the case. I think he was snooping around the Kennedys' house and got caught. He must have made a run for it, and it seems to be beyond that tree where they're all hanging out."

"How are we supposed to find him? He could be hiding anywhere, or could have run two miles away. I don't see Felix as one to take the risk of hiding in a bush to watch what's happening. He'll put his head down and keep running until he can't."

"I agree. We need these cops to leave, and possibly the kids. Who knows what they might say if they see us."

"We can't sit here. The police will make rounds through this neighborhood all night now."

"I think we're fine. Look." Arielle nodded to the group of kids. The two officers had started back toward their car, some kids following close behind, others branching off in their own direction. "Cops broke up the party. Probably don't want any of the kids outside if they think something's going on. We just got really lucky."

They watched for the next few minutes while everyone

dispersed to their homes. The police were the last to leave, but did so without wandering deeper into the field.

The neighborhood fell silent aside from the chirping crickets.

"I think we're clear," Arielle said. "Let's go."

# Chapter 33

They shuffled toward the field, opting to walk at a normal pace. Moving too fast or slow, or even staying crouched while they scampered down the sidewalk, would only make them look suspicious.

Fortunately, they only needed to worry about their appearance underneath the street lamps. Otherwise, their black attire helped them blend into the shadows.

Once they reached the field, they felt exposed outside of the coverage of surrounding houses. Surely anyone peeping from their front windows would spot them standing in the field.

"We need to move fast," Arielle stated the obvious.

She broke into a near sprint, Selena following close behind. The field stretched about fifty yards along the nearest home's property before reaching a concrete path. Arielle stopped at the path, well out of sight from the neighborhood.

Both directions led to different neighborhoods, and it was impossible to know which way Felix might have run. She decided left, since that was more toward where the tall kid had pointed.

"You sure about this?" Selena asked. "He could be nowhere near here. He might have even circled the area and arrived back to his car."

"Well, we're parked behind him, so he'll know we're looking for him. He's plenty observant to realize that."

"Maybe. He also gets flustered really easy. I can't imagine how his mind is right now. He might have tunnel vision to his car just to get out of here as fast as he can."

Arielle had already considered this possibility, and it didn't bother her. Felix getting home safely was the only concern. And if he did that while they were out looking for him, then so be it. "You know this is all the past. It has to be."

"I wondered that, but wasn't sure. How do you know?"

"It started this morning when I was following Kennedy into the mountains. I'm pretty sure it's been a domino effect since then. We were so close to finding that concrete evidence tying it all to Kennedy. And the past just won't let us. I was ninety-eight percent sure Kennedy is responsible as of this afternoon. I'm gonna say ninety-nine."

"What's holding back the last one percent?"

"Seeing the proof with my eyes. *Everything* points to Kennedy. Here we are two nights away from the robbery, on Kennedy's block, and we're going the opposite direction from his house. That's no accident."

"You don't think Felix just made a bad decision and got caught too close?"

"Well, sure, but that's not really the point. I've been sitting across from Kennedy's house for two weeks now, and I've yet to have anything like this happen."

They walked in silence for the next thirty seconds before Selena spoke. "I'm terrified for tomorrow. Just thought you should know that."

"Why? You have a really sound plan."

"I'm worried I'm going to get caught. I went into that

storage room this morning just to look around, and Dawkins saw me go in from the security camera. He just came right up and started knocking on the door. How can I expect to waltz in there tomorrow evening and act like everything is normal? My crew doesn't work weekends. The guards know that. They'll see me and wonder. And there's nothing stopping them from coming into that storage room to see what I'm up to. It's not like there's a lot of activity in the building to distract them on a Saturday. They'll probably notice every person who walks into the building."

"That's probably true, but we have to take the chance they'll forget all about you once you disappear from the cameras. If you get caught and kicked out of the building—which I don't think they'll do—then you'll come home and we can figure it out from there. Besides, the building is massive. There might be more going on than you realize. And if not, their boredom just might be the reason you're able to slip in undetected. I'm sure some of these guys fall asleep at the wheel on the weekends."

Selena let out a nervous laugh. "I'm not going to count on *that*, but hopefully you're right."

"Look, Selena, I know this mission has been all over the place. But you've both stepped up to the occasion. For someone who has worked on hundreds of missions by myself, I think it's safe to say this would be a guaranteed failure if I were here on my own. You've both stepped out of your comfort zones, and I'm grateful for it.

"Look at what we're doing, looking for Felix. Would you have thought for a moment, at the beginning of this mission, that he would have even dared stepped out of the apartment?"

"You're wearing off on us more than you realize. Once we

got past the intimidation of working with you, it's become impossible to not match your passion."

Arielle shrugged. "I don't do anything special—I just get the work done. That's all I've ever done."

Selena chuckled. "It's so much more than that. Anyone can clock in, do the work, and clock out. This is your life. There is no clocking out with you, and that's why you're the best. Me and Felix see that, and want it. We want to be the best, too."

"And you are both the best at what you do."

"Yes, but there's another level above that, and that's what we've never realized until working with you. The best will come and go—there's always someone to fill that spot. You're already greater than that, though. You're a . . . legend. You have this mythical perception that people just don't understand. And they never will, unless they get to work directly with you."

Arielle stopped and turned to face Selena. "Where is all of this coming from? You never sing praises to anyone, and you just showered me in them."

Selena looked down, embarrassed. "I guess I've never praised anyone because I've never been grateful to have anyone in my life—besides my mom, of course. And I'll admit, I came into this team closed-minded and skeptical. I thought you were overhyped and overrated. Just some bossy bitch—sorry—who wouldn't care about me. But I was so wrong. You've brought so much clarity and structure to my life with just these two missions we've done together. I've always felt like I've been wandering through life with no direction, but I finally know where I want to go. What I want to make out of my life."

"And what's that?"

"A legacy." Arielle noticed Selena's bottom lip trembling. "That's the difference between you and everyone else. Your name is going to remain in discussions long after you retire from the Angels, long after the day you die. I know that might sound weird to hear, but it's beautiful. Powerful. You've changed this organization and the world for the better, and nothing can take that away from you. I'm going to pursue my dream of one day winning an Oscar, even if it exhausts me to death. I want that to be my legacy."

Arielle smiled. "And I'll be right there in the front row to hear your acceptance speech. Now, shall we get back to finding Felix?"

A subtle grin touched the corners of Selena's mouth as she nodded.

They continued forward, and only after a dozen steps, Arielle came to a sudden halt, sticking out an arm in front of Selena. "Is that him?"

She pointed toward a ditch filled with tall weeds.

Selena squinted her eyes. "Is that a body on the ground?"

That's all Arielle needed to hear before dashing toward the lump. The body lay on the edge of the ditch, limbs splayed out in every direction.

"It's him!" Arielle shouted once she was within range to make out Felix's face, crouching by his side. "Holy shit!"

Selena caught up, and they each grabbed Felix from under his arms and pulled him completely out of the ditch and onto the grass.

"Felix!" Arielle shouted, squatting over his stomach so she could shake him by the shoulders. "Felix, wake up!"

His head rolled from side to side while she shook him. Arielle eased him back to the ground and stepped to the side, planting her knees into the earth and pressing her ear to his chest.

"He's breathing! Thank God, he's breathing!"

Tears had welled in her eyes and she wiped them away before sitting back up into a kneeling position at his side.

"What do we do?" Selena asked, panic completely overtaking her voice.

Arielle didn't hear Selena and kept nudging Felix in the side. "Wake up, dammit. Wake up, Felix!"

Felix moaned like a teenager refusing to wake up during summer break.

"Yes!" Arielle shouted. "C'mon!" She grabbed his head and rocked it.

"He has blood on his leg," Selena said, pointing to the dark splotches that had long dried up.

Felix moaned again, this time his eyelids fluttering as he attempted to come back to consciousness.

"Felix," Selena said in a nearly normal tone. "We're here. Wake up."

A few seconds passed as he bobbed his head from side to side, and he finally opened his eyes all the way. He looked to Arielle, then to Selena, then to the stars high above. "Jesus," he whispered.

"What happened?" Arielle asked. "Why are you bleeding?"

She scooted down to his ankle for a closer examination, but it was too dark, and the blood was too dry and caked on the skin to see a wound.

"Help me up," Felix said, his voice cracking before he cleared his throat. "Please."

He lifted his head off the ground, looking down at his feet.

Arielle and Selena grabbed him by the arms and pulled him into a seated position. He swayed for a moment before finding his balance, and planted his hands in the grass to keep from tipping back.

Felix drew a deep breath. "I was hiding in this ditch and got bit by a snake."

"What?!" Arielle gasped. "Do we need to get you to a hospital? Was it venomous?"

Felix closed his eyes and tilted his head back, clearly dreading his next words. "No . . . I sort of have a . . . phobia. I fainted from panic. The snake wasn't poisonous."

"Are you serious? How do you know that?"

"I know almost everything you can about snakes. I knew the snake wasn't harmful before it bit me. But once it happened, my mind just couldn't process it and shut down entirely. I haven't been this close to a snake in years, and just seeing its fangs sink into my leg sent me into a shock I've never experienced before."

"Christ, Felix. We thought you were in serious trouble when we saw you on the ground next to a ditch. I thought the worst had happened."

"So you're totally fine?" Selena asked.

Felix nodded. "I could use a bandage maybe, but yeah, I'll be good."

"Good," Arielle exhaled in relief. "Now, can you tell us what the hell happened? There were cops looking around the neighborhood. Had a chat with the Kennedys, and they kept pointing this way. I think your position behind this ditch saved you, or else they would have seen you from that tree where the kids were playing."

Felix recounted the events that had led up to him being caught by Mrs. Kennedy and having to run for his life.

"Why the hell would you step on Kennedy's property?"

Arielle asked. "That's reckless at this point in the mission."

"I don't know what came over me. I got greedy, I guess. It was dark, the block was busy with kids, Kennedy was clearly inside his house, relaxing. It's not like I haven't had stealth training—I break into people's houses regularly. It was just terrible timing on my part."

"This could have ended so much worse," Arielle said in a rather motherly tone—the old *not angry, but disappointed.*

"You're telling me. All I was imagining was Jacob Kennedy hunting me down with one of his guns. And the worst part is I got nothing out of all this. Didn't learn a damn thing to help the mission. A completely wasted evening."

"Nothing is ever a waste," Arielle said. "This is just one more reinforcement that Kennedy is responsible. The past wouldn't have thrown all this your way unless you were close to finding something out."

"Now we'll never know," Felix said, finally getting to his feet, brushing off his shorts and legs.

"You're fine, and that's all that matters. We need to get back home, and prepare for what lies ahead."

# Chapter 34

On Saturday morning, Arielle had originally planned to start the day at six o'clock. After last night's events, however, she told everyone to sleep until eight. They were already running on fumes and needed to muster all the energy they could for the final two days of the mission.

They gathered in the kitchen around 8:15, Felix with his laptop open to a live-feed of Peter Young's apartment, where the security guard remained in bed.

"Morning," Selena said as she made her way to the refrigerator to pull out all the fruit they had.

"Good morning," Arielle said. "How's everyone doing?"

Felix yawned and stretched his arms above his head. "Slept like a boulder. Really. I don't think I made a single movement all night. How about you?"

"I had a hard time falling asleep," Arielle said. "But still got about seven hours. I'll take it. What are you doing, Selena?"

She had chopped up fruit and tossed it all into a bowl. "Everything I'm going to eat for the day needs to happen within the next hour. I'm going to fill up on fruit and veggies, take a laxative at one, and be cleared out before I head to the office at four. I *refuse* to shit in a corner of that storage room like a zoo animal. Not happening."

"And water?" Arielle asked.

"I'm going to drink as much as I can before noon. It should all be out of me by four. I'm pretty hydrated, so not too worried about going thirsty while I'm in there."

"And you're going to pee in a corner of the room? Your body isn't going to make it that whole time, even if you stopped drinking right now."

"I'm allowing myself one pee while I'm in there. There's a bucket I can use. Otherwise, I'm going to do some exercises to sweat out some of the water. That should help reduce the urge. I've studied all of this to understand what needs to happen—I'm not too worried about it."

"You're taking snacks to have toward the end of your stay, right?" Arielle asked. Her phrasing made it sound like Selena was about to check into a luxurious package at the Brown Palace Hotel instead of a dusty storage room.

"Yep. I have applesauce, cans of soup, pudding, and chocolate bars. All low-risk for choking hazards—I don't trust the past."

"Very good. To be fair, I've never heard of the past actually killing someone—that would create a change in a timeline elsewhere—but I appreciate the thought you put into it."

Felix chuckled. "Well, if there were ever a time for the past to start killing, it would definitely be this mission."

"Thanks a lot," Selena said. "Death is exactly what I wanted to hear about this morning."

"You know we don't mean it like that," Felix replied, guilt immediately seeping into his voice.

"Of course, but I have to give you a hard time for it." Selena grinned while she shook her head and started popping grapes into her mouth.

"So," Felix said. "Are we even going to bother going near Kennedy's house today?"

Arielle rubbed her forehead. That same question had kept her up at night. "We kind of need to."

"I'm not going back," Felix said sternly. "I mean it."

"I'm not expecting you to. I'll go—I just don't know when, or for how long I should stay. I'll need to think about it. I can't just sit here all day and do nothing."

"You can, though," Selena said. "No one would fault you. We've done everything we can. It all boils down to tomorrow morning."

"She's right," Felix said. "Weigh the possibility of you actually finding something useful against the risk of going near his house again. If you ask me, it's not worth it."

"But it's the day before the robbery. If there were ever an opportunity to find something, it's gotta be today. I'm going, even if just for a couple hours."

Felix shook his head. "I know we can't tell you what to do, but I think you're making a mistake, Arielle. At least reconsider. Please."

"I've done plenty of thinking. I'll head there and park where you did last night. But I'm not going to step out of the car, no matter what I might see. And I'm sure the past will try to tempt me in plenty of ways."

"You think the past pulled me out of the car last night?" Felix asked, his face looking like he had just eaten something sour.

"Well, sure. You had no plans of going anywhere near Kennedy's house, but you did. I'm not saying the past can physically move you, but I believe it could have set up things to drive that temptation."

"That's lovely," Selena said, stuffing more fruit into her mouth and washing it down with a gulp of water.

"We just need to be extra aware. Our plans today can get tossed out the window in a split second. It's like I was telling Selena last night—we have to be ready to go with the flow."

"That should be easy for me today," Felix said. "I'm not leaving this apartment for anything."

Arielle checked her watch. "That's fine with me. In fact, we should plan for an early dinner so we can get to bed around eight. I want to head over to Kennedy's at six tomorrow morning, in case I run into obstacles."

"All while I'm having the time of my life," Selena said, grinning, "Just make sure we grab some margaritas when this mission's over."

"Oh, we most certainly will. Let's gear up for today."

# Chapter 35

Arielle left at noon, sure to give Selena a long, tight hug before departing. As much as everyone liked to worry about the prospects of the day, Arielle trusted their hard work and knowledge would keep everyone out of harm's way. Felix's placement had virtually no risk, and Selena was low-risk, at least for tonight.

Arielle had the most to worry about. She'd been in countless of these high-pressure situations before and had learned how to navigate through the minefield of obstacles and temptations the past would throw her way.

She would not make eye contact with Jacob Kennedy. She was mainly hanging around his block to follow him in case he left. Should he stay home all day, that was fine with her.

During her drive across town, Arielle thought back to the prior missions that had been as difficult as this one. Saving a high school baseball team from a fatal bus accident. Preventing the kidnapping of a judge's daughter. Countless missions of blowing up their old rival's properties as part of their decades-long war in the underground world of time travel.

*But I'm better now compared to back then,* Arielle thought.

By the time she turned onto Juniper Street, confidence had

swelled within Arielle. But not the type of confidence that would make her do something stupid like park across from Kennedy's house again.

No.

Confidence in her ability to stay disciplined. The past would continue its games to preserve itself, and she was ready for it.

Arielle parked her car in the exact spot Felix had just last night. She hadn't realized how much stress the darkness had caused them, finding the neighborhood peaceful under the afternoon sun. There were no kids playing in the field—the forecast called for ninety-eight degrees of brutal sunshine. Arielle felt the heat already brewing.

A gentleman six houses down from Kennedy washed his truck in the driveway, a cigar pinched between his lips, a bucket full of ice and beer bottles sitting on his front porch, rock music blaring from a boom box stationed on a table in his open garage.

Arielle studied the man, trying to figure out if he had noticed her. He seemed off in his own dimension, banging his head to the music, taking puffs from his cigar without a care in the world.

Over the next hour, the truck was clean, the cigar spent, the beer gone, and the man returned inside. A few people had emerged from their homes, families stuffing into their cars to drive off for whatever weekend events awaited. A teenage couple set up a picnic under the lone tree in the field, enjoying sandwiches and an extended make-out session under the shade.

Seeing it made Arielle think about Kevin. And his opioid addiction.

*If I had just seen the signs sooner.*

Arielle shook her head free of the self-inflicted blame. Fortunately, she was on high alert since waking up this morning, and was ready for anything that might throw her off her game. Who knows if that couple really had a picnic in the Original timeline, or if the past had placed them there to spark emotional vulnerability within her.

For added assurance, Arielle locked her door and reached over the passenger seat to lock the other. One more step to keep her inside the car should she decide, against her will, to step out.

Another hour passed. The couple had vanished back toward the path where she and Selena had found Felix just hours earlier.

It was 2:15 and Arielle felt satisfied with making it to the halfway point of her stakeout without seeing Jacob Kennedy.

At 2:18, a car turned onto Juniper Street and parked in front of Kennedy's house, the driver remaining in the car while the engine kept running, faint clouds of exhaust puffing out of the muffler.

The car was a light brown Nissan Sentra, probably an '88 or '89 model. It had parked with its rear facing Arielle, so even through a pair of binoculars, she couldn't make out the driver. She could, however, read the license plate, a California tag she jotted down to call in later.

"Who the hell are you?"

Kennedy appeared from his front door, dressed in gym shorts and a raggedy t-shirt, clearly without plans to leave his house. He waved at the car before making his way down the path, where he squatted to poke his head through the open passenger-side window.

Arielle held her gaze through the binoculars, unable to see

much thanks to a brutal glare off the car's back window. The figure in the driver's seat wore a ball cap, so she figured it was likely a man—thought she couldn't confirm this with confidence.

She watched for ten minutes while the two talked, wondering what they would have to speak about for so long, and why the driver never stepped out. Kennedy's head bobbed every few seconds, and he only stood up once to stretch his back before squatting back down to lean in through the window.

After those ten minutes passed, Kennedy returned inside, but the car and driver remained. Arielle wanted nothing more than to drive by to see who was in the car. She felt like a caged lioness salivating over a piece of meat just outside of paw's reach. There had been too many close calls in the past couple of days to justify driving down the block right now. With her luck, Kennedy would step outside again right when she was in front of the house, and recognize her car from yesterday.

Kennedy returned outside after a couple minutes, this time with a brown paper bag clutched in his hand.

Arielle returned to her binoculars to watch Kennedy hand the bag over to the driver. They chatted for a few more seconds before the car took off and Kennedy waved them farewell.

*Don't do it,* Arielle told herself, her hand having subconsciously moved to the key she left in the ignition. *The past wants you to follow that car—don't fall for it. It was probably just one of his kids.*

"He wouldn't have his own son wait in the car. That was a suspicious conversation and delivery of that brown bag."

Every cell in her body burned with overwhelming curiosity. She knew if she followed that car out of the neighborhood to find out who was driving, everything would fall into place and make sense. She also knew it would expose her to highly risky matters once back on the road. The best she could do was hope the encounter had no relation to the pending robbery.

"Dammit!" she screamed, and punched her steering wheel. She could count on one hand how many times she had felt completely helpless while on a mission. And this was one of the worst instances.

Arielle lifted the lid to the center console and rummaged through the car's paperwork until she found the packet of gum she had tossed in there on the first day. She never would let a car she was driving go without an emergency pack, and she popped two sticks into her mouth.

She still had ninety minutes until four o'clock, when she had vowed to leave to meet Felix at the apartment for an early dinner.

The thought of sitting in the car for another hour and a half shredded her psyche, knowing the car that drove away had some sort of tie to the robbery.

She watched Kennedy return inside the house and close the door, leaving the neighborhood motionless under the baking sun. Arielle threw her head back and silently screamed.

# Chapter 36

While Arielle spent the next ninety minutes stewing in her car, Felix watched Young on his laptop while Selena flushed out her insides in preparation for her long night ahead.

She stepped out of the bathroom and joined Felix at the dining room table, floorplans of the bank's basement and subbasement levels splayed out.

"Still doing nothing?" Selena asked.

"Honestly, it's incredible the man isn't 600 pounds. He does *nothing*. It's really looking like he has no involvement. He should be doing something today if he was, right?"

Selena shrugged. Diving into the mind of a potential bank robber was not something she had ever considered. Then again, if she had ever been asked to portray a bank robber, she'd have no choice, but that opportunity had yet to arise. "I suppose we'll know tomorrow morning just how involved he is."

Selena had her own growing suspicions about the mission, but had opted to keep them to herself. While it may have been risky to keep her thoughts to herself, she wanted to practice the skill that Arielle had taught them about withholding that information from the past. But would there ever be a right time for such an attempt? Her theories had formulated over the past few days, and so far nothing had happened out of the ordinary aside from Dawkins spotting her in the storage room early that morning—something she chalked up to his evolving infatuation with her.

"He's involved in some capacity," Felix said. "How else do you explain the secret meetings with Kennedy?"

"They weren't really that secret, though. Sitting at a sports bar is hardly a place to discuss a private matter like bank-robbing plans. Maybe they genuinely wanted to hang out and have some drinks. Think about it—the past didn't even resist you taking his notebook. That alone makes me think he's not involved."

"Unless the notebook has nothing to do with this. He could have made those ramblings months ago and not touched it since. I've yet to see him open that closet door during this whole time. I suppose that would be too much work for him."

Selena heard the frustration in Felix's voice. "You're just feeling helpless after what happened last night. It doesn't help that Young gives you nothing of substance. Just stay patient and trust that we're all in the right places. We have less than twenty-four hours until this robbery. Eliminating a suspect is just as important as anything else. If you have to spend all day watching Young eat himself within an inch of his life, then so be it. If we can cross his name off the list, then it's worth it—because he's still very much a serious suspect."

Felix rolled his eyes and nodded toward the monitor that showed an empty living room. Young had disappeared into the bathroom after slipping into a robe. "At least he takes showers."

"I know what you're thinking, and it's not true."

"Oh? What am I thinking, Selena?" Felix spoke in a mocking

tone before clenching his jaw shut.

"You think you're a failure because of last night. You're beating yourself up way too much. You're alive and well, and that's all that matters."

Selena saw the sides of his jaws bulging out as he clenched tighter. She was right, and Felix knew it. She could see the confirmation in his eyes.

"I *am* a failure. This has got to be my worst mission ever. I've been in Kennedy's house twice and haven't been able to set up any successful monitoring. That's literally my only job. I've been watching Young for two weeks and haven't learned a damn thing outside of his notebook. And even that's been as useful as a drop of water in the middle of a desert. I'm afraid of getting kicked off this team for failing to do my job. These last two missions have been so high-pressure working with Arielle."

"And whose fault is that? Arielle doesn't really put pressure on us. It sounds like you're putting it on yourself. Guess what? This has probably been the worst mission for all of us. Even Arielle. She's lost and confused on this one, even if she doesn't seem like it."

"Did she tell you that?"

"Not verbatim, but yes. And if this mission ends in failure, it's going to be on us as a team. No one is going to individually get thrown under the bus. We've all had some shortcomings along the way—it will be impossible to pinpoint the fault on any one of us."

Felix fell silent while he doodled on the table with his finger. Selena knew this was his way of processing everything she had just said. After a minute, he spoke. "Are you ready for tonight?"

"I am. I finished a gallon of water by noon, and should pee out the last of it by four." Selena checked her watch. "About another hour. Then I'll be on my way. Got my backpack loaded with the snacks I'll need, and two blankets. I'm going to roll one into a pillow—figured that would be easier than squeezing a pillow in. And I'm going to stop at the store on my way to grab some sleeping pills."

"Is that a good idea? What if you sleep longer than you should?"

Selena raised a calming hand. "I'm gonna take this pill at, like, six o'clock tonight. And on an empty stomach, it's going to process through my body much faster. At worst, I'll sleep until three in the morning. But I'll wake up with plenty of energy and be ready for all the action at nine."

"And what exactly are you planning on doing? You can't just pop out of the room and scare the robber—you'll get shot."

"I'm aware. I'm not planning on stepping foot outside of that room until the robber is in the vault. I'll have the door propped open an inch or two and will just be watching through the crack. Just trying to see if I can make out who it is. That's all Arielle asked me to do. Once the robber is out of sight, I'm going to sprint the other way."

"Seems like a lot of work for something that probably won't yield any results. The robber is in a disguise. How are you supposed to see anything looking through a cracked open door?"

"Well, the good thing is I've spent time in person with Kennedy and Young. Most of the security team, in fact. Arielle is relying on my instincts to pinpoint the robber."

"That sounds like nonsense."

"But it's not. You can sense someone's presence. Kennedy

definitely had a strong presence that night at the bar. Besides, even if it's just through a door, I'll have a much better idea of the robber's size and build. Kennedy and Young have two very different bodies—it shouldn't be that hard to tell who is who." Selena checked her watch. "I'm gonna get going."

She stood up and left Felix at the table to stare mindlessly at his laptop showing Young's empty living room. He'd plan to sit there until Arielle arrived home.

It only took Selena five minutes to use the restroom one final time and gather her backpack full of goodies for the long night ahead. She slung it over her shoulder and returned to Felix. "I'll see you in the morning, okay? Don't be so worried about me."

"I worry about all of us—you should know that by now."

"Of course, and we appreciate that. But just rest assured, I'll be fine. I'm not taking any risks. Hell, I might get caught and end up back here in a couple hours—that's still a very real possibility."

"I won't hold my breath."

Selena left the apartment and started on her usual route she had been taking to the office every morning. Around the midpoint was a convenience store where she planned to stop for sleeping pills.

Once she reached the store, she found the place swarmed with six police cars, all lights flashing under the afternoon sun. This same area was where the scenic views of the natural beauty surrounding the neighborhood started giving way to the jungle of concrete that was downtown Denver. A laundromat was next to the convenience store, and that's where she was forced to stop behind a police car serving as a barricade.

Three people huddled outside the laundromat entrance, all facing the scene with arms folded over their chests.

"What's going on?" Selena asked.

"I guess a homeless man walked into the store with a gun," a middle-aged woman said. She stepped forward, brushing back sandy hair behind her ears. "Tried holding up the place. The owner refused to open the cash register and ducked a couple of shots. Grabbed his shotgun, and the two got into a shootout. Cops said the bum ended up shooting himself."

The woman paused and shook her head. "I feel so bad for Bohdan—he's the owner. Must be so shaken up."

"Do things like this happen often around here?" Selena asked.

"No. Not at all. For a big city, it's pretty safe. In this part, at least. That's why this makes no sense. I suppose the world grows a little madder each day."

"I stop here almost every day on my way to work. Was just on my way and was going to grab something. Can't believe this is happening."

"You must have an angel looking after you. That's what I think. If you came a few minutes earlier, you would've been caught in the middle of this. Lord knows what could've happened."

*An angel looking after me, or the past?* Selena thought. Someone would have tried to draw a parallel, even if the homeless man had taken his own life and couldn't have possibly been involved in the bank robbery. *That's how I know this whole thing is from the past. But why? The past doesn't want me to sleep this evening.*

"Well, thank you for filling me in," Selena said. "I still need to get to work. Hope you all have a better rest of the day. Glad you're okay."

"Me too, hon. See you around."

Selena crossed the street to get around the patrol cars. She craned her neck for a look inside the store, but could only see huddles of police officers through the windows.

Dread settled into Selena's gut. She had left the apartment with so much optimism about their final leg of this grueling mission. She had a plan that would work, dammit, but matters were already getting pushed off-course thanks to the past's interference. If this much could happen before she even arrived at the office, what might await during the evening ahead?

Selena walked the rest of the way to the office, glancing over her shoulder every few seconds, paranoid that the past itself might jump out from a corner and suck her very existence away.

Once she reached the building, enough negativity had consumed her mind. She tapped her badge to the card reader and stepped inside.

# Chapter 37

Only ten minutes after Selena had left, Peter Young emerged from the shower, clean and dressed in a pair of jean shorts and a raggedy Metallica t-shirt.

Felix was grateful, seeing as Young typically paraded around his apartment naked after bathing. Some times for an entire hour.

When Young grabbed his wallet and stuffed it into his rear pocket, Felix jumped out of his seat. He hadn't expected Young to leave the apartment.

Felix didn't even have his shoes on, scrambling to find them in his bedroom before dashing back to his computer to see Young still in the kitchen, helping himself to a can of Coke.

"C'mon, you son of a bitch. Where are you going?"

Young placed the can on the counter, patted his pockets, and left the apartment. Felix noticed he didn't grab the car keys hanging on a hook next to the door, meaning Young was going somewhere on foot.

Felix grabbed his pistol and tucked it into the back of his waistband. He rarely carried a weapon while on missions, but he no longer felt safe and was in no position to take any chances.

He dashed out of the apartment and sprinted to the stairwell, knowing Young had never taken the stairs and always opted for the elevator. This would buy him just enough time to get outside first.

He hurried down the stairs, swinging around the corners and nearly sliding off balance a few times. But he reached the first level in record speed and made a mad dash for the building's exit. The elevator chimed right as he passed it, but he was out of sight before the doors parted.

Felix scampered around the sidewalk, panting for breath like an exhausted dog, while he searched for somewhere to hide and wait. Not knowing which way Young planned to go, Felix started walking down the sidewalk to look natural. There was no one else outside the apartment, and Young would likely notice a shady character hiding behind a trash can or tree.

Felix went south, and after ten paces heard the complex's doors close. He took three more steps before taking a casual look over his shoulder, seeing Young headed north. He sighed relief. Being in front of Young would have been awkward to finagle his way back behind him. This way allowed him the ease of simply turning around to follow Young and stay a safe distance behind.

He spun around and didn't need to hurry. Young moved at the pace one would expect of an obese middle-aged man with heart problems. *No way* this *guy robs the bank,* Felix thought. A bank robber would need to be a lot quicker on their feet. Even if Young could break into a sprint, how far could he reasonably run before stopping to catch his breath?

Young moved with no urgency, kept his gaze forward as he unknowingly led Felix four blocks to the nearest gas station. He cut through the lot and rounded the small building where a pay phone stood next to an outdoor storage bin of windshield wiper fluid.

"Shit," Felix muttered under his breath. The pay phone was too out in the open for him to sneak behind Young to listen to his phone call. The best he could do was stand around the corner and hope he could hear it.

Young picked up the phone off the receiver and popped coins into the slot, promptly dialing a phone number he appeared to have memorized. Felix inched his way to the corner, peeking around the brick exterior of the building where he saw Young facing his direction. He didn't notice Felix, however, so he quickly retreated out of sight.

"Dammit." Felix truly had no angle and already knew he was too far away—about thirty feet—to hear the conversation clearly. It didn't help that the occasional vehicle hummed by and drowned out the silence.

He peeked again, seeing the bin of wiper fluid bottles only ten feet away from Young at the pay phone. Young was talking. Felix could hear the mumble of his distant voice, but couldn't make out anything.

"Please don't let anything bad happen to me," Felix whispered, then stepped out from the corner, strolling calmly toward the bin of fluid. How he wished the bin was full of something that required more inspection. All the bottles of fluid were the same, so he couldn't justify standing there for over fifteen seconds. When he reached the bin, Young's voice became plenty clear.

"Everything is set," Young said. "You're clear."

Young paused when Felix reached into the bin and pulled out a bottle of fluid. Felix's heart froze as he pretended to read the bottle's label, paranoid Young had stopped talking because of his presence. He couldn't bring himself to look over to see what Young was doing. What if Young recognized him from the apartment?

*Don't be a fool. He's never seen your face. You're just paranoid. Like always.*

Relief flooded over Felix when Young spoke again, no suspicion in his voice. "Sounds good. It's been a pleasure. Good luck."

Felix sensed the conversation coming to its brief close and rushed away with the bottle of fluid in hand. Realizing he'd have Young behind him now, he went inside the store and disappeared down the candy aisle, keeping his eyes glued to the window, waiting for Young. The phone call must have not ended as soon as he thought, as a whole minute passed before Young walked by the window, returning the way he had come.

Felix went to the cashier and placed the fluid on the counter. "Sorry. Decided I don't need this."

He bolted out to find Young already crossing the street to return to the apartment. He wished he would have stayed longer reading the bottle's label, but he thought his head might explode with panic had he remained another second. There were thousands of possibilities for the words he heard from Young's mouth, and he kept repeating them in his head.

*Everything is set. You're clear. It's been a pleasure. Good luck.*

Those words could have easily been related to a potential bank robbery as they could have been intended for a friend or family member. They were nothing of substance, but Felix already felt the dials turning in his mind to crack the code. These words were just another puzzle he needed to figure out. And even though he knew they would likely lead nowhere, he wouldn't be able to help but stew over them for the rest of the evening. Fortunately, the robbery occurred the following morning, so this puzzle had a short window of relevance.

*Everything is set.*

Felix mulled over this phrase, figuring things might make more sense if he broke Young's words into smaller pieces. Was everything set for the robbery in the morning? If that was the case, then surely he had spoken with the robber. Why would someone who owns a home phone need to stop at a pay phone to make a call a mere four blocks away? That alone made it seem like a sensitive matter, and not just a discussion about dinner plans.

*You're clear.*

They had long suspected Young's involvement stemmed as an insider with the security team. What he might have cleared was the lingering question that needed an answer. Young didn't work during the robbery, nor did he today. If he made any type of preparation at the bank, it would have been completed on Friday. But what could he have done?

*He could have taken the tapes out with no one realizing in time before the robbery.* Felix didn't know how often such a task was the norm for the security crew.

*He could have left the vault unlocked, but was that even possible? Standard bank security systems cued an alarm if the vault was left unlocked for a particular amount of time.*

Felix shook his head, hoping the answer would fall into his mind, but no mission was ever that convenient.

*It's been a pleasure.*

This line from Young might have been the most troubling to peg. Would someone really say that with such normalcy under the circumstances? It was definitely possible, especially if the person was expecting a large sum of money to arrive because of the fruits of their illegal labor. *Thirty-thousand dollars,* Felix thought. *To take out some tapes and leave a door unlocked? I'd definitely give that proposition some thought.*

Felix never had issues remembering his humble roots of his family scrapping together enough money for meals, no matter what his bank account said these days, courtesy of the Road Runners. Thirty-thousand dollars for a blue-collar worker could change their life tremendously. What Peter Young would do with all that money was another question. Drink it away? Eat it away? He'd probably go to Vegas and get the best of both worlds, plus an opportunity to donate it to a charming casino.

*Good luck.*

The last phrase from Young before he hung up. The one that stirred those damned butterflies in Felix's stomach. The one that suggested more was to come. You didn't wish someone good luck for something they had already accomplished.

Felix had gained too much ground on Young during his mental calculations, and was glad he regained some focus in time to slow down once they reached the corner of the apartment complex.

He stopped and watched Young return inside, oblivious to the man from the future following him. Felix no longer felt the urgency to watch Young's every move. All he could do at this point in the mission was gamble on the knowledge they had available. Despite the horrific notebook and violent rantings of Peter Young, those last two words he had spoken summed everything up.

The call was made at a public pay phone. No home call log that could be pulled up in court.

*Good luck.*

It was as open-ended as it was definitive. Those two words implied Young was done with his part, and Godspeed to whoever was stepping into that bank in the morning, armed and ready.

Felix returned inside the apartment complex, a stale odor seeming to linger in the lobby, with one thought swelling in his mind.

*Young isn't our guy.*

# Chapter 38

Whatever fear had lingered in Selena during her walk into the office—never mind the stress that had accumulated after seeing her favorite local convenience store barricaded by local police—vanished once she pulled open the door and stepped into a deserted lobby.

Employees sometimes took the freight elevator—the same one the robber would use the next morning—but it wasn't required. As a member of the cleaning crew, Selena had a master key to get into the building from any door.

She figured the skyscraper's main entrance might draw the attention of the security team, but they'd quickly dismiss her presence once they realized who she was.

*Okay,* she thought. *I'm in the building.*

She strolled across the lobby, its marble floors finely polished, the leftover lemony scent still present. A pair of couches surrounded a small coffee table in front of the main reception desk—staffed by security guards during the weekdays. Fake plants lined the windows in the lobby, providing just enough privacy from any wandering eyes roaming down the sidewalks outside.

To Selena's right was the glass wall and door that customers used to enter the bank. Selena went forward to the main elevators and pushed the down button. This task could take an entire two minutes during the bustle of the work week, but a door opened immediately.

Selena stepped in and took the elevator down to the sub-basement level.

She stepped out, further relieved to find the long hallway also abandoned. The locker room waited roughly fifty feet ahead, and she felt her feet floating across the dust-covered concrete floor as she thought she had a clear path.

If the past had ever wanted to toy with her, it did so when a guard stepped out of a side room and started down the hall toward Selena.

Time screeched to a halt as her temples pounded with adrenaline. And fear.

Selena squinted for a clearer view of the guard, but still didn't recognize him. The two kept closing in on each other, Selena bracing for the worst.

*Act normal. You're working today. You belong here. Hold your ground, no matter what he says.*

Selena rarely had issues sticking to her guns, but something about this entire situation felt off. She wasn't herself. Was a lack of confidence something the past could plant into one's mind? Arielle had mentioned the past had never actually killed someone, but that didn't mean it couldn't render someone useless on a mission by rewiring their brain.

*You're overthinking. Just shut up and handle this.*

The two were within ten feet of each other, Selena now confident she had never seen this older gentleman before. He was at least seventy with snow-white hair protruding from a solid black ball cap, the word *SECURITY* embroidered across the center. He walked with a slight hitch in his step, as if he had a bad knee.

*Is the weekend crew like the junior varsity team around here?* Selena thought. No wonder the place got robbed. They left this poor old man, who would struggle to chase down a turtle should one decide to empty the vault, without a gun. What exactly did the security team think he could do to fend off an actual armed robber?

"Good afternoon, doll," he said with a lopsided grin, voice gentle and warm. "You're working today?"

"Hello, sir," Selena said, calculating every word and how it might be received before it left her lips. "Yes. Would much rather be out with my friends tonight, but here I am."

"Ah, yes. Saturday night. Not exactly a nightclub here, is it?" he asked, and let out a hearty chuckle. "Don't work yourself too hard, you hear?"

"I won't. Have a good evening."

"You too, doll. Take care."

Selena hadn't noticed it, but the old man never actually stopped walking. She had, but he kept moving along at his ginger pace, not a single plan of stopping his momentum.

She couldn't help but smile as she looked over her shoulder to see him inching his way toward the elevator she had just come from.

"See," Selena whispered to herself. "Nothing to worry about."

She pressed forward to the locker room and slipped in before anyone else spotted her. She flipped the light switch to blast the long fluorescent bulb above, buzzing a bit too loudly for her liking.

Selena sat down on the bench for a moment to make sure her thoughts were really as calm as she had thought. She wasn't lying to herself, and truly felt at peace after her encounter with the guard.

*Is the past throwing me a bone? Is there a depth to it—that it doesn't want such bad things to happen to innocent people? Could the past actually be rooting for us to succeed, while still doing its due diligence for appearances?*

She laughed at the thought. Of course none of that was true. The past wasn't a human with emotions. The past was an extension of time, which was an extension of the universe. And the universe simply *existed.* It didn't care if you were Mother Teresa or Adolf Hitler—what you did during your time in the universe was your business.

"Then let's own this moment," she said to help snap her focus back into place.

Selena pulled her t-shirt over her head and stepped up to open her locker. When she saw a small gift box inside, propped on top of her folded uniform pants, her blood froze.

*What the hell is that? Who's it from?*

Any tranquility she had composed within quickly vanished, her mind racing like a bat out of hell.

*This is it,* she thought. *This is the past finally waiting for its chance to make me turn around.*

Her thoughts quickly moved into paranoia—the box was a bomb planted by the robber, in her locker, of course—then moved into a panicking logic. *Someone knows all of our plans and is sending a message to stop. We were the ones being watched this whole time. That's the punchline the past has been waiting oh-so-patiently to deliver.*

That thought seemed a stretch, but not one she wanted to rule out completely.

Then she moved into a more reasonable logic.

*Dawkins.*

The guy clearly had feelings for her, even after a faux date. Dawkins had access to the women's locker room after hours, and could even find out which locker belonged to Selena. The box inside her locker was solid red with a black bow tied across the top of the lid. It was square-shaped, and no bigger than six inches on the sides.

*A romantic gesture?* she wondered, part of her hoping it was true, the other still sensing a trap.

She debated touching it. More harm than good could come from it. Opening the box might very well lead to the mission unraveling, and it seemed an unnecessary risk to take at this stage. She was in the building, only spotted by one guard who had likely already dismissed their encounter.

"One more step and I'm where I'll need to be for the rest of the mission."

Selena at least wanted to know what was in the box, and the thought of leaving it behind completely untouched and returning home after the mission would eat at her for the rest of her life. The box could be tied to the mission, or have no relevance to their work at all.

She needed to move the box, as it rested on top of her folded uniform pants.

Selena reached out with a trembling hand, forcing herself to get the shaking under control. If there was a miniature bomb inside the box, her nerves would certainly do no favors when handling the package.

She picked it up carefully and noted how light it felt between her fingers. Selena didn't dare shake the package, instead placing it gently on the bench behind her. She gawked at the box through the entirety of her changing outfits, refusing to break eye contact.

Once dressed in her work uniform, Selena stuffed her clothes into the top of her backpack and looked into her locker. All that hung was a second uniform shirt—one she'd never wear again.

It finally occurred to her, that even if they were still in 1991 on Monday morning, Selena wouldn't be coming into work. The whole building would be a crime scene—work would definitely be called off for at least a week while the authorities gathered evidence from every square inch of the skyscraper.

*I'm not coming back here. Ever.*

The reality was both calming and unsettling—mainly because of the mystery package. If she left it in the locker, they would discover it on Sunday afternoon. Selena already expected her name to float around during the investigation, seeing as she was a staff member who would essentially disappear from the face of the planet after the crime.

Perhaps the legend would change after their involvement. Maybe Selena's name would long stand as a mystery suspect for the bank robbery, assuming it all went through as it originally had. How else could anyone explain her brief employment for only two weeks before a robbery, followed by her vanishing act?

The thought sent chills down her back. Being accused of a bank robbery was no light accusation. A charge like that, even if unproven or lacking a shred of evidence, could tarnish one's name and reputation.

"But I don't exist in this timeline," she whispered.

Living the life of a time traveler, always in different years, made it hard for Selena to remember the simple fact that she wasn't on the grid during most missions she worked. If the authorities wanted to stress over her name after this robbery, it would only be a waste of time. While her name was real, her social security, ID's, and any other form of identification they might try to research were all false.

The realization always left her humbled. If Selena disappeared entirely, who would notice? Her parents, after a few weeks of no calls. Arielle and Felix, certainly, and the rest of the Road Runners organization. But who else of actual significance?

She was renowned in the time travel world, but what about the real world? The world everyone else lived in. The one where achievements were celebrated—across the globe, sometimes.

They might complete this mission and have all the answers to the questions that went unsolved for decades. Selena might even end up being the one directly responsible for discovering who the monster was behind the robbery and murders. But what did it mean for her? A quick pat on the back and a follow-up assignment to get back into the past.

This constant lifestyle of hustle and bustle didn't bother her too often, but now and then these same thoughts forced their way into her mind and planted themselves there for anywhere from a couple days to two weeks. More often than not, these thoughts caused her a severe bout of depression that led to hiding in her house, lazing around in her pajamas while every ounce of motivation to exist drained from her body like a hidden waterline leak.

She didn't quite feel that level of self-hatred creeping in yet, and it could all vanish after the mission was complete—that had happened more than once.

Selena closed her eyes and imagined the glamorous life of a

Hollywood star. Galas, award shows, flashy outfits, handsome actors, and a life traveling the world doing what she loved more than anything. Buried in the depth of these missions, her dreams felt like they lived on a different planet entirely.

*One day, I'll chase it all. I'll have it all.*

She stuffed the mystery box into her backpack and left the locker room behind for the last time, heading for the storage closet on the basement level above.

# Chapter 39

Arielle arrived back at the apartment about fifteen minutes after Felix had returned. She found him sitting at the dining room table, laptop flipped open to the live-feed of their suspect.

"How'd it go today?" she asked, pulling out the seat next to him. The laptop was pushed back, a glass of lemonade standing in the space between Felix and the computer. His focus was on the liquid ring that had formed around the base of the glass. He traced the fluid with his finger in a circular motion.

Felix explained everything that had happened, building up to his convincing proposal that Young's involvement did not carry into the day of the crime on Sunday.

Arielle shared the few details she had on the random visitor who had stopped by Kennedy's house. She pulled out the note with the car's license plate as a reminder to call it in. It could sometimes take hours to get a result back, even for the top-ranked Angel. While her requests took priority over many other Angels, she couldn't jump to the top of the line, no matter how urgent the information might be.

"So what are we supposed to plan for in the morning?" Felix asked.

Arielle shrugged. "The same plan we've had all along, I suppose. I agree with you about Young not being further involved, but we can't take that leap of faith without concrete evidence. You'll still need to keep your eyes on him in the morning before making your way to the bank. I wouldn't put too much weight on it, though. Maybe plan to leave around 8:30, assuming he shows no activity."

Felix nodded, his eyes quickly dashing to the screen that showed Young in his typical spot on the recliner. "Okay. And you're still going to Kennedy's house?"

"I'll be there around seven, ready to watch anything that might happen. From a distance, of course."

"And you're going to follow him? Won't tomorrow be the riskiest day to do that, considering everything that's happened already?"

Arielle nodded. "It sure is, but it's what we're here for. Sometimes you have to push fear and worry aside and just get the job done."

Felix allowed a moment of silence before speaking. "That doesn't mean you should risk your life for the job. Past all the glitz and glamour of being the top-ranked Angel, you're just a person doing a job. If you die tomorrow, I'm sure there will be a week of festivities to celebrate your life and achievements within the Road Runners. But then what? The number-two Angel becomes number one. Everyone shifts up a spot, then life goes on. No matter how much you accomplish in this role, you're only going to be a name in the history books. And only for the Road Runners, at that. I hope you keep this kind of perspective."

"I do," Arielle said. And she did, to an extent. Her biggest fear was dying before her grandmother. She couldn't bear the thought of leaving her closest relative alone in the world. She may have not had as many opportunities to visit her abuela as she'd like, but the thought of her grandmother somehow being the last member of the family left seemed a torturous way to end her final days on the planet. Would the Road Runners even inform her grandmother if Arielle passed away? Or would they would leave her to count the final days wondering why Arielle stopped reaching out and visiting? "I know I talk a big game, but I really proceed with caution. I'm not reckless, and I always weigh the potential death traps that can happen. I suppose I've just been doing this long enough, where it all comes natural to me now."

"Don't let that comfort twist into your downfall. That same story has been repeated plenty of times throughout history. Comfort leads to letting your guard down. Thinking you're invincible is probably the deadliest belief someone can have."

"I don't think that at all."

"Really? Who's the number-two ranked Angel behind you?"

Arielle bit her bottom lip. Why did Felix seem so hell-bent on pushing her buttons?

"Marcus Conners," she said confidently.

Felix shook his head. "He hasn't been number two for at least six months. Has it really been that long since you've looked?"

"I don't see how that's relevant."

"But it is. Don't get me wrong—I'm not one who puts a ton of stock into rankings of any sort. However, if I was, say, in the top ten, you can bet I'd be looking at those rankings daily, trying to understand how to move up and also how to avoid falling down the list. Someone who hasn't looked at the list in six months means they're comfortable with where they are and don't have a worry in the world about falling down the list."

Arielle sat up straight. "Wait, are you saying that someone is closing in on me? Who's in second?"

"None of that matters. That's beside the point. You can look that up after the mission."

"What happened to Marcus?"

Arielle had met Marcus Conners on multiple occasions, often to swap strategic ideas. The Angels at the top of the charts never worked together, the organization preferring to keep the talent dispersed evenly across multiple teams.

"Marcus suffered a serious injury on a mission. Tore an ACL, Achilles tendon, broken ribs, and messed up his spine. He's no longer in the top 100 while he's been in an intensive recovery."

Now Arielle stood up, and Felix joined her, the two looking like they might be about to break into fisticuffs instead of a heated discussion. "How did I not hear about this?!"

"Because you don't care. You're not worried about those below you on the rankings. They shared this information in the weekly emails from the Commander's office."

Arielle wouldn't admit it to Felix—at least not right now—but she rarely opened those weekly emails. They provided high-level happenings and occasionally spotlighted a Road Runner for some achievement. She thought of it more as a basic newsletter with information she never found interesting.

"I care. That's not fair of you to say I don't."

"I'm not saying you don't care about Marcus—of course you do. But you live so focused in your own world, that you're not aware of everything else happening outside of it. You might call that tunnel vision, but I see it as a dangerous level of comfort. You like it in your world. Nothing bad can happen to you in it. You control every aspect of your own universe. And you're certainly not worried about some other Angel barging in and taking your place on the throne. Why would you? It's *your* world."

Arielle felt a pang in her stomach that she wasn't sure was hunger or anxiety. "Why are you saying all this? I don't understand why tonight, of all nights, you'd want to plant this in my head?"

"I say it because I care about you. It's weird. I consider you pretty humble. But that doesn't mean your awareness is where it should be. Maybe your humble when dealing with others, but hold yourself on a pedestal within your own mind."

"I hold myself to high standards. I wouldn't say it's a pedestal."

"Whatever it is, it's good to be reminded of the big picture some times. I'd hate to see your downfall. You've done a lot for me and Selena, and we're in this for the long haul. But our team can't succeed if you make a mistake that costs everything."

Arielle's throat tensed shut. Part of her wanted to cry. The other part wanted to scream. "Thank you," she muttered, taking a big gulp to open up her throat. "I've never had someone care for me within the Road Runners the way you and Selena have. I'll be the first to admit how skeptical I was hearing about the plans for these permanent teams. But I'm glad it happened."

Felix grinned. "Our team is going places. It's only a matter of time before they rank the teams instead of the individual Angels. I wonder where we'll end up on that list." Felix looked to the ceiling and stroked his chin to feign deep thought.

This earned a giggle from Arielle, who felt a sense of relief she hadn't known she needed.  A weight was lifted off her shoulders.  Her team had her back through everything.  An unconditional love she had never felt from anyone besides her family and Kevin, once upon a time. It had been building up over the past few weeks, but Arielle now fully believed that it was okay to *not* be alone in the Road Runners.

"Thank you, Felix. For all of your words. I needed to hear all of that. You're exactly what this team needs. A calm, unbiased perspective on everything we do. It's invaluable."

Felix held his tight-lipped grin, never one to enjoy a shower of compliments in any setting.  He checked his watch.  "We need to have dinner and get some sleep. Tomorrow's the big day."

# Chapter 40

Arielle woke up on Sunday morning at 5:06, twenty-four minutes before her alarm, feet hitting the ground with a nervous anticipation of the day ahead.

She had broken her own rule last night, consuming two glasses of wine after dinner. But she needed it. She was in sync with her mind and body, her thoughts out of control. Without the wine, she probably would have been awake until midnight, likely later. With it, she lay down and dozed off minutes before eight o'clock.

Arielle had passed the time by packing her suitcase while she sipped on the wine. She had encouraged Felix to do the same. If all went smoothly this morning, they would return to the apartment, grab their bags, and never look back. Felix offered to pack Selena's bag as best he could. They had taken a peek into her bedroom to find clothes tossed all over the place and toiletries scattered across her nightstand. Arielle was grateful Felix bit the bullet to clean up her mess—doing so would have caused her serious stress.

Arielle fought off jitters while she dressed for the morning. It was nothing new—she typically experienced some level of nerves on the morning of the ultimate showdown. Thankfully, her anxiety didn't stem from a lack of belief in her abilities, but rather from the unknown. Would all their hard work over the past two weeks pay off? This mission, in particular, had brought up more doubts than most in the past.

Arielle could count on one hand how many times she had started the final day of a mission with no clue how it might turn out. Today was one of them.

Jacob Kennedy, Peter Young, now an outsider they were previously unaware of. Who slips into the bank and kills four people?

While Kennedy was still the obvious suspect, difficulty in finding concrete evidence made Arielle wary of fully committing to him.

Once her bag was packed, she left it on the foot of the bed. Arielle had dressed in her standard mission-day attire of black spandex over her entire body. She put a pair of athletic pants over, along with a baggy jacket that would allow room for a bulletproof vest underneath, should she desire.

She headed downstairs to find Felix at the kitchen table, laptop open, a glass of orange juice in front of him.

"Good morning," Arielle said. "Any action yet?"

Felix shook his head, an elevated level of seriousness consuming him. It was go-time, and Felix Francisco wasn't one to fuck around. "He's sleeping. I went back and checked the footage. He stayed up until 1:30 last night, watching late night television shows while he dozed in and out. Slammed six beers between ten and midnight."

"Doesn't sound like someone who needs to be awake early on Sunday morning."

"Not at all. He's gotta be passed out drunk still. I'm not counting on seeing a trace of him."

"It just doesn't make sense."

"We'll have a better idea by the end of the day."

"No breakfast this morning?" Arielle asked, nodding to the glass of juice.

Felix laughed through his nose. "A bit early, no? If you want something, I can make some toast real quick. I know you're trying to get out the door."

"Don't worry about it, I'll grab a banana on my way out." Arielle would have plenty of time to eat once she arrived at Kennedy's neighborhood.  She didn't exactly expect an eventful morning until around eight o'clock. Before leaving, she filled a short glass of water, chugging it instantly. "I'll see you down at the bank around nine o'clock. . . assuming Young really isn't involved today."

Felix glanced at the screen still showing a dormant living room. "Yes. I'll be there."

Arielle nodded, the tension heavy in the air. It didn't need to be said, but they both understood the risks they would all endure throughout the morning. Felix's words from last night still lingered heavily on Arielle's mind, and she felt obligated to proceed with an extra level of caution.

"I'll see you soon."

# Chapter 41

As Arielle drove across town, Selena awoke from a long night of tossing and turning. The lack of sleeping pills proved costly. Aside from an already flustered mind, Selena endured drastic temperature changes within the storage room throughout the night. From too hot to cold, her blanket ended up twisted into a spiral. Even with the makeshift pillow and blankets, sleeping on the concrete floor left her with plenty of back and neckaches by the time she woke up.

Shortly before four o'clock, she heard what she thought was a buzzing sound. An alarm blared for only a couple of minutes before cutting off.

*Was that something with the robbery? An early setup?*

It was possible the entire security team was in on the heist, each with a role to play to ensure a smooth robbery. But that didn't explain how four guards wound up dead before lunchtime. Unless the robber reconsidered before entering the bank. Killing off accomplices only made the surviving participants richer with a bigger cut of the money. This also seemed likely, but Selena sensed herself slipping down a dangerous rabbit hole of unproven theories. She shook her head free of all the thoughts, focusing on her simple task of keeping an eye out for the moments following nine o'clock.

On a positive note, her planning around food and drink was correct. Even upon waking, she had no urge to relieve her bowels or bladder. With her body tense and sore, Selena spent twenty minutes doing yoga stretches. The area had remained quiet all night, not that it mattered. She calculated roughly five hours of actual sleep.

*I've done a lot bigger tasks on a lot less sleep before,* she thought once she added up the time.

She had slept in her work uniform overnight and now changed into her mission outfit—nearly the same thing as Arielle—and stuffed a black ski mask into her back pocket. That was only to be worn if she felt in danger of being seen by security.

After stretching, Selena rummaged through her backpack for a pack of pudding, her stomach growling the instant her eyes fell on it. It wouldn't fill her by any means, but she welcomed any small boost of energy. She peeled the lid off, licking the chocolate goo before folding it into itself, and dug in with the plastic spoon she had brought.

Footsteps clopped down the hallway, freezing her for a moment until they continued past the storage room. Selena had to remind herself that she was on the security team's floor, and they still had a job to do. There was probably someone walking around overnight, but she had either been too occupied or sleeping to notice. In just a few hours she'd listen to Bill McDowell's final march to his death in the elevator.

*I wonder if that's him,* she thought. He would likely start his shift around this time, according to their notes.

Selena still had her nagging suspicions about the mission, and thankfully the distractions throughout the night helped keep those thoughts at bay. It was a lot harder than it sounded, keeping her mind oblivious to its own thoughts, but Arielle insisted this was the skill that made her great.

From Selena's viewpoint, she was perhaps the safest one on the mission thanks to her hiding spot. Aside from someone barging into the storage room, there was little the past could do to interfere with her snooping.

She checked her watch to find a time of 5:45, less than four hours until the robbery. If there were happenings within the bank from any potential insiders, those would unfold in the coming minutes.

"Today's the day," she whispered as she rolled up the blankets and stuffed them into the backpack. She had pulled out all the snacks and replaced them on top for easy access. Her stomach spun after the measly pudding it received, clearly desperate for more.

She originally planned to hold the door open while peering out, but with plenty of time to kill, Selena searched the storage room for something to ease that task.

She sifted through cleaning supplies, both old and new. Old radios the security team likely used in the past. Boxes of uniforms. Light bulbs. Toilet plungers. She even found a dusty six-pack of beer bottles.

Selena considered using the toilet plunger's handle to prop the door ajar, but thought it might leave the crack *too* open—it was an inch in diameter. When she found a pyramid of six small paint buckets hiding in the corner, she immediately rummaged the pile of supplies. Paint trays and rolling brushes were well in stock, and when she found the stirring sticks, she had exactly what she needed.

"Need to test it out," she said, grabbing three of the sticks and holding them together in a tight bundle about half an inch thick.

Selena shuffled toward the door, examining the sticks for any cracks and vulnerabilities that might prove them ineffective. She even gave them a slight bend to make sure they were sturdy.

The door handle stared at her, prompting a hesitation. The latch made an audible clicking sound when turning the knob and would surely catch the attention of anyone in the hallway. That was why she needed to have the door propped open before the robber arrived. Silence was the most critical aspect of remaining hidden.

She pulled the door handle, its click echoing around the storage room. She hadn't even pulled the door open, waiting for a reaction from the other side.

None came, so she squatted down, keeping a tight grip on the handle so the latch wouldn't pop back into place and make her do this all again. Her arm wavered as she pulled the door open, an intense focus on not pulling too quickly.

With two inches of space, she saw the cold grayness of the hallway's concrete floor. In just a few hours, a robber would make his way down that very concrete, one murder already under his belt, as he sought the vault.

Selena slid the bundle of stirring sticks into position, standing them vertically inside the doorjamb. Once placed, she inched the door closed, keeping her finger between the gap to hold up the sticks. When the door touched the sticks, the gap it left was just wide enough to pull her finger out.

"Holy shit," Selena whispered, standing up. "It worked."

She took a step back and crossed her arms, admiring her work. The door was ajar by the half-inch provided by the sticks. She stepped forward and pressed her face against the door, one eye peering through the small crack.

The hallway was still empty, but all that mattered was that she could see it. Knowing the robber would come from the left side of the hall, she'd have a clear view of most of his trek from the elevator.

Her only concern was not knowing how the door looked from the outside. There was still a little over three hours to kill, and if any of the guards ventured down the hall, would they notice the door slightly open?

Selena returned to her backpack, and sat on top of it, anticipation growing heavier with each passing second.

*We're almost there.*

# Chapter 42

At 6:17 A.M., Arielle arrived to Juniper Street an hour earlier than planned, the neighborhood silent and still. A light fog lingered over the grassy field. The clouds glowed in a purplish haze, sunrise only thirty minutes away.

She parked next to the field, facing Kennedy's house at the opposite end of the block. If Jacob Kennedy didn't step foot outside of his home before 8:57—the absolute latest time he could leave to arrive at the bank by 9:14—where would that leave them?

Arielle braced for both possibilities and was equally prepared for either outcome. She expected Kennedy to step outside sometime between 8:30 and 8:45, leaving time for a leisurely drive across town. Kennedy had so far proven himself a patient driver who followed the law—not surprising for a former police officer.

Once he got in his truck, Arielle's job was pretty straightforward: follow Kennedy to the bank and watch him call for the security team to let him in.

What she *didn't* have planned was the decision to spring into action or not. The mission called for only finding out who was responsible for the robbery. Unlike the hundreds of missions she had completed before, they did not ask her to intervene and prevent the tragedy from happening. However, that didn't mean she would pass the opportunity if it presented itself. Nor did the mission report say anywhere that she *shouldn't* intervene. It was a loophole. One she could only presume Commander Briar had left open on purpose.

Arielle didn't have her usual slew of weapons as she did when preparing to stop a heinous crime. She had only her pistol and a couple of throwing knives.

She needed to shake off the thoughts. Even if the mission would be deemed a success for the elementary task of finding out who the robber is, walking away without trying to stop four murders from happening went against every grain of Arielle's instincts.

But there she sat, still without enough proof to definitively say Kennedy was responsible for the morning's robbery. Had that been the case, she would interfere right now. Every Angel was to never act off an assumption.

Interfering with the past was delicate business, and every move should be pre-meditated and calculated to avoid problems. Arielle had once tested the boundaries of this theory on one of her early missions, and paid dearly.

It was a situation not too different from the one currently in front of her. She had to stop a liquor store robbery, and had narrowed down the suspects to two potential men. One she deemed less likely to be the culprit based on a minimal amount of evidence. She went with her gut feeling, and sat outside the wrong house the night of the robbery. The suspect she had become so convinced was responsible ended up spending his entire night at home, drinking a bottle of wine while watching soccer on TV.

By the time Arielle realized he had no plans of robbery, she hurried to the store, much too late. They marked the mission as a failure and assigned her to work with a special team who dissected every step of her mission to determine where things went wrong.

Failing a mission wasn't a call for punishment by the organization—dozens of failed missions occurred on a weekly basis—but Arielle beat herself up over the fiasco, vowing to never trust something as abstract as a gut feeling again. Perhaps the misstep had made her too literal of a person since then, but she only failed two missions in the years since, both extremely complicated matters with several factors beyond her control.

With Young all but eliminated as a serious suspect, Arielle still refused to go all-in on Kennedy. They lacked that final piece of the puzzle to fuel complete confidence in her decisions.

She ate her banana while passing the time. At 7:08, the front door of Kennedy's house swung open, and out he stepped, dressed in raggedy shorts, a t-shirt, and a pair of white sneakers with green grass stains smeared across the bottom. He had his hands on his hips as he examined the front yard, drawing in a deep breath full of the fresh morning air.

"What the hell?" Arielle asked as she watched him trudge along the house, disappearing into the backyard for several minutes before returning with a lawn mower. The echoes of that past failed mission rang loudly in her mind. "Why would someone planning to rob a bank worry about cutting his grass before leaving?"

The task, though normal for a warm summer morning, made absolutely no sense in the thick of their investigation. She wanted to drive off to find a pay phone to call Felix to alert him of the unfolding matter. However, Kennedy still had ninety minutes before needing to leave. Even if the chore made little sense at the moment, Kennedy could still be right on schedule for the robbery.

*Maybe he's doing it to distract his mind,* Arielle thought. She had fallen victim to mindless housecleaning in the days leading up to a big mission, all to keep her mind occupied. Sitting in a room and dwelling on an intimidating task had only ever driven her mad. And she had done hundreds of missions.

It would be Kennedy's first robbery, making it highly un-likely he was numb to the dangerous undertaking. There had to be a healthy amount of nerves consuming him. He was still human, after all.

But the more she watched him, the less she believed he would soon drive to the bank. Before he started on the lawn, Kennedy reached into the passenger side of his truck, popped a cigarette into his mouth, and lit it up. Only after a couple of drags was he satisfied enough to rev up the mower.

*Is he just preparing the lawn for a relaxed Father's Day with his family?*

The possibility had certainly crossed her mind, but she didn't rule out the chance of Kennedy being twisted enough to rob the bank in the morning, stash the money in a hiding spot—presumably the hole he dug in the mountains—then return home by lunchtime to spend the rest of the holiday with his family.

She had been in this business long enough to know some people simply lacked souls. And sometimes those same people hid behind seemingly normal lives.

For the next fifteen minutes, she watched Kennedy go up and down the front lawn, cutting the grass in near-perfect lines. When he finished, he went to the backyard and did the same. Arielle could only hear the humming of the motor while he was in the back for another fifteen minutes.

When the motor fell silent, Arielle saw the time was 7:43. Kennedy still had an hour before leaving for the bank. That thought quickly vanished when he returned to the front yard with a gas-powered lawn trimmer.

"Are you kidding me?" Arielle whined from the car.

She crossed her arms, shaking her head as she watched him landscape the front lawn. There was still time for him to pack everything away and head to the bank, but the window was closing.

Just when she thought it couldn't get any stranger, Kennedy's next-door neighbor stepped outside. She was a woman perhaps slightly younger than Kennedy, pink curlers in her hair, a long teal bathrobe swaying at her ankles with each step. She had walked out of her house and waved to Kennedy before shuffling over to their shared fence.

Kennedy killed the trimmer and met her. They conversed for a minute, swapping laughs as Kennedy stood with his arms crossed over his chest. The neighbor returned to her pathway and strolled to the sidewalk where she picked up the Sunday morning newspaper and returned inside.

Kennedy studied his lawn before taking the trimmer to the backyard. Arielle listened to the piercing roar of its motor for about five minutes before the neighborhood fell back under the blanket of silence.

*That was his alibi,* she thought. The mission files had mentioned he had an alibi in court who testified that they had seen Kennedy working on his lawn in the morning. Even wished him a happy Father's Day like a caring neighbor would do. Either the woman had no sense of time, or she was in on the secret. Kennedy could have easily offered his neighbor some money to testify in his favor in court. But was that agreement already in place before this morning, or had it just happened?

"Stop it," Arielle told herself. *You're letting your mind drift all over the place. An agreement like that would have been settled indoors. It's not something you casually mention to your neighbor while you're mowing the lawn.*

The frustrations swirling around the mission seemed to reach a boiling point for Arielle at this precise moment. She wanted to scream. She wanted to sprint down the street and attack Jacob Kennedy, barge into the house and get all the missing answers.

*Why is the truth refusing to show itself?* she wondered. The past was winning this battle, and easily. Nothing pissed off the top-ranked Angel more than a lack of knowledge.

Kennedy finally returned from the backyard at 7:56 and moseyed back into the house without a single shred of urgency. The realization that Kennedy might not be responsible made Arielle sick to her stomach.

She had thirty long minutes ahead until she'd find out for sure if Kennedy would head off to the bank.

# Chapter 43

At eight o'clock, Felix dressed in his uniform. Peter Young remained asleep, not so much as stirring in bed.

Felix would give the man until 8:30 to show any sign of life. He could technically wait longer, mathematically speaking, but if Young wasn't out of bed by 8:30, the odds were entirely against his involvement in the day's events.

Felix was already convinced of this. Watching Young snooze the morning away only cemented this belief. If Young was involved, it wouldn't have been so easy to take his notebook. The live-feed wouldn't have been running flawlessly this entire time. There were virtually no obstacles for his spying on Young.

"Listen to the past," Arielle had told them one night.

And that's exactly what he was doing. All the resistance so far had surrounded Jacob Kennedy and his house. Kennedy dug a mysterious hole in the middle of nowhere. Kennedy had bank floor plans in his basement. Plus guns and ammo.

But Young had to be involved, at least to a degree. He had the thirst for revenge. The police scanner. And he was the other half of the private meetings with Kennedy. It seemed impossible for someone as lazy as Young to be the mastermind behind the operation, but any other explanations otherwise were becoming less likely. Could someone who crafted such a brilliant robbery scheme simply sleep in the morning of the big day?

Felix had to remind himself that people were unfathomably complex. Just because *he* wouldn't dare get caught sleeping had he planned a robbery of his own, didn't mean other people thought the same way. In fact, this very mission proved just that.

"We all live in our own little worlds," Felix said to the empty apartment. "All trying to do what we think is right, no matter how far off course that might actually be. The world is an odd, robust jumble of chaos. Where everything makes perfect sense, yet somehow makes absolutely no sense, all at the same time."

It was 8:15, and still nothing from Young's bedroom. Setting up in this apartment complex had now seemed like a mistake. They would have been better off trying to buy a house on Kennedy's block, or at least somewhere in his neighborhood. Felix didn't want to write off Young as a waste of time, but felt their efforts could have been better spent pursuing someone else of interest.

Felix's stomach growled. He hadn't eaten breakfast—his mind was too occupied. Even after their prior mission working together, he still hadn't grown used to remaining involved on the day of an actual crime. The days of bouncing from mission to mission, setting up surveillance, and disappearing were over.

"I'm a full-fledged Angel," he muttered. He played an important role in today's events, no matter how irrelevant Young had become in the past few hours.

By 8:20, Felix lugged the suitcases out of everyone's rooms

and parked them next to the kitchen table, where he had spent what felt like the last three years of his life sitting and watching Young do absolutely nothing. At least he'd have a scar from the snake bite to remind him of the lone exciting moment on this mission.

If all went smoothly, the team would be back in this apartment by ten o'clock to grab their bags and return home to the present. No one had said it aloud, but it had become clear all three of them longed for that moment. This mission had emotionally drained each of them, every day somehow more complex than the prior.

At 8:25, Felix rummaged through his backpack for his pistol. He hated pulling it out, a reason he thoroughly enjoyed his old mission work of never needing it. But he was an Angel, and every Angel was trained in the fine arts of firearms. Preferring peaceful resolutions, Felix rarely took his weapon with him, even when breaking into random people's homes.

Today, however, he tucked it into the back of his waistband. He also despised this move, likening it to something criminals did. But he couldn't simply walk around with the gun on his hip holster, not when he'd be feet away from a robbery in progress. Preparing a mission, even something as gutsy as breaking and entering to set up bugs and cameras, posed little risk if he had a trusted schedule to follow.

The day of an actual crime was an entirely different beast. They had to factor the past and its wrath. After two weeks in the past, minor things had changed, trajectories moved, and there was no predicting how the crime would ultimately unfold. Felix understood this elevated risk, and that's why he carried his pistol.

Everything functioned at a high-risk, high-reward level for

the entire day of a crime. And this fine Father's Day would prove no different.

The clock struck 8:30, and Young remained snoring.

Felix shook his head. "Unbelievable."

As much as he knew this moment would come, it didn't disappoint him any less. It was officially safe to eliminate Peter Young from consideration as a suspect for the Father's Day Massacre.

"Off we go," Felix said, slamming the laptop shut and quickly shoving it into his suitcase.

He hurried out of the apartment building, nothing but the pistol tucked into his waistband. He was to meet Arielle at the west side of the bank, where they would watch the area for the robber to arrive.

When he stepped outside, he found the weather perfect. The morning sunlight kissed the nearby skyscrapers. A couple strode down the sidewalk with their dog leading the way. Birds sung cheery tunes over the quiet neighborhood while a father and his young boy sat on their porch across the street, watering their lawn without a worry.

The calming utopia of the world made Felix that much more uneasy, knowing what was about to unfold just a half-mile away.

He started down the block, having budgeted twenty-minutes to walk to the bank. After three blocks, he had already passed a half-dozen people out for a morning jog through the neighborhood.

*Just try to look normal,* he told himself, the biggest secret in the world wanting to burst out of him as he attempted to take regular strides. He even offered a small grin to one jogger, who paid him no attention.

Felix was ready to cross one more block when he saw a car swerving across the intersection. His legs immediately locked, mind kicking into high-gear as he watched the vehicle jerk left to right as it made its way down the road at a lethal pace. They were still in the neighborhood, the posted speed limit at twenty-five miles per hour. Felix figured the car was going at least double.

"Hey! Watch out!" a voice shouted from across the intersection, fear suddenly growing heavy in the air.

Felix remained stuck in a virtual staredown with the berserk car veering toward him. The thought of death numbed his entire body. He tasted the saliva flooding the back of his mouth, thick as his throat clenched shut.

*Is this really how it ends?* Felix thought. *Some drunk driver is going to crash into me. Poof! Drive home safe, folks.*

The sensation of facing death straight on rattled Felix. In a matter of seconds, hundreds of thousands of memories flooded his thoughts, each one of them crystal clear for the millisecond they displayed in his mind. The human brain was not built to process thoughts at such a deadly velocity.

The car strayed right—Felix's left—then skidded back left, smoke puffing from the screeching rear tires as the car lurched onto the sidewalk, narrowly missing a telephone pole before connecting squarely with a fire hydrant. The hydrant split the car's front end directly down the middle of the hood. More smoke oozed from the wrecked engine, spreading a thin, transparent fog across the neighborhood block.

Felix felt and heard his heart pounding in his ears. He hadn't even realized he'd been holding his breath, panting as he recovered.

Water erupted into the sky. It fell on the crashed car, the

driver leaning head first into the steering wheel, not moving.

"Holy shit!" Felix cried, taking a step forward, then stopping. His basic instincts were to run over and help the driver get out of the car before it became flooded from the hydrant water. But in that moment, he understood that if he approached the vehicle, he'd be stuck as a witness for this chaotic accident.

*Exactly what the past wants,* he thought. There was someone on the sidewalk further down the block, where the car had come from, who could likely testify they had seen the car swerving across the road, but they didn't have the up-close look at its final resting place on the hydrant.

Homes lined the block, and one resident stepped out to see all the commotion. It was only a matter of time before more followed suit. Felix returned his attention to the car, the street now with a half-inch layer of water pooling across it, and looked at what he assumed was a dead body behind the wheel. The driver still hadn't moved despite the amplified white noise of water crashing onto the car's hood.

Dread ballooned inside Felix as he knew what he had to do. It was going to look cowardly, but he started running across the intersection, leaving the scene behind.

"Hey!" the man who had stepped onto his porch shouted. "Hey, stop!"

Felix kept his head forward, running at a brisk pace, the back of his mind so badly wanting to turn around to help. He didn't even look at the man through the corner of his eyes, hearing the terror in his voice.

"Hey!" the man insisted. "What happened?! You can't just leave the scene of a crime!"

*It's not a crime. It's an accident.*

Felix had to assure himself of this simple fact. It's not like an innocent bystander had been harmed. Just the driver, who could have been drunk or suicidal, for all Felix knew. Perhaps he could send in an anonymous letter to the police station explaining what he had witnessed. It wasn't his fault he had to run to learn the truth about a decades-old cold case.

The adrenaline remained steady throughout his body as he dashed through the neighborhood. The shouting man's voice had continued but faded into obscurity.

Sirens wailed in the distance, followed by flashing police lights coming from the direction Felix was running. The police cars were about two blocks down, probably a few hundred yards away from where the bank was about to get robbed.

Felix reached the next intersection and broke left. He ran halfway down the block, another quiet neighborhood minding its business. He still panted as his lungs tried to catch up from the excitement. Once he heard the cop cars zoom by behind him, he stopped to let out an exaggerated sigh of relief.

*Good one, past,* he thought, trying to brush aside the overwhelming fear he had just endured and refocus on the task at hand. He was still three blocks away from the bank and had to make up for lost time.

Felix checked his watch to find the setback had only cost him ten minutes, including the small detour he was now taking. The skyscraper stood tall in the distance, its cash-register-shaped roof seeming to pull Felix toward it, daring him to intervene with the past's disturbing plans.

He put his head down and ran the rest of the way.

# Chapter 44

It was perhaps the longest thirty minutes of Arielle's life, waiting for Kennedy to step out and get in his truck. And she had once sat frozen in time during Commander Briar's mission to confront Chris Speidel.

At exactly 8:40, Jacob Kennedy reappeared in his doorway. This time he wasn't examining the lawn or taking in a lungful of fresh air. He went straight to his truck after closing the door behind him. No goodbye kiss to his wife, at least not from the doorway. He no longer moved with the casualness he had displayed all morning. He moved with purpose, taking shorter, confident steps toward his truck.

Kennedy sat down behind the wheel and fired up the engine within seconds.

*This is it*, Arielle thought, relieved all of her doubt was vanishing. She could see his thick mustache through her binoculars. The only things missing were the sunglasses and fedora.

Kennedy pulled out of the driveway and drove away from where Arielle sat at the other end of the block. She flipped her car around and circled around the block to find Kennedy turning right toward the eastbound Sixth Avenue on-ramp that would take him downtown.

Arielle felt no pressure to keep up with Kennedy as he drove—she already knew where he was going. And with how much time remained before the bank was to be robbed, she doubted he'd have time to stop anywhere else before. She kept the most distance she had compared to any of the other stalking during the mission. But Kennedy always remained in sight.

She expected little resistance from the past. Her tricks of masking her intentions weren't even needed, because she truly didn't know what she would end up doing once they arrived at the bank.

Every move, every decision felt so delicate. Like a child holding a newborn chick in the palm of their hand, terrified of crushing or dropping the fragile creature. Arielle felt this same sensation as she followed Kennedy across town for the next twenty minutes. Every touch on the brakes, every turn signal, every lane change were treated with an exaggerated caution.

It was easy. Kennedy drove as he had been—committing zero violations. When they exited the highway, arriving downtown, he even slowed down in anticipation of the light turning yellow. Traffic had been light, but enough cars had gathered at the stoplight for Arielle to remain six vehicles behind Kennedy. He had no angle of making eye contact with her from his position at the front of the line.

When the light turned green, he took his time proceeding forward, the tall buildings of the downtown skyline directly in front of them as they turned onto Lincoln Street.

Tension crept into Arielle's body, starting in her arms, forcing her to tighten her grip on the steering wheel. *This is really happening. We're two miles away from the bank. It's*

*Kennedy.*

She felt an odd sense of glee. Perhaps relief. While the odds and little evidence they had found had all pointed to Kennedy as their main suspect, there had been plenty of doubt around that theory.

Each block they drove killed that doubt one piece at a time, until they finally arrived at the corner of Seventeenth and Sherman. Kennedy sat at the red light, his turn signal flashing on the left.

Arielle pulled over before turning onto Seventeenth, wanting to keep a safe distance behind Kennedy. Downtown was deserted, not another vehicle visible in their immediate vicinity. They were smothered in the shadows of the concrete jungle blocking the still-rising sun.

At 8:59, the traffic light flashed green and Kennedy turned left. Arielle crept forward, taking her time to reach the same light Kennedy had just left. In time-sensitive matters, she liked to keep a mental count of the passing seconds—because even one second could change the outcome of an entire mission.

She wanted thirty seconds between herself and Kennedy, so she didn't even touch the accelerator, letting the car coast up to the light at a mere five miles per hour. The light turned red, and she happily stopped, spotting Kennedy's truck parked on the curb right in front of the bank's main entrance. To the right, she saw Felix hustling down the sidewalk, stopping in front of the Last Drop's front doors. There were a handful of cars parked at the meters in front of the diner, the place bustling with a breakfast crowd full of families and fathers to kick off the day's festivities.

Felix saw Arielle and tossed his hands in the air in a *what-*

*am-I-supposed-to-do* manner. Arielle rolled down her window and waved him over. He clasped his hands behind his head and stood tall, drawing in a deep breath before jogging toward the intersection. The light was about to turn green, but there was no one behind Arielle, so she waited for Felix, tossing her backpack into the rear to clear the passenger seat.

Felix reached the car and pulled open the door, huffing and puffing like he had just run a marathon. "You . . . will not believe . . . the morning I've had," he said between gasps for air.

"Shhh!" Arielle pressed her finger against her lips. "He's right there." She nodded to the left. "I'm not sure of the best place to park so we can still see him and he won't notice us."

"Why is he in front of the main doors? The robber didn't escape through there."

They sat through the green light and watched it turn yellow, then red again. Arielle hoped Kennedy wasn't noticing them sit through two green lights. Ideally, he had bigger things to worry about.

Arielle tapped the clock on the car's radio. It read 9:02. "He still has twelve minutes before he's set to call security from the freight elevator. Maybe he's going to pull up closer that way."

The entrance to the building's parking garage, where the freight elevator was, stood open halfway up the block on Sherman, between Seventeenth and Eighteenth. Arielle could see where it normally had the drop-down fence was now a dark, open space. *He knew it would be open today.*

Arielle shook her head. Felix looked around. "Park in front of the diner," he said.

"But I won't be able to turn around and follow him up

Sherman from there. Once I pass this light, I'd have to circle completely around the building to get back here. It's all one-way streets."

Felix rolled his eyes and stretched his hand to Arielle's shoulder. "If I can survive a near-death experience this morning, I think you can handle making an illegal U-turn to get back on Sherman. It's not exactly rush hour out here." He chuckled and leaned back in his seat, still breathing heavily.

"Excuse me. . . Near-death? What—"

Felix raised a finger. "We'll discuss it later. Kennedy's on the move."

Arielle swung her attention back to Kennedy's truck, now treading up the street toward the parking garage. The light turned green and Arielle drove forward, parking in the first spot on the corner of the intersection in front of the diner. She still had a clear view of Sherman Street and could see Kennedy's truck. The brake lights were on as he stopped in front of the parking garage entrance.

"It's 9:10, and he still isn't making a move," Arielle said, brow scrunching while she gazed out the window.

"9:14 is the time of the first call to security, right?"

"Correct."

The brake lights flicked off, and the truck rocked as if Kennedy had put it into park.

"Who's that?" Felix asked, leaning over the center console to watch over Arielle's shoulder.

Arielle didn't know what he was talking about at first, then noticed a figure walking down the sidewalk toward Kennedy's truck. She reached back into her bag and whipped out the binoculars. "It's the robber!" she gasped. "I don't understand."

She saw a man dressed in a fedora and sunglasses, a thick mustache above his lip. He looked a lot like Kennedy. Granted, the disguise left plenty to the imagination. The mustache was Kennedy's signature, yet Kennedy remained behind the wheel.

The man hustled and made no eye contact with Kennedy's truck before turning into the parking garage. Just as he did, the truck came back to life and veered off, turning right on Eighteenth Street and out of sight from Arielle and Felix.

"What the *hell* is going on?" Arielle asked. "Who do we follow?"

"Well, we can't exactly follow the robber. He's on his way—it's too late."

Arielle knew this, but that voice in her inner psyche screamed at her to disrupt the robber before he lay a finger on the intercom. "Hang on," she said, throwing the car into reverse and peeling backwards to face northbound on Sherman Street.

In one swift motion, she flung the gear into drive and floored the accelerator. The move might have been exaggerated, considering she came right back to a screeching halt after a half block, but the adrenaline was overflowing her senses.

When they came to their stop outside of the garage entrance, Arielle noticed Felix's hand white-knuckling the grab handle above his head, legs fully extended as if he had been slamming on an imaginary giant brake pedal. The little color he normally had in his face had vanished, his lips pressed tightly into a ghastly paleness.

Arielle craned her neck to see Kennedy around the corner, but he remained out of sight. She had a second to decide what benefited the mission more: tailing Kennedy or the robber.

"Felix, snap out of it!" Arielle slapped her friend square in the chest.

He jolted back to focus.  Whatever had happened to him earlier clearly had some lingering effects. He looked down at his locked knees and pushed his shins down to force a bend in the legs. "I think Kennedy is the getaway driver," he said in a distant tone. Felix might not have appeared fully there, but even through the tension, his mind remained focused on the mission, putting together all the pieces of this troubling puzzle.

Arielle agreed. It explained Kennedy disappearing around the corner and not approaching the garage entrance. "Young's at home, right?"

The clock showed 9:12. They had less than two minutes to decide their next move.

"I can't say if he's still home right now, but he's not here. I know that much. He still wasn't out of bed when I left."

"So who the hell just walked into the garage?"

Felix shrugged.

9:13.

Arielle opened her door, stepping one foot out before Felix grabbed her arm. "What are you doing?!"

"I have to. I can't just sit here and hope Selena gets a better view than us. I need to at least try."

She could feel Felix's hand trembling beneath his tight grip. He held her arm like a scared child not wanting to let their parent go. And he surely didn't want to be left alone outside of an unfolding bank robbery.

Arielle looked at the clock, knowing only seconds stood between the robber's finger and the call button that would change everything. "I have to do this."

Felix's grip weakened. He nodded, staring absently toward

the floor. "Just keep a safe distance."

"Of course." Arielle stepped all the way out and closed the door behind her. Downtown was eerily silent, the air still. Somewhere around the corner, Jacob Kennedy waited in his truck. That no longer seemed like a priority now that she took silent steps toward the garage entrance.

The clock struck 9:14 in her mind as she entered the garage, the disguised robber just having pressed the call button.

Everything was right on schedule.

# Chapter 45

About forty feet remained between Arielle and the robber. He had his back to her, a long jacket swaying to his knees. The fedora was parked so low on his head that she couldn't quite make out the color of his hair. The lighting in the garage wasn't the best, either, adding to her difficulties.

She crept toward the first parked car she saw and crouched behind the rear wheel. The robber wouldn't see her if he turned around, but the garage was quiet enough to hear his echoing voice as he spoke into the call box.

"Hello," the robber said, his voice unrecognizable. It sounded as if it were being disguised. Like someone younger was trying to sound older by deepening their tone. "This is Robert Caldwell. I've lost my keycard and need to get up to my office. Will you be able to let me in?"

Arielle nodded, satisfied she could hear everything. Robert Caldwell was the bank's vice president. Even during Kennedy's trial, they mentioned the robber had used this alias to gain entrance. So far, everything was on track with how it had originally played out. Their tampering with the past had changed nothing.

"Good morning, Mr. Caldwell," a voice crackled from the intercom. "We're sorry to hear that. We'll be right there to let you in. Should be about one minute."

"Thank you," the robber replied, taking a step back and swaying from side to side while waiting.

The urge to sprint forward and take him down had reached its peak. If only this mission hadn't proven so difficult up to this point, Arielle just might have done it. Her inner motivator had given way to another voice telling her it was a bad idea. There was simply too much ground to cover to hope the robber wouldn't turn around and see her.

Instead, she pulled out her gun, cocked it, and waited.

The guard coming down the elevator would be Bill McDowell. If Arielle didn't stop this from proceeding, Bill would be dead within the next two minutes.

She lined up a shot and pulled the trigger.

The gun made a faint clicking sound, but nothing else happened. Arielle clenched her jaw, half expecting this to happen. It wouldn't be the first time the past had conveniently jammed her gun, and it wouldn't be the last. Changing the past could never be that simple.

The elevator chimed, its doors parting to show a relaxed Bill McDowell with a coffee cup in hand, face scrunching in confusion when he first saw the man standing outside the elevator.

Arielle hadn't noticed from her angle, but the robber had already pulled out his gun and extended it toward McDowell.

The security guard dropped his coffee cup, the hot liquid splattering across the elevator floor, as he whipped his hand to the baton handle on his security belt.

"Don't even *fucking* think about it!" the robber shouted. "Swing that thing and I'll blast your brains all over this elevator."

McDowell obliged, dropping the baton and raising his open hands above his head.

"Better," the robber said, looking over his shoulder and making direct eye contact with Arielle Lucila through his sunglasses. She had no way of knowing his expression behind the disguise, but he suddenly shoved McDowell toward the back of the elevator and hurried inside.

"Stop!" Arielle shouted, stepping out from behind the car. Her hands flailed to her utility belt, grasping one of her throwing knives.

The robber frantically pushed the button to close the elevator doors, and they took their time gliding shut. Arielle flung the knife, watching it clang against the steel elevator doors, the black sunglasses watching her through the crack just before they shut.

She raced to the elevator, sure to pick up her knife.

A muffled bang rang out from the other side of the door, and she knew Bill McDowell was now the first victim.

"Fuck!" Arielle screamed, punching the elevator door. She had waited perhaps two seconds too long, assuming her knife would have even landed successfully on the robber. She clenched her fists, fighting every urge to press the call button to alert the rest of the security team of what was unfolding. But she had already decided beforehand that would be the wrong decision. Doing so would likely lead to the police getting called already, leaving Selena trapped inside where they would soon sweep the building.

After one more punch on the elevator's doors, Arielle spun around and fled the scene. Felix remained in the car, leaning out the passenger-side window, gawking toward the garage entrance.

Arielle ran to him. "He's in."

"Did you see who it was?" Felix asked, his eyes studying Arielle for any clue.

Arielle pursed her lips and shook her head. "No one I could recognize through the disguise. It's *not* Young or Kennedy—that much we know."

"What do we do?"

Arielle placed her hands on her hips and looked to the clear skies. "I have no idea. We can't exactly get into the building at this point. That elevator was our only way in."

"So we just sit here and wait for Selena to come out? Does she even know which side of the building we're on?"

"I told her where we'd be. She's going to take the stairwell that comes out next to the freight elevator—no keycards needed for her to exit."

"Can we not get that door pried open?"

"You want to pry open a door during a bank robbery? You're smarter than that, Felix."

Arielle learned that Felix's mind worked in overdrive and could sometimes overlook common sense.

He leaned back. "So we sit and wait. Welcome to my world."

As much as Arielle hated hearing it, he was right. All other options had vanished as soon as those elevator doors closed. Whether that was bad timing or an act of the past, she'd never know. It was a moment that would haunt her over the next few weeks as she digested the happenings of the mission.

Defeated, Arielle circled the car and returned to her seat behind the wheel, where the helplessness would eat at her for the next fifteen minutes.

"It all comes down to Selena."

# Chapter 46

Selena had been glued to the storage room's door from the moment her watch struck nine o'clock. She needed to know all movements that had taken place in the minutes leading up to the robbery.

When Bill McDowell had meandered by, on his way to the elevator, Selena felt a gnawing in the depths of her soul. Watching a man go unknowingly to his death was not something she was used to. Much like Felix, she typically did her work before the day of a crime—or she at least had no reason to be present during the act.

Even her involvement in their prior mission working together didn't involve her coming this close to the action. She and Felix had the luxury of watching Arielle take care of business from a distance.

Seeing McDowell sparked feelings she had never faced before. While most missions involved a death, she had never gone through seeing it all play out.

Only days ago she was at the diner chatting with McDowell, getting to know the kind and decent human being he was. Before that, he had welcomed her with open arms into the security office when she had lied about needing to clean their space. He was a trusting man who saw the best in people.

As he took his final walk to the elevator, she knew with confidence that he believed the bank's vice president really was outside and had forgotten his keycard. He hadn't once considered a potential threat waiting for him outside. If he had, he wouldn't have moved with a calming casualness down the hallway.

Even as a spectator, Selena felt like everything was going to be alright. And that was all thanks to McDowell's presence, despite what lied ahead for his own fate.

In the seconds she had to process all these thoughts, and her personal tug-o-war of jumping out of the room or not, she understood just what made Arielle stick out from the rest. With enough practice anyone could elevate their skills of driving, shooting, and even espionage to match Arielle's level. It was her decision making that separated her from the pack.

Every mission was a series of decisions that needed to be made, based on the information available, while also factoring how the past might play into the equation.

Selena had nowhere near the knowledge of the past and its stubbornness as Arielle, but she suspected if she had leapt out of the storage room to stop McDowell from continuing to his death, there would certainly be hell to pay.

She further understood Arielle's unbreakable discipline. Any person with a normally functioning conscience would justify jumping out and stopping an innocent man from his brutal murder. But that was why the Road Runners didn't recruit the average Joe off the street. Knowledge and discipline was the combination they looked for in recruits. Anyone with those two intangible skills could be groomed for any role the organization desired.

Now, in the thick of the most critical moment of the mission, Selena had to dig deep within herself to tap into that same discipline. It was unlike anything she had emotionally experienced before in her life.

Dedication can often be confused with discipline. Staying up late to cram in a study session while friends were out partying on a Friday night was dedication. Forcing herself to *not* stop McDowell—something she believed was absolutely the right thing to do—was a level of discipline she hoped to never face again. The mission was bigger than herself and her personal desires.

Making that type of decision was sick. And wrong. And flat-out excruciating.

But once McDowell passed, and she realized she couldn't undo her decision, she could move forward with the next phase of the mission: waiting once more.

McDowell left, which only meant the robber would return minutes later.

Selena mentally prepared for the moment. Spending the last seventeen hours in solitude left her on an island of wonder. The lack of communication had proven troublesome. It was entirely possible that Arielle and Felix had already figured everything out, but they had no way of relaying that information to Selena within the building. They had floated the idea of Selena carrying a radio, but they all agreed the risk outweighed the reward. If one wandering security guard heard the crackle of a radio, all plans would collapse within moments.

All she could trust was they hadn't solved the mystery yet, and she needed to follow through with her task. Identify the robber and get the hell out. Don't wait around for the fireworks to begin. She knew the exact route she needed to take out of the building.

Her job was easy, yet extremely difficult at the same time. Selena hadn't anticipated all the added stress that had already presented itself. And she only hoped more wouldn't come once the robber started his journey down the hallway. She had plenty of doubt.

Her heart started beating faster than its normal pace, and she leaned into the meditation practices she had long mastered to attempt getting it back under control. It was 9:19 according to her watch, and she had expected the robber to appear at any second.

Perhaps Arielle and Felix had prevented any of it from unfolding. Despite what the mission report called for, she knew Arielle was incapable of resisting the urge to stop the robbery from happening. And knowing Arielle, she just might have pulled it off.

All that hope vanished, however, when Selena heard the distant chime of the elevator doors parting at the far end of the hallway. Every muscle in her body tightened, her breath held in an overwhelmingly anxious anticipation.

The world fell still and silent, and she focused her hearing on the approaching footsteps.

*Who am I kidding?* she thought. *I'm not Arielle. I don't know what I'm listening for. A footstep is a footstep.*

Arielle likely could tell the height and weight of a person by the simple sound of their footsteps.

That didn't stop Selena from at least trying. The footsteps sounded heavy. They already knew the robber was a man. So that's what she envisioned while listening. She tried to keep Kennedy and Young out of her thoughts, wanting as neutral of an eye as she could have. The robber would be in full disguise, and she'd have a second, maybe two, to process everything through the sliver of the cracked-open door.

Over the past week, she had counted the amount of steps from the elevator to the storage room multiple times. Arielle had offered her this tip to anticipate exactly when the robber might appear. That decision was paying off huge dividends.

She had run this experiment using different strides each time, not knowing how long of a step the robber had. She found a range of twenty-eight to thirty-six steps.

The robber had already taken sixteen since she heard the elevator doors open, give or take a couple. The steps neither slow nor fast.

By the twenty-fifth step, Selena crouched, sure to remain below the robber's line of vision should he glance toward the door. What she saw froze her blood.

*It can't be,* she thought.

The robber wore the attire she had expected: sunglasses, fedora. And the mustache.

Only the mustache didn't look real. Even in those few seconds, she clearly saw it was slightly off-center, like an amateur makeup artist had glued it on.

The mustache, however, was only a distraction. She immediately recognized the robber's body. Tall, yes, but slightly slender. Way too thin to pass as Young or Kennedy. What stood out the clearest was his chin, the only part of his face she could truly see.

She had stared at that face for hours not too many days ago. And the chin connected with a chiseled jawline she found rather irresistible.

*It can't be.*

Once those two seconds passed, she could only see the

back of the robber, and that only made things worse. She knew, without a doubt, the man behind the disguise was Brian Dawkins.

Just days ago she had plotted out a complex plan to continue a potential relationship with the young security guard from California. Now her body broke into gooseflesh. The idea she had even sat with him through a whole dinner made her sick to her stomach.

Selena had actually suspected Dawkins had some minimal involvement after their dinner. He had freely admitted he wouldn't be working during the robbery, and that alone had propelled him as a suspect in her eyes. All the chatter he had offered about how the guards discussed the ease of robbing the bank had turned the dials for her to consider it all a team effort.

Now she dreaded she hadn't shared these thoughts with Arielle and Felix. Compared to them, she felt intellectually out of place. She doubted herself, didn't trust her own instincts. All out of fear of being wrong.

With this revelation, Selena felt a weight of responsibility for letting it all reach this point. She should have trusted her gut. Maybe she could have veered Dawkins off the path that led him to breaking into his own bank and murdering four of his colleagues. She had long considered herself a sound judge of character, but knowing a cold-blooded killer had slipped right through her filters made her doubt everything she knew.

Selena picked up her backpack and slung it over her shoulders. It was time to leave and never look back.

Dawkins was no longer in her line of sight through the cracked door, so she pulled it open all the way, staying low to catch the paint stirrers before they clanged to the ground.

She stuffed them into her back pocket, not wanting to leave anything behind that had her fingerprints on it, and stepped out to the hallway.

She let the door glide shut, bracing it with her arm so the latch clicked as faintly as possible. It was quiet enough, and Dawkins continued down the hall where he'd soon enter the guardroom and shoot the poor souls who had no idea what was coming.

*I can't just sit here and let him do it. This is all my fault.*

She knew it wasn't what the mission called for. Nor was it necessarily the smartest thing to do, but the guilt was already eating at her, and she needed to rein it in as best she could.

Selena dashed toward the elevator, not caring how loud her footsteps might have been. The forty steps between her and the elevator dissipated in seconds. The door to the stairwell stood immediately next to the elevators.

She pushed open the door and spun around to hold it open with her back, and shouted down the hall.

"Dawkins!"

The robber froze and pivoted in a swift motion.

Selena would never see the emotion swimming behind those sunglasses, but she could only imagine how startled he must have been. He said nothing, didn't move, and they had a stare down that felt like several minutes, despite only being a few seconds.

"Don't do it!" Selena shouted, her words echoing down the empty hallway, bouncing all around them. She saw the gun in his hand, but it never wavered. He wouldn't dare harm Selena. Would he?

"Hey!" a voice hollered from the far end.

A guard had stepped out of the office, baton elevated as he

charged toward Dawkins.

If only Selena had called out Dawkins's name later, she might have saved the guard's life.

Instead, Dawkins swiveled around and promptly shot the guard square in his forehead. The guard went from a crouched, running position to looking like someone had electrocuted him, limbs jolting out in every direction. The baton flew from his grip and clattered on the ground, rolling in a circle before coming to a complete stop a few feet from the security office door.

*Oh my God!* Selena thought. *I just changed the past.*

And she had.

Two guards were supposed to have been killed in the security office, while a third would later enter, oblivious, and also get shot in the open doorway. Now, a guard lay dead in the middle of the hallway, and Dawkins broke into a sprint toward the security room.

Before he reached it, the other guard who had been inside stepped out. Dawkins lunged toward him, whipping him across the face with his pistol to send him spiraling to the ground. Once down, Dawkins hovered over him and shot him twice in the back.

The guard lay lifeless as Dawkins entered the security office, its door unable to close shut as it rested against the dead man's splayed out feet.

Selena's legs locked. She had never seen someone get murdered, and she had just witnessed two within seconds of each other. She knew Dawkins entered the guardroom to strip away all evidence. But she wondered if he would still go through the same process once he knew someone had seen him. And not just anyone, but Selena, who knew exactly who he was.

Selena debated following him down the hallway, only because she couldn't help but wonder if the changes she had just made in the past would cause Dawkins to kill all of the employees in the vault. Originally, he had not, sparing six lives while he robbed the vault. Why, they never understood, and Selena hoped that would still be the case.

Dawkins was rattled, however, and sure to lash out by any means necessary to spare himself being caught and arrested. Selena thought she might vomit, the mixture of death and guilt becoming too much for her to handle.

*Run,* the voice in her mind pleaded. *Run before you get sucked into this. Run before you become a suspect. Run before it's too late.*

Once more fighting her own will, Selena turned and dashed up the stairwell. Her hurried footsteps echoed, the door closing shut with an aggressive bang that made Selena squeal. She tripped twice on her way up the stairs, legs shaking out of control as they had turned to Jell-O.

She caught herself both times, hands clutching the steps ahead to keep her face from slamming into them. By the time she reached the top landing and flung open the door to the parking garage, Selena was nearly hyperventilating.

The cool air of the outdoors, albeit dank within the garage, injected Selena with rays of hope. She was free from the storage room.

She hadn't realized how bothersome the isolation had been until she took that first step outside. Death had been on her mind plenty during her stay in the basement, and she couldn't help but wonder if she would spend her final moments staring at its gray ceiling .

She had a new sense of life and hope, plus a greater appreciation for her work as an Angel Runner. It wasn't the great Arielle Lucila, or even the brilliant Felix Francisco, who had learned who the killer was. It was Selena Nicole. The vibrant actress-turned-Angel who had no faith in herself to perform at the highest level for her secret organization.

All the self-doubt that had brewed over the past decade of her life had taken a huge blow today. Selena smiled, proud of herself—something she couldn't recall having ever felt.

She looked around the parking garage, saw no one, and let the door close behind her. There was no going back into the building to stop whatever mayhem might unfold, and she had to be okay with that.

Selena bolted out of the garage to search for Arielle and Felix.

# Chapter 47

Arielle sat like a statue behind the wheel, refusing to break her gaze from the garage. Every second that Selena hadn't appeared made Arielle grow a little more nauseous.

She had been beating herself up ever since returning to the car, and now wondered if her actions changed how everything was playing out inside. It was possible Selena was in danger because of Arielle's actions, but she had no way of knowing. All she could do was trust the past to keep things as close to the same trajectory as the Original timeline.

Hearing the gunshot blast that killed McDowell was both a tough blow to take, but also relieving. McDowell was supposed to die in that elevator, so everything had remained in place up to that point. Arielle might have been more worried had she not heard the weapon discharge.

Felix had been rambling about all the facts they had come across during the last two weeks, trying to make sense of who the killer could be if it wasn't Kennedy or Young. He ran through every name of the security guards who worked in the bank. He had even entertained the idea that Kennedy was working with someone else on the outside. Young covered matters from the inside, Kennedy was the mastermind (and getaway driver), while a third-party had been hired to do the dirty work. The actual robber could have been anyone, in that case, and they were only hurting their cause by assuming it was someone who worked inside the bank.

His voice droned into the background for Arielle. She had given up trying to identify the robber through the little evidence they had. If it had been that easy, they wouldn't be sitting outside the bank while murders occurred just inside.

No, she wouldn't dwell anymore on what they could have done differently, or who the robber was. That ship had sailed.

The elevator ride from the garage to the basement only took thirty seconds, according to Selena. To walk from the elevator door to the security office was roughly another forty-five seconds, possibly a minute if the robber was taking his sweet time.

Selena was to exit the storage room once the robber entered the guardroom.

That was all she needed to do. The whole thing should have taken less than two minutes once the robber descended in the elevator.

When the clock struck 9:21, five minutes had passed, and Arielle could only assume things were not playing out as they had originally.

There was still no reason to believe Selena was in any true danger. She was hidden, out of sight from the robber. Even if the other guards on duty had somehow realized what was playing out and confronted the robber at the elevator, Selena would still be safe within the confines of the storage room.

*Maybe she's just needing to wait it out a little longer than planned.*

By 9:23, Arielle fought the urge to find any way she could to get inside the building, no matter how reckless of a decision that might be.

That's when Selena spilled out of the garage, head spinning around frantically in every direction. Felix finally stopped talking and stuck his hand out the window, waving it silently.

Selena scanned over the car twice before seeing Felix, and dashed toward them, practically jumping into the back seat.

"We need to get out of here!" Selena wheezed through sharp gasps for breath. "GO!"

Arielle fired up the engine and sped away, no questions asked. They reached the end of the Lincoln block, screeching to stop at the red light. She looked right, as was Felix, and they both spotted Kennedy sitting in his truck further down Eighteenth Avenue.

"He's right there!" Felix cried.

Arielle looked both directions. She could only turn left onto Eighteenth, as it was a one-way street that ran east to west. Kennedy was parked facing them, the correct direction. Not seeing any cars, she floored the accelerator and blazed through the red light, flying up Lincoln and taking a sharp right on Nineteenth Avenue. Selena tumbled around the backseat like a bowling ball, banging on one door before being flung to the other.

Nineteenth allowed two-way traffic, and Arielle blew by the couple cars present as she approached Sherman Street, again turning hard enough to flip the vehicle, had it been an SUV. Sherman was clear, so she gunned the car to return to Eighteenth in record time. Kennedy remained parked in his same spot as she approached the intersection.

The block between Sherman and Lincoln was less than three-hundred feet, and Kennedy was parked at the midpoint. Arielle turned the car onto Eighteenth and pulled over immediately, staying roughly one-hundred feet behind Kennedy. They were certainly close enough to be noticed by Kennedy, but he didn't appear to pay them any attention.

"Okay," Arielle said, as if she had just completed a menial task. "Tell us what happened in there."

Selena recapped the uneventful night, sure to mention the guard who had seen her upon arrival.

"Is he going to remember your face?" Arielle asked.

"Hell if I know. He looked straight at me, but didn't really stare at me, if that makes sense."

"Shit. The police will seek anyone who was in the building over the weekend. If this guard mentions seeing you, it's going to make you a suspect. They'll find out easily enough that you weren't supposed to be there."

"Well, the good news out of all this is that we can leave. Dawkins is the robber."

Selena said this in an almost uninterested tone.

Felix spun around in his seat to face Selena. "Dawkins?! Are you certain?"

Selena nodded. "The one person I ended up spending the most time with on this mission. I could tell it was him, even through the disguise. I called out his name." She lowered her head as if ashamed to admit this.

"You *what*?!" Arielle spun around, taking her eyes off Kennedy's truck. "You tinkered with the past by doing that."

Selena nodded, keeping her head low. "I know," she whispered. "I shouldn't have done that. But I had to be certain, you know? What if I was wrong?"

"You can still be wrong," Arielle said. "I'm sure he turned around not because of the name you said, but because you said anything at all. Selena, what happened?"

She finally looked up, shaking her head, tears welling on the surface of her eyes. "The other guard came out of the office. Dawkins shot him. Then he shot the other. I left before seeing what would happen to the fourth."

"Holy shit," Arielle said, turning back forward and rubbing the sides of her head. "Okay. We're okay. Right?"

Arielle knew she wouldn't have botched this part of the mission had she been the one inside the bank. But was it truly a mistake? Selena discovered the robber's identity—that was the goal. But Arielle would have saved as many lives as she could, given the opportunity.

The robber, presumed to be Dawkins, appeared at the far end of the block ahead of them. He had run to the corner of the intersection, looking from left to right until he saw Kennedy's truck. The sunglasses, fedora, and mustache all remained.

Arielle saw him, but Felix was the one who shouted, "There he is!"

All eyes in the car narrowed on Dawkins, scampering down the sidewalk like a panicked zombie.

"He doesn't have a bag of money," Arielle said, pulling up her binoculars for a better look. Now that she had Dawkins in her mind, she could definitely see the resemblance on the little she could see of the bottom half of his face.

"Where's the money?" Felix asked, squinting as Dawkins had run into the street, making a direct line for Kennedy's truck. "It's supposed to be in a large black bag, right?"

Dawkins had nothing but the clothes on his back, and presumably a gun hidden somewhere within the layers.

"It's not there," Selena said, a hint of relief slipping into her voice.

"So, the robbery didn't happen?" Felix asked.

Dawkins reached Kennedy's truck and leaped into the passenger seat. Kennedy sped away immediately. Arielle dropped her hand onto the gear, but didn't move further.

"What are you doing?" Felix asked, urgency clinging to every word. "Aren't we going to follow them?"

Police sirens wailed in the distance.

"No," Arielle said. "We're not."

"What?!" Felix and Selena cried in harmony.

"The mission is done," Arielle said, still refusing to move the car. "We got what we needed. There's nothing more we *need* to do. Trust me, I'd love to follow those two wherever they're going, and beat the shit out of them. But what does that accomplish? It only gets us further tangled in this mess—and this has been a *messy* mission. I had my chance to stop it all, and that failed. The dead are already dead. Nothing we can change about that. Let's stop while we're ahead. When anyone looks back to this mission, all they'll see is that we accomplished what was asked. A success."

"We can't just leave without knowing what happened in there," Selena said.

"I agree. Let's head back to the apartment to get our things, and we can watch the news. It shouldn't take long for this to become a breaking story. I'd say as long as we leave the apartment by noon, we shouldn't have anything to worry about. Can we all agree on that?"

"You really don't want to know where Kennedy and Dawkins are going?" Felix asked, his mouth still agape from amazement.

"Sure, but it's not worth putting us at risk. We know they're *not* going to that hole he dug in the mountains—they have no money to hide. They're probably just going somewhere to get cleaned up and hideout for the rest of the day. Dawkins is about to be wanted for at least three murders."

Arielle finally moved the car into gear and drove forward, the sirens growing louder as they approached the building. She circled the block once more to get back east, leaving the Cash Register Building in the rear-view mirror.

# Chapter 48

They practically barged into their apartment, Arielle and Selena rolling their eyes while Felix struggled with the key getting the door unlocked.

"Put the TV on!" Selena commanded as soon they stepped inside.

The suitcases had already been lined up neatly next to the kitchen table, courtesy of Felix. He hurried to the TV, which he couldn't recall having been turned on at all during this mission, and pressed the power button. It turned on to Channel Four; the feed distorted. Felix adjusted the antennas above the box until it showed a clear image of two news anchors, a man and woman, with sorrow splayed across their faces. A headline flashed across the bottom: *BREAKING NEWS: FOUR DEAD IN ATTEMPTED ROBBERY AT UNITED BANK.*

"Four dead," Arielle said, crossing her arms as she stood in front of the TV, mesmerized.

Selena watched her, worried Arielle might still hang on to the fact that she had shouted Dawkins's name.

The woman anchor spoke in a concerned tone. "We've just been informed that three of the deceased were security guards for the building. The fourth was a bank employee. There was a small group of employees there to count and sort money that had arrived earlier this morning, something they did every two Sundays. The rest survived, along with a fourth guard who heard the gunfire and immediately phoned the police. The security company had revoked the possession of firearms from their guards a year ago."

"They haven't said anything about missing money," Felix said, stroking his chin.

"The money isn't important," Arielle said. "The same amount of lives were lost."

"Don't sound so down about it," Selena said. "Like you've said, our goal was never to stop the murders. Unfortunately, we have the same amount of victims. On the flip side, it won't become a cold case. We know Dawkins was behind that disguise. What do we do now with that information?"

Arielle turned the volume down on the TV, standing in front of it as she faced Felix and Selena. "We don't have to do anything. We'll hand over our findings to HQ, and they'll take it from there. I'd assume they'll have someone from this era worry about finding the best way to deliver that information to the authorities. But you're right, Selena. Justice will be served to all three men involved. Kennedy, Young, Dawkins. They're toast. Possibly even other guards who could have been involved—we don't know."

"I can't wait to read the Futures Report on this one," Felix said, his eyes still drawn to the TV that was showing different pictures of the interior and exterior of the United Bank.

"I wish we could know how Dawkins originally did it," Selena added. "How did he get away with it forever? How come his name was *never* mentioned in any of the investigation?"

"I'm surprised Kennedy never outed him," Arielle said. "They could have sentenced Kennedy to death had the trial played out differently. And he, what, followed some code of not ratting out his accomplice?"

"He had to have felt very confident about the lack of evidence in the trial," Felix said. "I looked through those trial notes. The prosecution's case was suspect. A real stretch of the imagination."

"It's not like Kennedy was innocent," Arielle argued. "Can't exactly say the prosecution was far off—they just had the guy running everything behind the scenes, not the one who pulled the trigger."

"Could Kennedy have planned to be found not guilty to get money?" Selena asked.

"I don't think you get compensated for time in jail," Arielle said.

Selena shook her head. "Not money from the state. Money from everything that probably followed the trial. Think about it. You stand trial for one of the biggest crimes in Denver history. You're found not guilty and released. You don't think people are going to throw whatever they can at you for an interview? Something like this can turn you into a local celebrity—if not more. If Kennedy was smart enough to plan this whole thing and not get caught, then I'm sure he was smart enough to think this through before throwing Dawkins under the bus. Kennedy had some serious debt and needed a way out. The money was never found originally. Maybe Dawkins ran off with all of it, never to be heard from again. Kennedy still could have understood the opportunities that awaited after an acquittal."

"That seems like such a huge risk for something that wasn't guaranteed. He couldn't know for sure how the trial would go. And if his idea failed, he faced death. I can't think of a reasonable person who would literally risk their life for a few thousand dollars.”

“Reasonable people don’t orchestrate bank robberies.”

“You guys are arguing about nothing,” Felix interrupted. “Look.”

He nodded to the TV that showed a police officer speaking in front of the bank. Arielle turned around and raised the volume.

“We believe this was an inside job,” the officer said. “It was all very calculated. The perpetrator knew exactly where he was going. Took the videotapes from the security room, ripped pages out of the security log book, and exited the building without any hesitation. We have not discovered any money missing, although we believe it was intended to be a robbery. The employees working in the vault heard gunfire and immediately hid the money they were counting. Five of them hid in a mantrap, but the sixth remained in the vault. The perpetrator shot this employee and escaped without any cash.”

“See, Selena,” Felix said. “You did make a positive impact. The gunshots occurred in the hallway because of you. You alerted those employees. Now, you couldn’t control what happened after that, but you gave them an opportunity to get to safety. Be proud of what you accomplished.”

Arielle nodded silently, Selena waiting for her potential praise. But none came. Instead, she turned the TV off. “I’ve told you both I have no interest in the Futures Reports, or seeing how things turned out. I’ll admit, I had plenty of curiosity, and that’s why we watched the news. But this mission is over, and I need you to trust me. I’ve played this game before. Selena, you’re probably going to dwell over these murders for the next few weeks. You’ll feed yourself a ton of guilt because four murders still happened. This is not healthy for you. I suggest you remove this mission from your memory as soon as possible. Start preparing for whatever the next one is. Are you satisfied with how this all turned out?"

"Yes."

"Good, then just leave it at that. With all the resources we have as an organization, not enough care and attention are given to our mental health. Especially us Angels. We witness death, evil. We experience the most drastic swings of emotions: hope, doubt, fear, guilt. If I can be open, I'm feeling a little of all that right now. It's impossible to reasonably process it all."

"But we accomplished what we needed," Selena said. "Why such a range of emotions?"

"It's not so black and white. I've seen Angels go into some dark depressions, even after a successful mission. The problem with what we do is that there is always something we look back on and think we could have done better. Obviously with this mission, we'd have loved to save all the lives lost. We could have, had we known Dawkins was our guy from the beginning."

"You can say that again." Selena still wasn't ready to admit to her team that she had suspected him for some time, and if being honest with herself, wasn't sure she ever would. Perhaps that was exactly the type of negative dwelling that led to mental health issues for Angels.

"All I'm saying is to not overlook how much these missions can eat at you." Arielle strolled away from the TV and grabbed her suitcase, pulling it toward the apartment door. "We face a dark road after each mission, and I'm so glad to have you both in my life to vent to about it. I've always gone into these strange moods in the few days between missions where I feel kind of empty. Unfulfilled. I haven't been able to put a finger on it until recently, and now that we all have each other as a tight-knit team, I encourage we all openly share our feelings to prevent any dark thoughts."

"What are you saying?" Felix asked. "Dark thoughts? Like suicide?"

Arielle shook her head. "No, not to that extreme. But I can totally see how people fall into that. For me, it's been more like thoughts of running away. Hiding from the world. Sometimes I wish I could hit the restart button on my life and do it all over again. I still have a lot of emotional scars I'm dealing with. Between losing my family and the love of my life . . ."

Selena crossed the room and threw her arms around Arielle, who was crying. "You don't need to hold anything in."

The scene unfolding in their borrowed apartment was becoming rather intense for Selena. She had come from a family who refused to show emotion, so she'd always thought that was just how people were. She expected nothing different from the most intimidating figure in their time travel universe, but over their last two missions working together, Selena had learned that emotions were far more complex than she ever understood.

She had always seen Arielle as a confident, powerful woman who had it all. Ask anyone within the Road Runners and they would likely all share the same opinion. Arielle sat on a pedestal. She set the bar others tried to reach. But now, getting to know the person—the human—behind the façade of power and greatness, Selena saw a strong but insecure person dealing with trauma that might never stop haunting her. Yet, Arielle still powered through it all with grace and an unwavering will for the success that had built up her image over the years.

Tears rolled down Arielle's cheeks as she stepped out of Selena's embrace. "I've always prided myself on being a loner. Completely independent. I didn't need help from anyone for anything. Losing everyone important in your life will have that effect. I figured I was meant to be alone in this world.

"I had long given up hope of finding anyone I could trust. Be vulnerable with. But it's you two. And I'm never letting you go."

Felix and Selena exchanged a look once Arielle's head hung low, and both encircled her, each grabbing an arm. "Are you saying we're friends?" Felix asked, causing a muffled laugh through tears from Arielle.

"I'm so impressed with you both," Arielle said, regaining her composure. "And you're not just phenomenal at your work, you're incredible human beings. You two carried this mission. You both risked so much to see this through, all while I was wasting my time following Kennedy's every move. Selena, why didn't you tell us you thought Dawkins was involved?"

The question caught Selena completely off guard, and she felt her face flush. "H-how did you know?"

Arielle cracked a grin, wiping away the tears with her sleeve. "I piece things together. Even when it seems like I'm doing nothing, like those brutal days spent outside of Kennedy's house, I'm always thinking. I think about everything. It was clear you had taken an interest in Dawkins, but I wasn't sure why. Possibly romantic, but unlikely. Maybe it was because he was one of the few people who actually spoke to you at the office. I don't know. But after you went on that date with him, I started piecing it together. You didn't have much to say that night. I could tell you were hiding something. Then yesterday, when I saw that California plate outside of Kennedy's house, it all made sense. I still didn't know how much to believe, so I wanted to see it play out."

"Play out?" Selena asked, her jaw remaining open for a few seconds. "What if I got hurt?"

"I trusted you.  I had complete faith in you to follow your hunch and see it through.  And you were right.  I still don't know why you kept it a secret, and I don't expect an explanation.  But next time, share your thoughts—they matter."

Selena's face remained red, but relief flooded through her just the same.

"Well, that was a lot to unpack in the last few minutes," Felix said. "We should probably get going. We have a date at D'Corazon. If I recall correctly, we deemed it as a post-mission ritual now."

"You mean margarita time?" Selena teased. "Absolutely."

They all grabbed their suitcases and lugged them out the door, leaving the 1991 apartment behind forever.

# Chapter 49

Instead of risking a trip across town amid an attempted bank robbery, they opted to step outside the apartment building where they waited for complete isolation before taking their swigs of Juice and jumping forward to 2022.

The apartment complex remained behind them, a whole new facelift given to it in the thirty years that had passed. Peter Young was long gone.

"This walk kind of sucked last time," Selena said. "We can call a Lyft to give us a ride."

She wasted no time powering her cell phone back on after it had been a useless piece of plastic for the last two weeks. She licked her lips like a ravenous dog in anxious anticipation as the screen flashed on.

Felix laughed. "Right back to our lazy ways, I see. Why not walk? It's a beautiful day."

That it had been.

"Well, sure, we can walk, Felix, but that means more time until we get those celebratory margaritas."

Arielle chuckled. "I have to agree with Selena on this one. If this mission hadn't been so grueling, maybe we'd walk. But I'd rather get to those margs and bowls of chips and salsa as quickly as we can."

Felix shrugged. "If you say so. I guess I find a quiet walk through nature more calming than a loud restaurant."

Selena tossed her hands up to gesture around them. "Bro, this is downtown Denver. There's nothing quiet or nature about this place."

"You know what I mean," Felix said, shaking his head in defeat while Selena called the Lyft.

They only had to wait a couple of minutes for a car to arrive, followed by a ten-minute drive through the heart of downtown to their final destination at D'Corazon.

It was 12:15 and the streets of downtown bustled with a heavy crowd for the lunch hour. A line filed out of D'Corazon's door, and Selena moaned when she saw it.

"Relax," Arielle said. "It's lunch, not dinner. People are in and out fast."

"Should we take our bags back to headquarters and come back?" Felix asked. "It's only three blocks down."

"I'd rather not," Arielle said. "If we show up there, who knows how long we'll get stuck in some conversation about the mission. I'd rather just wait it out here and deal with all that after."

Their wait only ended up being fifteen minutes, where they passed the time watching the hordes of business people hustling up and down the sidewalk of Blake Street. Cars sat at a standstill on the road, adding extra heat to an already sweltering day.

Arielle looked at her team. Felix yawned. Selena gazed mindlessly into the distance. They were beat.

Once they settled at a table near the back of the restaurant, Arielle asked, "What are you two planning to do with your time off?"

"Sleep," Felix said with a laugh. "I'm going home after this, getting into bed, and will wake up whenever my body so desires."

"I haven't thought about it yet," Selena said. "Definitely going to shut myself inside my house for the rest of the day. But maybe a trip somewhere tomorrow. I could use a couple days on a beach with drinks being delivered around the clock. You're more than welcome to join me."

"I'll consider it," Arielle said. "I need to touch base with Commander Briar to see what we have coming up next. And I'm going to have a long talk with him about never assigning a mission like this again."

"Good luck with that," Felix said. "We completed the mission. The bottom line is it was a success. They won't care about all the trouble we had—that's just part of the mission, they'll say. If anything, I think we'll get *more* missions like this."

"All I can do is try. He listens to me. If I voice this concern, it'll at least be taken under consideration."

"Arielle standing up to the commander," Selena said, grinning. "That's so . . . Arielle."

They all broke into laughter, a server finally coming to take their drink order. Selena ordered a round of strawberry-mango margaritas for the three of them.

"You're going to get a big boost in the rankings," Felix added. "It'll further cement your place at the top."

"I'm sure Arielle is just fine with her ranking," Selena said. "What are you planning on doing with your time off, anyway—assuming you don't join me on the beach?"

Arielle sat back and crossed her arms. "I don't know. I wasn't planning on leaving town, but maybe I should. Especially since the mission was in Denver. Would be nice to go somewhere else, even for a few days."

"Are you going to call Javonte?" Selena asked, shooting a devilish smirk across the table.

Arielle blushed. "Haven't decided yet. Maybe I will."

"Well, he is an NFL player. I'm sure he can afford to join you on a trip at the last minute."

"Unless he has training camp," Felix added. "That's more important."

Selena rolled her eyes. "I'm sure he can take a weekend off. I think you should call him. No harm in seeing where it might go."

"I don't know," Arielle said. "I've been thinking it over, and I don't think he's my type. A professional athlete. Aren't they just looking for trophy wives?"

"You don't think he can handle you," Selena said.

Arielle grinned. "Well, I could probably kick his ass and make him cry if I wanted to. Can a macho football player be okay with having a woman like that in his life? Besides, I probably shouldn't see someone in the public eye. I don't exactly live a life I can flaunt around. It's still top-secret. Keep in mind, I haven't dated anyone since becoming a Road Runner. I don't know how it would work with someone on the outside."

"Sounds like a romance story waiting to happen."

The margaritas arrived and everyone wasted no time in pulling theirs in and chugging long sips from the orange-and-red concoction.

Arielle pushed her drink back, satisfied. "A romance? Not likely. But I feel ready for something more in my life. Maybe not a relationship. Perhaps a new hobby. Maybe even a dog."

"Well, jeez," Selena said, sarcasm clinging to every word. "Why date an NFL running back when you can adopt a dog?"

"I think that's wise," Felix said. "We're all still young and crushing our careers—our lives, I suppose. I've never considered the complications that come with dating a non-Road Runner. The Bylaws clearly state that we can only share our secret with spouses and children. You'd essentially have to date someone, go through an engagement and wedding, then drop the bomb on them. That doesn't seem like a great way to kick off a marriage, but what do I know?"

"You guys are too serious," Selena said. "Who said anything about engagements and weddings? I just suggested it for Arielle to have some fun, not to marry the guy. You can have a handsome, athletic man on your arm. Get suite tickets to the games every Sunday, eat at the fanciest restaurants in Denver. And, yes, maybe go on some obnoxious vacation with the guy in paradise."

"I can already do all of that stuff myself," Arielle said, shrugging.

"Suit yourself. I wouldn't pass up the opportunity, but I suppose we're all different."

"I don't know why you're so concerned about this, Selena," Felix said. "Don't you have something you were going to show us from the mission?"

Selena's eyes bulged as she sat up straight. "Oh my God, I almost forgot. Yes, I need to open it here with you both."

"The present from the locker room?" Arielle asked. "Who do you think it's from?"

"I'm pretty sure it's from Dawkins. I don't know who else it could be."

"Well, that's disturbing," Felix said. "Let's see it."

Selena reached under the table and pulled her backpack onto her lap, unzipping it with vigor and dropping the gift on the table before shoving the bag back underneath.

"What would he have given you?" Felix asked.

"No clue, but I wouldn't have gotten it until Monday, the day after the robbery—assuming the cleaning crew would even be allowed in the building."

"They definitely would not."

"Enough," Arielle said. "Open it."

Selena nodded, fingers crawling over the box and pulling at the seams. She tore the gift wrap completely off to reveal a box of chocolates, frowning in confusion as she flipped it over and found a folded piece of paper taped to the bottom of the box.

She pulled it off, opened it, and started reading.

"Selena. You have been such a wonderful addition to our team. I know this isn't fun work, so here is a little something to show my appreciation for everything you have done in your first few weeks. Looking forward to working with you. Olivia."

Tears welled in Selena's eyes.

"Olivia?" Felix asked. "Your boss from the cleaning crew?"

Selena nodded, wiping away tears. "I don't know why that hit me so hard. I wasn't expecting that."

"It's because you've touched someone," Arielle said. "And they showed you appreciation. Few people do that, but it seems you left quite the impression on Olivia."

Selena smiled, unable to look away from the gift.

"We may not get much visible appreciation," Arielle said. "Not in this sort of sentimental way, at least. But it's what we do. We touch lives. We help people. Many of them will never know it."

"I'm understanding that," Felix said. "I've never felt my work has made a huge difference, but seeing it all in motion has shown me that every little detail matters."

"We should never feel like we're just going through the motions of some job," Arielle said. "Our missions aren't busywork. They serve a purpose. Even when it doesn't feel like it. Even if they fail. They aim to make the world a better place."

"I feel awful," Selena said. "Olivia will never hear from me again. I'm just vanishing from her timeline."

"You're probably going to be a suspect for a little while because of it," Arielle explained. "The chatter will eventually die down once they find zero evidence linking you to anything, but rumors will fly. It's impossible to say what will happen to your reputation."

"Just until they pin it all on Kennedy and Dawkins," Felix added. "Once they have those two in prison, everyone will forget your name."

"Except Dawkins," Selena said.

"Doesn't matter. Them being locked up will clear your name."

"We're wasting our breath," Arielle said, taking a sip of her drink. "This is all speculation—don't play that game. Wait for the Futures Report and see exactly what happened. And leave me out of it—I don't care. We're here, back on our home turf in our Original Time. Let's celebrate what we accomplished, relax, and prepare for the next one."

"Cheers to that," Selena said, raising her glass. "God knows the world still needs plenty of cleaning up."

# READ THE FUTURES REPORT

Just because Arielle Lucila doesn't want to look at the Futures Report to find out what happened after the mission, doesn't mean you can't!

Enjoy an exclusive look at the official Futures Report for the Father's Day Massacre mission that is prepared for the Commander's office following each mission.

All you need to do is join my e-mail Reader Club by signing up at BookHip.com/SAWCWDH

# Author's Note

Thank you for reading Secrets in the Vault. This was an interesting story to write, and one that required perhaps the most research I've had to conduct while preparing a novel.

The Father's Day Bank Massacre was a real-life crime that remains a cold case today. However, there isn't a ton of information available on the topic, despite the trial being one of the first to be nationally televised on CourtTV. A quick search online will find plenty of similar articles outlining the timeline of events, but there isn't much that takes a deep dive into the happenings of this massacre.

My search, however, led me to an out-of-print book called *Murders in the Bank Vault*, a detailed look at the trial of former officer James King, written by the defense attorney, Walter Gerash.

I understand there was likely a slanted view presented by Mr. Gerash, seeing as he represented the defendant and won. But the amount of information available was unmatched, as it contained testimonials from witnesses, officers, and everyone in between. Not to mention the hoards of evidence presented at trial.

After reviewing all the information available, I still can't say I have an opinion on who ultimately carried out this attack. As it's laid out in the book, I believe it was a team effort to pull off this heist. I have a hard time believing one man could have planned this from start to finish, especially considering King no longer worked in the bank and had easy access.

It's entirely possible the whole security team was in on it, and whoever they dubbed with physically robbing the bank had a change of heart and killed his fellow guards to earn a bigger cut of the pot.

I'm not much for plotting a story, but I had to for this one, considering all the moving parts. But even so, I left the ending open, wanting to see where the story took me. I never decided from the beginning who it would be, and I was just as surprised as you (hopefully) to find out the man behind the disguise.

This book took a lot out of me. It was as stressful as it was fun to write. But in the end, looking back, I'm pleased with how it all came out. Aside from the mystery surrounding the robbery, I enjoyed reuniting with Arielle, Felix, and Selena, and watching their relationships continue to grow. I look forward to spending more time with them in future books and diving deeper into what makes each one of them tick.

I owe a few thank you's for this book. First, is for Bruce Yates. He presented me the idea of writing about this tragedy, more in an investigative manner than fictional. That's not really my style, however, and I thought it would be more fun to explore in a fictional world with multiple characters all working on the case. Regardless, I'm forever grateful for the idea!

Thank you to my editor, Stephanie Cohen-Perez, for her continued work on my novels. I feel we both elevate our skills to the next level with each one, and I can't wait to see where we'll be ten books from now.

And my final thank you is for my family. My wife Natasha, for running so much of the publishing business behind the scenes, so that I'm free to write the stories. And to Arielle,

Felix, and Selena for the daily motivation to keep going. We are on the verge of a whole new life, and I can't wait to share it with all of you!

Thank you again for reading, and I look forward to the next adventure. Until then, happy reading!

Andre Gonzalez

November 22, 2021 – June 28, 2022

# Enjoy this book?

You can make a difference!

Reviews are the most helpful tools in getting new readers for any books. I don't have the financial backing of a New York publishing house and can't afford to blast my book on billboards or bus stops.

(Not yet!)

That said, your honest review can go a long way in helping me reach new readers. If you've enjoyed this book, I'd be forever grateful if you could spend a couple minutes leaving it a review (it can be as short as you like) on the site you purchased you this book from, or on Amazon if you bought it in-person.

Thank you!

# Also by Andre Gonzalez

**Arielle Lucila Series:**
Secrets in the Vault (#2)
Angel Assassin (#1)

**Wealth of Time Series:**
Time of Fate (#6)
Zero Hour (#5)
Keeper of Time (#4)
Bad Faith (#3)
Warm Souls (#2)
Wealth of Time (#1)
Road Runners (Short Story)
Revolution (Short Story)

**Amelia Doss Series:**
Salvation (#3)
Nightfall (#2)
Resurrection (#1)

**Insanity Series:**
The Insanity Series (Books 1-3)
Replicate (#3)
The Burden (#2)
Insanity (#1)

Erased (Prequel Short Story)

**The Exalls Attacks:**
Followed Away (#3)
Followed East (#2)
Followed Home (#1)
A Poisoned Mind (Short Story)

**Standalone books:**
Snowball: A Christmas Horror Story

# About the Author

Born in Denver, CO, Andre Gonzalez has always had a fascination with horror and the supernatural starting at a young age. He spent many nights wide-eyed and awake, his mind racing with the many images of terror he witnessed in books and movies. Ideas of his own morphed out of movies like *Halloween* and books such as *Pet Sematary* by Stephen King. These thoughts eventually made their way to paper, as he always wrote dark stories for school assignments or just for fun. Followed Home is his debut novel based off of a terrifying dream he had many years ago at the age of 12. His reading and writing of horror stories evolved into a pursuit of a career as an author, where Andre hopes to keep others awake at night with his frightening tales. The world we live in today is filled with horror stories, and he looks forward to capturing the raw emotion of these events, twisting them into new tales, and preserving a legacy in between the crisp bindings of novels.

Andre graduated from Metropolitan State University of Denver with a degree in business in 2011. During his free time, he enjoys baseball, poker, golf, and traveling the world with his family. He believes that seeing the world is the only true way to stretch the imagination by experiencing new cultures and meeting new people.

Andre still lives in Denver with his wife, Natasha, and their three kids.